A SECOND REVOLUTION

Dedicated to Corey, Colby And to Mr. Jim Murphy

This book could never have been written without help from those around me.

For Corey - You encouraged me to rediscover my love for writing. You have taught me that we can chase our dreams and make them come true. The words, "I can't do that" aren't even in your vocabulary. Thank you, my love. To Colby - Your love and devotion have been an inspiration throughout all my writing endeavors. I love you. To Mr. Jim Murphy – As a shy high school student, it meant the world to me when you squatted by my desk, one of my stories in hand, and told me I had real talent. You asked me if I ever thought of becoming a writer. I have always dreamed of being able to tell you how much that moment meant to me. Teachers may not always know the impact they have on their students, but what you said that day, stuck with me forever. From the bottom of my heart, thank you! To my dad and mom, Julie and Lynelle – You provided me with a life of never-ending love and support. Thanks for always being in my corner. I love you! To all the rest of my family and friends; thank you for your unwavering support! I wouldn't be who or where I am now, without each one of you. I hope you have fun finding the surprises I left for you in the book! There will be more to come. To the Lancaster County Writers group -Your encouragement, suggestions, advice and support were invaluable. Jacinda, Gary, Clay, Diane, Barb, Marcia, the Suhrbiers, and all the rest – I thank you!

Thank you to all who read and critiqued my work - Lynelle Caber, Angie Hauck, Suzy Rivera, Leon Fox - I appreciate your willingness and insights. Marla Robinson- Your suggestions made me a better writer and your kind words gave me the courage to put myself out there. Thank you! To Alix Daniel and her team at Cybirdy publishing, UK. Thank you for seeing something special in my book that captured your heart. You have made my dream come true!

A SECOND REVOLUTION

by

Kelly Noll

First published in paperback special edition, 2024
By Cybirdy Publishing
101 Camley Street, London N1C 4DU, UK

Designed by Cybirdy Publishing
Illustrations by George Barrell from Cybirdy Publishing
Photos by Mathias Reding, Alexandra Kollstrem, Matteo Basile
from Pexels.com
Edited by Bernadette Sheehan, for Cybirdy Publishing
Printed by Hobbs the Printers Ltd

This book is typeset in minion, Proxima Nova and Copperplate.
A CIP record for this book is available from the British Library

ISBN: 978-1-0686309-9-6

A SECOND REVOLUTION

Kelly Noll

CHAPTER 1

At the Races

Jerrett could feel the warm sun on his back, while a steady breeze rustled the banners. Colors and voices swirled all around him as he wove through the crowd and past the booths. The sounds of engines screaming down the track were a constant drone in the background. Dirt bikes perched precariously on stands, lining the lane through the pit area.

Jerrett felt a much-needed peace, like a breath of fresh air, and a break from the stress of the work week. Today he would enjoy the races with his family, cheer on his kids, visit with friends and forget about everything else.

At least he would try to.

As hard as he tried, the ominous dread was always there, shoved down and buried as best as he could manage, but it never vanished completely. It was an uncertain time they lived in and he never quite knew what to expect next. He'd gotten pretty good at faking being carefree and relaxed so his wife and kids wouldn't worry. It was as if he was hovering above two completely different worlds. He wondered if anyone else felt the same as he did.

His gaze caught the Elite Guard at the front gate. The man had been there all day, patrolling the main entrance. There were Guards at all the races nowadays; a true sign of the times they lived in. Every time he passed one of them, a cold fear gripped him. He'd heard too many stories about the Guards not to believe at least some of them were true. It was best to stay away from them and off their radar.

Jerrett lowered his gaze, and pulled down his hat brim, trying to make himself unnoticed. Guards would look for any reason to exert their power; it was how they controlled the masses, and it worked effectively.

Voices raised in anger registered in his brain, and instinctively he turned to see what was going on. His first thought was that two motocrossers were arguing over a race, but as he scanned the crowd, he realized someone was actually confronting the Guard. That caught his interest immediately and he froze, trying to figure out what was going on. Others in the crowd did the same, turning towards the raised voices.

An overweight man, in a motocross jersey with 'Dad of 117' written on the back, chugged a final gulp of his beer and tossed the can to the ground. He wobbled a bit, off balance, but quickly regained his footing as he faced the Guard. "Yeah, I said it, and I meant it." He jabbed his finger towards the Guard. "Get out of my way!" He staggered towards the Guard and gave the man a push.

In seconds, the father found himself thrown to the ground, with a knee in his back. "Umph!" grunted the man, now struggling to get the Guard off him.

The sound of a gun being cocked made him freeze. The Guard growled at him menacingly, "Don't move a muscle or I will shoot you in the head, right here and now." He pressed all his weight into the man's back.

Jerrett felt his stomach clench at the sight, tension roiling through his body. Would the Guard actually kill him, right here and now? Everyone around the scene had frozen, no one daring to intervene. Jerrett found himself wishing there was something he could do, but what? If he tried to stop the Guard, it would only bring unwanted attention to himself and he'd be on the ground right beside the dad of 117.

The Guard thumbed his radio, calling for backup. "I need help at the main gate, right away!" Then he looked up, glaring at the crowd gathered around him.

"Everyone stay back!" As one, the crowd took a few steps away.

"Please," the man on the ground begged, his voice muffled and strained, "please let me up." He gasped for breath, "I'm sorry … I was out of line. Can I just go?"

"Don't even think of moving," threatened the Guard, with a growl. He pressed even harder into his back. The man on the ground groaned. Within minutes, two more Guards joined the first one, guns drawn.

"Don't move!" one repeated.

"What happened?" asked the second Guard. The first one explained the situation and they hauled the man up to his feet. Two of the Guards hauled him away; one resumed his position at the gate.

"Please, please let me go! I'm sorry! I wasn't thinking!"

"The only place you are going is with us!"

The father looked around frantically at the crowd. "Please, someone, please, find my wife. Tell Colleen what happened!" The Guards pulled him away roughly and his cries faded as they left the area.

The crowd began to slowly disperse, looking around at each other and talking in low voices about what they'd just seen. The Guard watched them, apparently not happy at how slow they were going.

"Move it! Get out of here right now!" He yelled, glancing around at the crowd. To get his point across, he scanned the crowd, his gaze landing on an elderly man slowly shuffling by. "I said, move it!" He roared, shoving the old man so hard he fell to the ground.

The crowd gasped collectively, but no one dared move to help the man.

Jerrett stood by, frozen in fear, his every instinct crying out to go help the man up. He swallowed hard, heart pounding, and clenched his jaw, attempting to reign in his feelings. *Do not intervene. Walk away,* he told himself. He gritted his teeth and clenched his fists. Everything within him wanted to go after the Guard.

On shaky legs, the old man managed to get himself upright and hurry away as fast as he could.

Jerrett bristled, fury racing through him. He tensed up; his nails digging into his palms and his heart pounding, ready to lunge at the Guard.

But then he stopped. No, he couldn't do this. He'd only be inviting trouble on himself. He couldn't do anything.

He had never felt so helpless in all his life.

Jerrett gritted his teeth, slumped his shoulders, and forced himself to turn around and move on. These days, you had to mind your own business and stay out of trouble. He breathed deeply, trying desperately to slow down his heart and temper his rage. *Deep breaths, in, out…*

He unclenched his fists, shaking out his hands slightly in an effort to release his rage. He rubbed his hand over his face, noting the tremble in his fingers. He couldn't go back to the pits and face his family like this. He needed a moment.

Turning down a driveway in the opposite direction of the pits, he walked briskly, face down, baseball hat pulled low over his eyes. He needed to walk; walk away from his anger, his frustration and his fear until he could breathe normally again.

He hated this. He hated living this way. Ever since martial law had been put in place and these awful Guards put everywhere, he'd lived with the tension and fear of one day doing the wrong thing and winding up just like that dad he'd seen.

People disappeared all the time nowadays, though that was the first time Jerrett had seen someone taken away right in front of him. The Guards rarely told family members where their loved one was after they were taken away. They would just release them on a whim when they were done with them. Or perhaps you'd be lucky enough to receive an official letter. That happened sometimes.

What would his wife, Gwennie, do if he had been the one to get arrested? It would crush her –not knowing what happened to him. His brothers and kids would be devastated. How would his business keep afloat? Sometimes when people went missing, they stayed missing for a month or more.

He shook his head, his face grim. How had America gotten to this state so quickly? It was as if he'd blinked and the 'Land of the Free' was gone.

His throat tightened and he blinked his eyes furiously. *No!* He was not breaking down, especially here. Drawing in a deep breath, he pushed it out slowly, straightening his spine and willing himself to calm down. Another lap around the pits was in order. As he walked, he forced his mind onto other things, anything but what he'd seen.

Once he felt calm enough, and somewhat settled, he made his way back to his family's pits. He needed to focus on them now, on why he was here in the first place.

"Jerrett! Jerrett Nolan!" A sudden shout pulled him out of his thoughts, and he looked around trying to see who had called him.

A man about Jerrett's height waved to him. He was trim and fit with a prickly buzz cut. He looked almost military in his black t-shirt, camouflage pants, and boots. Jerrett wondered if he had been in the armed forces. A small smile crept across the man's face as he whipped off the dark sunglasses he wore.

Jerrett had a moment of uncertainty as he thought he recognized the man but couldn't place where from.

"Hey, Jerrett. How've you been?" The familiar stranger stretched out a hand.

Jerrett hesitated a moment, trying to place him. The name of a high school classmate suddenly popped into his head.

"Mitch? Mitch Carson?"

Mitch nodded vigorously as he pumped Jerrett's hand. "That's me. How've you been?"

"Fine, fine. What brings you out here?"

"I was here to see the race, but I was looking for you, too. I heard you have your own cycle shop. Is that right?"

"Sure is."

Mitch cast a sidelong glance around them and moved closer, dropping his voice. "Listen, I've got a job for you." His eyes flicked in the direction of the Guards. "I can't talk about it here. Can I stop by your shop later in the week? So, we can talk in private?"

Jerrett was perplexed but nodded. "Sure, but what is this all about?"

Mitch shook his head and whispered, "I can't say more here. Later in the week, OK?"

"OK, then." Jerrett agreed. "See you later this week." They shook hands and Mitch left. Jerrett watched him as he drifted away down pit lane. His brow furrowed. What on earth could Mitch have meant? His mind spun with possibilities, and he felt uneasy. Was Mitch into something illegal? He didn't know Mitch very well, so there was no way to tell what he might be into.

This day was getting stranger and stranger. He shook his head wearily. Glancing up at the moto on the gate sign, he realized he needed to hurry. It was almost time for his son, Troy, to race.

Jerrett picked up his pace, breaking into a jog.

A few minutes later, he made it to his family's pits. Gwennie stuck her head out of the window of their delivery-truck-turned-camper. Her brown hair was secured in a high ponytail, wild strands falling loose.

She was beautiful, even with the messy hair. After all these years, his heart still skipped a beat at the sight of her.

He could see her eyes light up as she caught sight of him. A smile spread across her face. Jerrett smiled back and waved to her.

She'd been his teenage sweetheart and they dated all through high school and college. It was hard to believe it had been eighteen years since they'd married. Gwennie was his rock, the one who kept him steady. She worked long hours as a nurse and was always tired, but still managed to keep things going around the house and oversee the kids' schedules. He could never figure out how she did it all. And on top of that, he'd dumped two brothers on her. Trevor lived in an apartment over their garage and Dean was always around. But she never minded.

She called out his name, which startled Jasper, the family pit bull. Jasper looked around and spied Jerrett. He began barking with excitement as he recognized his master. His crooked tail, once broken and re-healed into a right turn, wagged furiously.

Jerrett called out, "Hey, hon! Is Troy down in staging yet?" He bent down to pet Jasper and untangle his tether. He scratched the dog's ears and kissed his furry head, which smelled like he needed a bath. He'd have to remind one of the kids to tackle that when they got home.

When he straightened up, he could feel Gwennie's eyes watching him. He was still feeling out of sorts about what he'd seen, and Mitch's mysterious conversation, but he needed to keep Gwennie from noticing … and worrying.

"Yes, I sent him down with Dean. He's waiting for you. I'll meet you on the viewing platform."

"OK, love you, babe."

"Love you, too!" She yelled, smiling at him before she turned back to whatever she was doing.

With a wave to his wife, Jerrett continued down the driveway to the staging area where the riders would meet and get ready for their race.

Once there, he quickly caught sight of his ten-year-old son, Troy. His bright yellow helmet stood out in the crowd.

Troy was an easy-going kid who got along with everyone. His obsession with dirt bikes and motocross encompassed his whole world. He did OK in school, never got in trouble, strived to be helpful, and enjoyed teaching younger kids how to ride. It had been Troy who'd taught his little sister all the basics. Out of Gwennie and Jerrett's three children, Troy was the most easy-going.

 Troy's attention was on something his uncle Dean was saying to him as he bent down close to the boy. Jerrett weaved his way through the dirt bikes, riders, and parents. He didn't feel like talking to anyone just now. To avoid questions, he plastered on a fake smile as people moved over to accommodate him.

Dean straightened up and spotted him, waving him over with a smile that looked much like his own. Along with the same dark -colored hair and green eyes, there was no mistaking they were related.

Making his way to Dean's side, Jerrett clapped his brother on the back. It was like hitting a brick wall.

Dean was the quintessential health nut; he was solid muscle and had excelled at every sport he'd ever tried. In contrast, Jerrett hadn't worked out in years and was distressed to notice a new softness around his middle.

"Hey, Jerr, good! , You made it! " Dean announced. But as he looked his brother over, his brow furrowed, as if he sensed Jerrett's inner turmoil. He cocked his head and wrinkled his brow, questioning his sibling silently. Jerrett just shook his head slightly.

Dean nodded, understanding that they would talk later. Dean could read him like a book; a talent that went both ways.

Troy turned and saw his father. "Dad!" he yelled, delighted.

"Hey, bud." Jerrett gave him a knuckle bump. The distressed, helpless feeling that had overwhelmed him slipped into the background – here was something he could throw himself into. His boy was about to race. "You all ready?" He asked as he looked over at his son. "Where are your gloves?"

Troy pulled them out from where he'd jammed them behind his number plate and waved them in Jerrett's face.

Nonplussed, Jerrett rolled his eyes and continued, "Goggles?"

Dean wiggled the goggles from where he had hung them around his neck, a cocky grin across his face.

Jerrett resisted the urge to smack the irritating smile off his brother's face and turned back to his mental pre-race checklist. "Check the gas?"

"Well, of course! Full tank. Would I miss that?" Dean answered. Jerrett's mouth quirked up in a partial grin, which he just couldn't seem to hold back. Shaking his head at Dean, he leaned down to his son.

"Watch the ruts on the inside sweeper after the backstretch. Stay to the right, OK?" He referred to a tricky corner another rider had told him about. Troy nodded in understanding.

Jerrett stood up and adjusted his cap while looking around. The familiar faces of friends surrounded him, all eager and apprehensive. The crowd was a swirl of bright colors and patterns. Jerrett soaked in the contented feeling of oblivion around him. No one knew what had just happened at the gate; their minds were on one moment only.

He wished his thoughts were.

Refusing to dwell on the incident at the track entrance, he distracted himself by mentally counting the work he had lined up for the next week. Jerrett had a small shop, with just himself and one other mechanic. He mentally ticked off the number of bikes that he knew were coming in on Monday for work. The day after a race was always busy, since racers break things all the time.

Jerrett's thoughts were yanked back to the present when the riders' numbers began to be called. He pushed Troy's bike to the gate and got him positioned. Dean moved in to give Troy his goggles, followed by a fist bump. Jerrett leaned in close to tell him good luck before he moved away.

The other racers lined up at the gate, waiting tensely for the race to start. Jerrett and Dean joined the other family members off to the side to watch. At the drop of the gates, the bikes took off, as fast as they could go, trying to outdistance each other to the first corner for the holeshot.

They watched as Troy took the lead. Jerrett whipped off his hat and waved it in the air, hooting and hollering for his boy. It was easier to put all the other things out of his mind as he allowed himself to get caught up in the excitement.

After the first corner, he and Dean ran to the observation deck, where they could see the rest of the track.

Gwennie was waiting on the platform with their other two children and his younger brother. "Jerrett! Dean!" She called, waving them over. "He's in the lead!" Her excitement was evident in her voice.

Jerrett hurried over to join them, their fervor mingling together as they cheered Troy on. Gwennie turned to him briefly, flushed with excitement with a broad smile splitting her face, her love and pride in Troy obvious to all. Jerrett moved in close beside her.

Seconds later, a sturdy little body pushed in between them, heavy motocross boots stomping on the wooden platform. A squeaky voice called out, "Daddy, look! Troy's in the lead!"

Jerrett spared a glance at his little daughter, dropping his hand onto her shoulder. Since Cami was racing later, she was dressed in her flashy pink motocross gear and Troy's old boots. Her blond hair was tucked into braids that were so long they nearly reached her waist. His little girl was a spitfire, precocious and sassy. She was a high-energy kid who reminded Jerrett of a busy little chipmunk.

He squeezed Cami tightly, "He's doing great!"

His oldest son, Dalton, blew a shrill whistle as his brother went by. The fifteen-year-old didn't often race, since he'd taken a break to play football this year, but still enjoyed cheering on his younger siblings. Trevor, Jerrett's nineteen-year-old, half-brother, stood by Dalton, quietly observing but with a proud smile on his face.

Together they watched the riders fly around the track. Jerrett smiled as Gwennie held her hands up to her mouth, her eyes glued on their son. He knew she couldn't relax until the race ended and Troy had safely finished. He took her hand away from her face, kissed it, and held on to it. She spared him a glance and a little smile before turning her head back to the track.

They watched as the riders swapped places, passing each other over and over, angling for the lead. Troy was in the front, pushing it for all he was worth, when suddenly he and another rider got tangled up and both went down.

Gwennie gasped, "Troy!" and started towards the stairs on the platform.

Jerrett grabbed her arm to stop her. "Wait! They're getting up." She stopped and watched, her body tense and her face anxious. They spied their good friend, Matt Kepler, who'd been flagging out on the track, lift Troy's bike off him. Troy scrambled up. They watched as Matt talked to Troy while kicking over the engine for him. Luckily, it started on the first try; Troy hopped on and took off like a shot.

"See? He must be fine or Matt wouldn't have let him continue," Jerrett assured his wife. Gwennie looked doubtful, but there wasn't anything she could do. Riders fell over all the time; they'd both learned to restrain themselves from running out on the track.

Gwennie sighed, "Oh, Jerrett, I'll never get used to that! My heart's pounding."

Jerrett chuckled and squeezed her, but his eyes never left Troy. Already the boy had gained back a position. "Look at him go! He's fine."

Troy finished the race in third place and the family headed back to their pits to meet up with him.

They reached the camper just after Troy. He was still sitting astride his dirt bike, waiting for Jerrett to lift it onto its stand. He had his helmet off and his face lit up with a huge smile.

"You did so good!" Gwennie gushed, kissing his face. "Are you OK?"

"Yeah."

Troy hopped off the bike and Jerrett swung it onto the stand. After high fives and congratulations, Dalton and Trevor left to hang out with the other teenagers and the rest of the family made their way into the camper.

Their camper wasn't really a camper; it was an old delivery truck that they'd customized. The truck came with a built-in heater and air conditioner, but the rest had been built by Jerrett and Trevor. Trevor was a skilled carpenter and was a willing helper in customizing the truck.

There were built-in bunks, a table, and benches that converted into a bed, cupboards, and a counter. A small microwave was nestled into the space above the table. A portable camping toilet was tucked in the back corner with a curtain around it.

It was a tight fit, but it worked. The family had shelter and a few comforts of home, but it was nothing like the fancy RVs that many other racers had.

"Are you hurt at all, Troy?"

Troy grinned at his mom, "Nah, I'm OK. Just a scrape." Gwennie pushed up his sleeve and examined the injury.

"Hmm, not too bad. Let me patch it up." Gwennie went in search of the first aid kit.

Jerrett fished out a bottle of water from one of the coolers along the wall by the table. Passing it to his son, he smiled at him and nodded his approval. "You did great out there, kiddo. Don't worry about what place you finished in. What really matters is that you didn't give up."

Troy beamed back at him, basking in his dad's approval and nodding with obvious pride.

Luke Bradford, a close friend, popped his head in the door and drawled, "How's the kid?"

"He's OK, Luke," Gwennie called out, flashing Luke a smile.

"That's good, beautiful." He winked at Gwennie.

Gwennie laughed naturally, "You big flirt!" She teased back, "What would your wife say?"

"She wouldn't mind! Neither does Jerrett."

"Hey, husband right here," Jerrett pointed to himself, "Least you guys could do is flirt behind my back!" Luke and Gwennie cracked up laughing and with a wave, Luke headed off down the pit lane.

Within minutes Troy had been patched up and was bouncing out the door with a gang of friends.

Gwennie watched them leave, sighing. Jerrett knew she was still reeling after the crash. It was hard to see your child get hurt. He took her by the shoulders and turned her to him, "He's OK, hon."

She smiled and nodded, melting into his arms. For just a moment, Jerrett forgot all about Mitch and the altercation at the gate. He sunk into Gwennie's arms, relishing the feeling of contentment and peace. It was an altogether rare feeling lately.

CHAPTER 2

Around the Campfire

As darkness fell, Jerrett, Gwennie, and Dean made their way over to the campsites of their friends, the Bradfords and Keplers. Tradition dictated that they gather with their friends each night after the races were over. The adults would congregate by the campfire, while the kids wandered in and out of the area in little gangs.

Crossing through the shadowy darkness, they entered their friends' pit area. A warm glow from the campfire cast a welcoming light in the darkness. Adults lounged all around the fire on folding chairs and the kids and dogs roamed among them. Tools and riding gear were scattered among the dirt bikes propped on their stands. The sound of chatter and laughter filled the air.

"Owen, pick up your stuff and put it where it belongs!" Matt Kepler called to his oldest son, while waving a spatula at the pile of riding gear on the ground. Turning back to his task, Matt lifted the lid of the grill and the savory aroma of juicy burgers filled the air. Sixteen-year-old Owen meandered over and began collecting his things. Jerrett spotted his son, Dalton, following along to help. The teen gave his parents and Uncle Dean a wave when he spotted them. His teenage uncle, Trevor, hovered nearby.

One of the kids yelled and as Matt turned to respond, he spotted the Nolans. "Hey, there you are!" He waved his spatula at them. "Just in time for dinner. You want a burger?"

Matt and his wife, Laura, along with their five children, were regular fixtures at the races. Several of their kids raced. The Kepler RV was always filled with the Kepler children and their friends. If you couldn't find your kid, they were usually at the 'Kepler Orphanage', as it had been dubbed. Laura and Matt's RV was brand new, as were their bike and gear. Laura often wandered the track in designer clothes. However, neither they nor their kids ever flaunted their money and they remained the kindest, most generous family at the track.

Luke and Jennica Bradford always pitted next to them, with the two RVs forming a compound of sorts.

Luke and Jennica's RV looked a bit different though. They had a bright red rug under their awning and colored lights strung from the top. A beaded curtain was stretched across the doorway. Inside, incense was always burning and crystals sparkled from where they hung by the kitchen window. Jennica wore her curly black hair hanging loose down her back. She favored ankle-length dresses in bright, lively colors that set off her dark skin perfectly. Luke usually could be found in torn flannel and jeans.

Their four children were each given 'earthy' names. The twins were Terra and Thalassa, which meant earth and sea, respectively. The oldest boy was Woody Oakes and was a good friend of Dalton's. At 14, he resembled a tree, with gangly limbs jutting out at every angle ready to trip someone up, but he was reliable and helpful. Marlowe, a friend of little Cami, was the youngest. He loved explaining that his name meant 'a hill by a lake' to anyone who would listen.

The two families, along with the Nolans, had formed a tight group. They frequented all the same races and looked out for one another.

Jerrett's gaze was pulled away from the campsite as a group of screaming, laughing kids tore past playing some kind of chasing game. Marlowe stopped to pet his dog as he passed. Cami ran by and stuck her tongue out at Marlowe as she wagged her fingers in her ears. Gwennie laughed at the sight and shook her head.

It was wonderful that they could all be together like this. The curfew that applied to them at home didn't matter at the track. As long as the kids stayed on the track's property, they were allowed to roam at will, though it had been drilled into them to never leave the grounds. The Elite Guards who were stationed at the track guarded the gates.

At home, you were not allowed to leave your property after 9 pm. The only exceptions to the curfew were for those traveling at night, but they needed to get permission from their local Elite Guard Unit and their travel papers would be examined at checkpoints. Years ago, motocross families would leave after a race, but the distance they sometimes traveled to race made it too far to get home before the curfew. Many found it easier to just camp for another day and leave the morning after the races. So it became a time to relax with their friends.

Cami wandered over and climbed into her daddy's lap. Jerrett adjusted his position to accommodate her, loving that she still was little enough to cuddle up with him.

Around 11 pm, the rest of the younger kids were corralled and sent off to bed. Gwennie took Troy to settle him in; Jasper would keep him company until the rest of them went to bed. Cami had fallen asleep in Jerrett's arms, so he motioned for Gwennie to leave her where she was. Cami was a warm and comforting weight on his lap. As Jerrett looked at her, he felt an overwhelming sense of love for his littlest one. He shifted his arm into a more comfortable position and settled in. He was in no hurry to end this moment by carrying her to bed. Jerrett smiled and kissed her head, glad she hadn't outgrown this.

The teens wandered in, looking for food and debating who had the best race that day. They stacked their plates high and drifted off again, the friendly argument continuing.

Jerrett looked at Luke and rolled his eyes at the kids' arguments. Luke chuckled, Dean and Matt, joining in. It felt good. Jerrett treasured these few moments of normalcy in a world that was anything but normal.

They needed these moments to uplift them, considering the web of laws and restrictions that suffocated them daily.

The conversation shifted then, as Luke relayed a rumor he'd heard about some mysterious camps that the government had built, surrounded by barbed wire fences. Supposedly they were reeducation camps and were being filled with political dissidents. Someone even said that children had been sent there – to brainwash them. It had piqued the interest of the others and they began debating the truth of the story.

It filled Jerrett with a sense of unease. The spirit of laughter from moments before vanished like the wind. He tightened his hold on Cami as if to protect her.

Jerrett let his mind drift back. "Remember, before the bombings, how different things were?"

Jerrett felt the others staring. It wasn't something that was often talked about. He went on. "There were always rumors of the government doing shady things and conspiracies, but, well you know, nobody believed them."

Dean joined in, "I remember. We didn't need travel permissions. Could come and go as we pleased." His voice took on an edge, the frustration evident.

"No curfew, no unwarranted arrests," Laura added.

Gwennie returned to the firelight just in time to add, "Yeah, but that was all before the April Bombings."

The April Bombings. Jerrett's mind flashed back to that terrifying time.

On Day One, seven major U.S. cities had been attacked. Bombs went off at intervals, several in each city. On Day Two, another four cities were hit. By Day Three, the entire country was looking over their shoulders, wondering who would be next. The terror of those days was still fresh in Jerrett's mind. By Day Four, most people were hiding in their homes, glued to the news and checking on loved ones. By the end of the week, Americans were clamoring for something to be done. They were practically begging for martial law and when it was put in place, they were all relieved – for a short time anyway. Once the bombs stopped exploding on every corner and reason returned, the Americans realized what they'd given away.

But the freedoms were gone, and there was little chance of them being restored. Life in America changed overnight in the days after the April Bombings.

"Do you think they will ever lift martial law?" Dean asked.

Matt shrugged his shoulders before answering, "I doubt it or they would have done it before now. The powers that be won't give up control that easily."

Jerrett felt heavy; weighted down. He gently twisted a finger in Cami's hair. He remembered when the president had called up the National Guard to quell the violence and then neglected to rescind the order. Then he created a new organization – the Elite Guards, who answered directly to him.

"Remember how happy we were when the Elite Guards were first formed?" Gwennie reminisced.

"Oh my gosh! Were we? I guess we were – right in the beginning." Jennica puffed out her lips and shook her head in disbelief as she twisted a crystal on her necklace.

"Not anymore."

"Do you think there's any truth to the rumors that the Guards are all ex-prisoners?"

Luke answered, loving a good conspiracy theory, "That's what I heard. They only picked the most brutal ones. Then they brainwashed them, so they'd be under the government's control."

Jerrett shrugged and shook his head. Luke's ideas were often farfetched, but how could they really know what was happening? No one told the truth on the news nowadays.

"Who knows?" Matt answered, "The Guards are a cold-hearted and merciless bunch, that's for sure."

Jerrett remembered how regulations had gradually increased, slowly – so as not to alarm the people. A temporary curfew was implemented, welcomed by people in hopes that it would keep the troublemakers in control. But the curfew stayed, becoming permanent. Then checkpoints appeared on the highways, random searches began, small surveillance drones were used in the cities, and you learned to watch what you said and who you met with.

"I'm so glad we can still sit and talk with people we trust," Gwennie said. "Whenever I meet a stranger now, I have to wonder what side they're on. Are they spying for the Guards?" She shrugged, "You just don't know who to trust."

Heads nodded in agreement all around the campfire. They all felt the tightening of their social circle. No one was eager to let anyone new in.

It amazed Jerrett how quickly people went from rejoicing at the inception of the Elite Guards to living in absolute fear of them. Everyone knew of someone who had been arrested or had simply disappeared. Judges, lawyers, and trials became a thing of the past.

Nowadays it was guilty till proven innocent.

Jerrett missed the old days. It had only been a few years since the restrictions had been put upon them, but it felt like a lifetime.

Jerrett sighed and scrubbed at his head with his free hand. He couldn't allow his mind to drift back anymore; it was just too painful.

Melancholy gripped him this evening, though, and he had trouble keeping it at bay.

He looked at the others sitting around the campfire. Matt, Luke, Laura, Jennica, Gwennie, Dean, Cami. Would one of them disappear one day? He wanted to weep at the thought.

Blinking furiously, he forced himself back to the conversation at hand.

They were talking about the man who'd been taken by the Guards today. Laura was in the middle of the tale when Jerrett interrupted.

"I saw that."

"You saw what?" Laura wondered.

"I saw it happen. I was right there when they took him." Jerrett explained. "I don't know what started it, but they hauled him away right then and there. They wouldn't even let him say goodbye to his wife." In his mind's eye, he replayed the memory of the father being hauled away and the old man pushed to the ground. The seething rage and shame built up inside him like a living force. Why hadn't he done something? He'd just stood there, letting it happen. Disgusted with himself, he suddenly found it intolerable to sit still and chat any longer. Cami was the perfect excuse. She was a dead weight as he moved her to his shoulder and pushed up off the chair.

"I'm going to put her to bed."

"Jerrett?" he heard Gwennie question. He waved her off and continued on. He could sense everyone staring at his back and could hear their murmurs, but he didn't care. Turmoil rolled through his gut, memories plaguing him. He hated himself at this moment, hated what he'd become: a scared, timid shadow of his former self. He tightened his grip on Cami and felt her comforting warmth against him. What kind of father was he? What kind of person? It used to all be so clear. The old Jerrett would have stood up for what was right; he would've defended those weaker than himself. Right and wrong were clear to him and he hadn't been afraid to act on it.

But not now. Everything had changed.

CHAPTER 3

The Shop

Jerrett's shop was a roomy two-bay garage with a large showroom attached. On the outside, the freshly painted building looked crisp and clean. A black stripe ran through the middle of the wall, with gray paint on the bottom and white on the top. The name JN Cycles was emblazoned in stark black letters. A pile of used, forlorn tires was stacked like a sentry beside the garage door. A couple of trashcans, one knocked over, sat beside the tires. Paper trash had spilled out of the toppled one and was floating across the parking lot in lazy swirls. Inside the shop, shelves were displayed neatly and were well stocked with oils, cleaners, and other supplies.

Jerrett finished stacking bottles of coolant on the shelf. He straightened up and dusted off his hands, made his way around a quad for sale, and headed towards the counter. He moseyed along behind it, pausing to flip through one of the giant books on top of the counter and scribbling down a part number. Digging through the heaps of paperwork cluttering his desk, he found the customer's number and called them to relay what was needed. Next on his to-do list was to give the showroom a good sweeping. It hadn't been done for ages and the dust bunnies were threatening mutiny.

The showroom was a bright, airy space; it had been remodeled only a few years before. Racks of hoodies, riding jackets, and motocross gear filled the space. Shelves full of shiny, colorful helmets lined the wall near the outer door. T-shirts were neatly folded and stacked below them.

Jerrett dragged the broom under them, disturbing the dust bunny colonies.

Leaning on his broom, he looked around the space at all the special touches his family and friends had helped add to the room. He remembered when Dean's ex-girlfriend had painted the edges of the full-length mirror with flames and added wall art here and there. Above the showroom counter, which was covered in diamond sheeting, Trevor had hung a pair of crutches, lights fastened across them, a tongue-in-cheek symbol of all the times they'd been used after motorcycle crashes. Matt and Luke had created lights from motorcycle handlebars, which were hung across the ceiling. Even Gwennie and the kids had helped by painting the walls and ceiling. Wherever he looked, he fondly remembered how everyone had contributed to this special place. It was his second home.

Feeling contented, he finished up the sweeping and put the broom away.

Out in the garage area, his mechanic, Barry Forrester, was keeping busy, with several new jobs that had come in after the race this past weekend. That was one nice little after-effect of the races – people broke things, which kept the work flowing in.

Jerrett joined Barry and the two were soon engrossed in their jobs.

Barry had worked for Jerrett for several years now. He was in his early fifties, powerfully built, with a long, gray ponytail hanging down his back. Dressed mostly in Harley shirts, jeans, and boots, he could chase off a threat with a look, but if you were accepted into his "family' he protected you just like a mother bear with a cub. It was comforting to have Barry at your back.

Today Barry was busy changing out a tire on a race bike while jamming to an 80s rock band.

Jerrett struggled nearby, with the carburetor from an '86 Yamaha Virago. He'd been at it for an hour already and it just wasn't cooperating. He slammed down his screwdriver onto the metal bike lift in frustration, running a hand through his hair and turning away.

"I need a break," Jerrett announced to Barry. "Maybe I'll do something relaxing … like paperwork, for a while."

Barry picked up on Jerrett's sarcasm, "'Bout time you did some real work anyhow."

Jerrett threw Barry a dirty look, which Barry promptly ignored. Leaning back against the lift, Jerrett asked Barry, "So, how was your weekend? You had Caitlyn, didn't you?" He referred to Barry's twelve-year-old daughter. Barry's girl had a reputation for hating everything Barry loved – motorcycles, the outdoors, mud, hunting, and hanging out in a greasy garage. She was just like her mother and it was still a mystery to Jerrett how Barry had ever gotten together with a woman like that in the first place.

"Yup, had her all weekend. We went to the mall." He made a face like he was in agony. "Oh, and guess what? She wants to move in with me."

"What? Why?"

"What d'you mean 'why'? 'Cause I'm her daddy!" Barry feigned indignation. "It's because of her mom's new boyfriend. Guess they don't get along, so she wants to come live with me full time."

Jerrett had a hard time holding back his laughter, and it burbled out in a barely concealed snicker.

"What's so funny about that?" Barry demanded, shaking a ratchet at Jerrett in a mock vicious gesture.

"I'm just picturing you two watching chick flicks all the time, going to the ballet, and getting your nails done together. Quite an image, really, ya know. ."

"Haha," Barry made a mocking fake laugh at Jerrett while scowling. Even though they joked about it, it was well known that Barry loved his daughter and would do anything for her, though painting his nails was probably over the line.

Hearing a noise, Barry tilted his head to look out the window. "Someone's coming, boss."

Jerrett angled his head to get a view out the window, wondering if it was someone he knew and hoping it was not an Elite Guard. Sometimes they stopped by businesses to check things out. Jerrett had yet to have one visit the shop, but he'd heard stories about how the Guards snooped around, looking for some violation to charge the business owner for.

Jerrett finally caught sight of the man headed his way. It was Mitch Carson, whom he'd seen at the track on Sunday. Maybe he would finally tell him the mysterious secret he'd hinted at. Jerrett rubbed his hands on a rag, heading for the counter to greet Mitch.

Mitch pushed open the door, setting off the jangle of bells that hung overhead and strode up to the counter.

"Hey there, Jerrett. Good to see you again." Mitch stretched out a hand and shook Jerrett's. "How did your boy do on Sunday at the race?" They chatted for a few minutes about the race, but Jerrett could hardly stand the small talk, eager as he was to hear Mitch's secret.

Finally, unable to wait any longer, he asked, "So, Mitch, what's the big secret that brought you here?"

"Well, I've got a Goldwing that needs an engine swap. Is that something you do here?"

Jerrett wrinkled his brow, "Umm, sure, absolutely … but what's so secretive about that?"

Mitch glanced furtively around the shop, lowering his voice and leaning in closer. "Jerrett, I need to tell you something else first, before you say yes to this job." His eyes took another spin around the shop. Satisfied that no one was listening, he continued. "I lead the Eastern Pennsylvania Militia."

Jerrett straightened, pushing back against the counter. This changed things. A lot.

Helping the militia came with an element of danger. The officials didn't like anyone who gave aid to militia members and would trump up charges against them whenever they could. It would seem like common sense for people to shun the militias because of that, but instead, they were joining them in record numbers. The militia represented a way to fight back against the martial law that had been forced upon them.

Noticing that Jerrett had pulled back, Mitch held up his hands, "Now wait, before you say no, I know some businesses have been busted for helping militias out or selling things to us, but it's not illegal to do so, no matter what you may have heard."

"Not yet," Jerrett interjected. "But you guys aren't painted too good in the news. You know they blame you for everything from inciting riots to organizing people in a revolt against the president?"

"You don't believe that, do you?" Mitch rested his hands on his hips. "The news is full of lies. All those media companies are owned by the government, so they only say what they're told to. We are perfectly within our rights to form a militia."

Jerrett rubbed his chin thoughtfully. "I know that, Mitch. And I know it's not illegal for me to take your job, but that doesn't matter to the Elite Guard. They get wind of me helping you out and I stand a good chance of being arrested anyhow. Guilt by association and all that. It's not that I think that's right, by any means, but I can't take the chance of being put in jail."

Mitch's head nodded in agreement. "Yeah, I know." He leaned in secretly, "But didn't you ever just want to rebel a little, to get back at them, even in a small way? By helping me out, you'll be doing just that." Jerrett was surprised to find himself intrigued. It *would* be a way to do something, even if it were a small something.

Mitch went on to tell him about the militia group he was leading. He even mentioned a meeting coming up soon. He went so far as to invite Jerrett to come and check it out.

Jerrett's stomach churned nervously. He flicked a gaze over to Barry, who was still busy working on his motorcycle, the radio blaring rock music in the background. He hadn't heard them talking.

That was good, it meant he couldn't be implicated, Jerrett caught himself reasoning.

Wait, what was he thinking? He couldn't take this job or go to some militia meeting. He'd wind up in jail, like that kid's father at the track.

But ... what if? What if by taking this job, he could finally feel as if he were somehow striking back at the injustices inflicted on them all? He would be playing a very small part in it, but it was a way he could maybe help.

Mitch seemed to sense Jerrett's potential cooperation. "The engine repair is a big job, too. A lot of money to just turn away," he added.

"I'll do it." Jerrett surprised himself by saying. He should be worried now, but he wasn't; instead, he felt a thrill shoot through him. He needed this.

CHAPTER 4

Home, Sweet Home

Jerrett pulled into the driveway at his house, the gravel crunching under his tires. Parking his truck behind Gwennie's SUV, he hopped out and stood for a moment, leaning on the door. Gazing at the house in front of him filled him with a feeling of safety, familiarity, and warmth. The soft glow of the kitchen lights shone through the windows, creating a homey, comforting presence. The smell of honeysuckle and hyacinth wafted on the air.

The building was a rustic, rambling farmhouse, its white siding going gray with age and the paint on its wooden window frames peeling up in strips. A wraparound porch meandered across two sides, like a set of arms cradling the house in a hug. Muddy shoes, Cami's hula hoop, and some dart guns littered the worn, wooden floor of the porch.

Climbing out and closing the truck door, Jerrett looked out over the yard. It was a little overgrown; Dalton hadn't mowed it last week. Jerrett made a mental note to remind him. The black rubber tire swing hung empty and forlorn from the giant, towering oak tree. Troy's bright green hoody lay forgotten under it, streaked with mud stains. Jerrett absentmindedly picked it up, along with a mangled one-legged Barbie that Jasper must have stolen.

Beams of light, from the windows, tickled the lawn like fingers, reaching across the grass. Pulled like a moth to a flame, he followed the light up to the porch and through the door to the kitchen.

Jerrett was greeted by the sight of Gwennie, dressed in her scrubs and leaning over an open textbook with Troy. Cami hovered nearby, toting a giant teddy bear. Gwennie looked up as Jerrett entered and flashed him a warm smile while tucking a loose strand of hair behind an ear. "Hi, honey."

"Hi," Jerrett replied. He made his way around the kitchen counter and planted a quick kiss on her lips, while Jasper danced around his heels, tail wagging frantically.

"Hi, daddy," Cami squealed, reaching up to him for a hug.

"Hi, baby," he said as he hugged her. She was wearing a hot pink tutu and black biker boots. Her hair was falling out of its updo and hung in tangled strands all around her face.

Jerrett moved over to Troy and kissed the top of his head, "Hey, bud."

Troy spared him a glance and a quick "Hi" before going back to what he was doing.

Jerrett glanced around the kitchen, its yellow walls as warm and soothing as honey on a sore throat. They had repainted the kitchen just the year before. Dishes, recently dirtied, were stacked haphazardly in the sink, awaiting attention. Scattered across the island in the middle of the room were school books, papers, pencils, and markers. Two lunchboxes and a mismatched pile of Tupperware containers lay on the far counter. Gwennie had been interrupted while packing tomorrow's lunches.

Jasper was in the corner now, ignoring everybody as he noisily crunched and slobbered over his dog dish, spilling bits of kibble out of his mouth and across the floor.

"How is everybody?" Jerrett asked.

Gwennie looked up from the books, "We're fine, but Trevor isn't feeling well. Maybe you want to check on him."

"Trev? What's wrong with him?" he asked, concerned about his younger brother, who lived in the mini apartment over Jerrett and Gwennie's garage.

"It's not too serious, just a fever, but I haven't been able to get away and check on him in a while." Jerrett nodded, grabbed an apple, and headed back out.

As he followed the path leading out to the garage, he quickened his pace. He wasn't really worried but needed to see for himself that Trevor was fine.

He hurried up the stairs and gave a soft knock on the door as he pushed it open. He glanced around the main living area. A tattered sofa and chair sat in front of an old TV. Posters covered the walls, and coats, books, and video games littered the floor. The kitchenette was tiny and dirty dishes crowded the single-basin sink next to the unused stove. Jerrett swiveled his head around, and seeing no one, he turned toward the bedroom.

"Trevor? Trev?" He called.

"I'm in here."

Jerrett followed the voice into the tiny bedroom. Trevor lay on the small single bed that took up most of the space. Dirty clothes were strewn throughout the room: on the floor, hanging on the bedposts, and cast on top of the dresser. More clothes spilled out of open drawers. Empty hangers hung on pegs that were driven into the walls.

Jerrett ran a hand over the hangers, rattling them together. "You know these work better with clothes on them, right?" A smirk danced across his face.

Trevor returned the grin, pulling himself up on an elbow. "Yes, *dad*." His voice dripped with sarcasm. It was refreshing to hear the humor in his voice. He couldn't be feeling too bad if he was cracking jokes.

"Don't call me that."

Trevor quirked up a corner of his mouth. "Did you come up here for something specific or just to give me cleaning tips?"

"As much as I think you could use them, no, I did not come to give cleaning tips." Jerrett paused, sitting on the edge of the bed. "Gwennie said you were sick. Running a fever. I came to see how you were."

Trevor's thin face was pale and sweaty. His dark blond hair hung damp and limp. Jerrett fought the urge to push back his hair and feel how hot he was.

"I'm fine."

"Heard that one before." Jerrett quipped. Trevor always said he was fine when he was hurt or sick. He never wanted to trouble anyone.

When he'd brought Trevor here to live, after he'd had that awful fight with their dad, Trevor had insisted he was fine, even though it took eight stitches to close the gap in his head.

Jerrett remembered that night, how he'd sped to his father's house after Trevor had called him for help. On the phone, Jerrett could hear their dad shouting in the background, and Trevor's voice, laced with pain. Afraid he'd been hurt, Jerrett had raced across town, worried sick.

Upon reaching his dad and stepmom's house, Jerrett raced up the steps two at a time, to the sound of screaming and crying. Flinging open the door, he entered a scene of chaos.

His dad, face red with anger, one hand twisting Trevor's shirt and the other an upraised fist, frozen in midair as he looked at Jerrett in the doorway.

Trevor was lying on the floor, bleeding profusely, and begging him to stop.

Cowering in the corner, Trevor's mom, Michelle, was crying hysterically but made no move to intervene.

"What're *you* doing here?" His father growled at him, hair wild and spittle flying from his lips.

Jerrett had then hurled himself across the room and punched his dad in the face, dropping him to the ground. Throwing a disgusted glance at Michelle, he'd pulled Trevor up and hauled him out of there.

Trevor had been living over their garage ever since.

In the five months since the fight, Trevor's mom had only called a handful of times to check on her son. They hadn't heard from their dad at all. Cutting off contact that way had left Trevor floundering, sad, and unsure. The boy had gone through a period of guilt, wondering if he'd done something wrong, but Dean, Gwennie, and Jerrett refused to let him accept that burden. Instead, they had rallied around him, protecting and guiding him ever since.

And taking care of him, like they were now.

Jerrett cast a critical eye on his sick brother. "Sure you're 'fine'," Jerrett commented smugly, "That's why you didn't go to work today, huh? How high's the fever?"

"Not bad. Just need to rest, ya know?"

Unable to resist any longer, Jerrett dropped a hand to Trevor's forehead. With an exaggerated groan, Trevor shrugged him off.

"Yeah, it's not too high," Jerrett conceded.

"Told ya."

"OK, smarty, you were right. You need anything?"

Trevor jerked a thumb towards the nightstand where a tray sat, loaded with medicines, a glass of water, and an empty soup bowl.

"Ah, so Gwennie the nursemaid has already been through," Jerrett quipped.

"Yes, so you see, I really am fine," Trevor smirked at him. "Quit your worrying."

Jerrett smiled warmly at the boy. He loved to hear the fire in Trevor's voice. In the past, the kid had hardly said a word, especially if strangers were around. But lately, he'd been much more open. It comforted Jerrett, knowing that Trevor was adjusting so well.

But quit worrying about him? Never.

● ● ●

Later that night, Jerrett and Gwennie lay cuddled up together in the privacy of their bedroom. Gwennie was enjoying the moment, relishing the feeling of Jerrett's arms around her, making her feel warm and safe. Too often their busy lives made them feel like they were like two ships passing through the night. Throughout the years, they'd come to cherish the moments when it was just the two of them.

After all these years, though, she knew when something was on his mind that he didn't want to share with her.

"What's bothering you?" She held up her hand at the inevitable protest. "Don't tell me 'nothing'. I can tell something is. Just spill it." She waited him out, staring at him until he looked away.

"I never could get anything by you, could I?" He straightened up, leaning against the pillows. She rested on her elbow beside him and listened as he told her about Mitch coming to the shop with a job, the militia ties Mitch had, and the meeting he'd been invited to.

Gwennie listened with growing trepidation. She could hear in his voice how much he wanted to be a part of the militia, even if he didn't realize it himself yet. Her thoughts flew in a thousand different directions. It was dangerous, they both knew that, but she knew her husband desired to do something, that he yearned to make things different.

Over time, she'd buried that knowledge and the accompanying fear. There was nothing he could do, no way to get involved in something revolutionary. But now? Now there was a way right in front of him and it could get him in a lot of trouble.

A shiver ran down her spine.

If he were to get involved, it could endanger them all. What if his brothers were to follow him and join up too? Or he got arrested? The children needed him … and so did she. What would she ever do without him? She couldn't bear to be alone. Her need for him was so great it was almost despicable. The thought of losing him was unbearable.

"Gwennie, what are you thinking?"

Gwennie felt a lump rising in her throat, rendering her unable to speak. Fear coursed its way through her system. Tears fled the corners of her eyes.

Jerrett turned to look at her, noticing the tears. "Gwennie, why are you crying? Come on, nothing's happened yet. I'm just thinking about it."

"Jerrett, the government is afraid of the militia, and they'll arrest anyone who is helping them. You know what happens when they arrest people, don't you? Julie, that girl I work with? Her neighbor, Kyle, was taken and they didn't let him go for eight months. Eight months! And his family got no word about where he was or how he was the whole time." She paused, choking back tears. "When he came back, he was so broken up; you know – in his head, not just his body. He was never the same after that." She sat up, her face pleading with his. "Don't you see that the same thing could happen to you? You could be taken away, tortured, and hurt! Jerrett, I can't bear the thought! How can you risk that happening?" The words tumbled out of her, without conscious thought. "We can't lose you, Jerrett! What would that do to all of us? You're what holds us all together." Gwennie felt all control slipping away, the tears pouring down her cheeks in earnest now. Her Jerrett, beaten and tortured! She could hardly bear the thought. Her overactive imagination conjured up the image of him curled in a ball, in a cell, bloodied and wounded, hungry and shivering.

"Gwennie, Gwennie!" Jerrett squatted on the bed in front of her and grabbed her arms, giving her a little shake. "Nothing is going to happen to me. I just want to go to the meeting, that's all. Get some information, some actual news. That's all, Gwennie. They won't arrest me. I don't know any secrets or anything. I'm just a guy at a meeting. Gwennie, I'll be careful. Nothing will happen."

"I couldn't stand losing you, Jerrett. I … I don't want to be … alone." Gwennie ducked her head in shame for thinking of herself. What a horrible person I am, she thought, to worry about being alone, when Jerrett could be arrested or hurt!

"Oh, Gwennie girl." He hugged her tightly, compassion in his voice. Pulling back, he reached out to brush the wetness away from her cheeks. "I won't leave you. I'll always be here for you." And he hugged her again. "You aren't getting rid of me that easy."

"Just promise me you'll be careful."

He smoothed her hair, "I promise. OK?" His reasoning and calm voice comforted her, and she chided herself for overreacting.

Though it was childish to cling to a promise they both knew he had no control over, she held onto it anyway. She nestled in his arms, holding tight to him, relishing the feeling of him there with her, breathing in his smell, hearing him murmur to her.

It would be alright, she told herself, he'd promised her.

CHAPTER 5

The Militia Meeting

Jerrett and Dean drove down the road towards Mitch's house. Never one to hide much from his brother, Jerrett had told Dean about the meeting, and of course, Dean had insisted on going along. He was curious as well as protective toward his big brother.

They parked Dean's Jeep Wrangler outside Mitch's house. It was a white rancher with blue shutters, which sat on the cul-de-sac of a housing development. Trees had grown thick around the house, shielding the building; party balloons were tied to the branches.

Jerrett hesitated a moment, battling his indecision. He may have convinced Gwennie that there was no danger, but he didn't really know. The Elite Guards could burst in here at any moment, hauling them away on some trumped-up charge. However, since the meeting was under the guise of a birthday party for Mitch's wife, it was highly unlikely.

Dean seemed to understand Jerrett's hesitation. He clapped a hand on his brother's back. "Come on, let's do this."

A grin ghosted over Jerrett's face as he flicked his gaze at Dean. He nodded his assent and the two made their way up the driveway.

They were met at the door by a woman with plain brown hair, cut into a blunt bob, bangs just above her eyebrows. She wore a lavender sweater set and sensible shoes, which made her look older than she actually was.

She smiled warmly, "Hello, I'm Caroline Carson, Mitch's wife." She announced, softly, meekly, while holding out her hand. Jerrett shook it while introducing himself and Dean. The handshake was limp, like shaking a dead fish. She led them into the house, through the hallway, and into the living room. It was tastefully decorated with everything in its proper place. Neat and tidy. Just like Caroline.

In the living room was a cluster of people, some sitting, some standing, and everyone sipping lemonade or coffee. Mitch stood by the fireplace mantle, a crowd gathered around him, with some heated discussion going on.

"OK, OK! Enough for now. Let's table this for a while and come back to it. It's time to get this meeting going," Mitch announced as a way of stopping the argument. He spotted Jerrett and Dean standing in the doorway and gave them a nod of his head. Jerrett felt a gentle nudge on his back and turned to see Caroline behind him, prompting them to move forward and join the group. She smiled demurely and then turned and left the room without another word.

"Alright, let's get this meeting going. We'll start by reading our mission statement." The group fell silent as Mitch pulled out a booklet and flipped it open. "This is a meeting of the PA Patriotic Militia. PPM for short. We believe in freedom, not tyranny. We believe in the Constitution and the Bill of Rights and all they stand for. We are law-abiding citizens. Our purpose is to train, educate and prepare for any emergency. We will defend our land against any adversary, foreign or domestic. We will promote the right to bear arms. We will act with the highest standards and honor. No one will be refused membership on the basis of color, race, or beliefs."

Mitch lowered the booklet and looked up. "Well, we still believe that, but we may have to do something more to preserve our mission. Training and educating may not be enough anymore. It may be time for action."

"Yeah, man, my neighbor got arrested last night for coming home after curfew when his car broke down," said a young, muscular black man. "What are we going to do about that?"

"What do mean, Ely? What *can* we do about that? You want us to get involved somehow?" The man who spoke was middle-aged, balding, and wearing a button-down shirt. Jerrett thought he looked like a banker or something. The balding man waved an arm around angrily. "That's none of our business. We can't do anything without getting ourselves arrested!"

Another man stepped forward from Ely's side, presumably a friend of his. His arms were covered in tattoo sleeves and his blond hair fell to his shoulders. "So, we just let stuff like that go, Andy? What if they come for you or your kid next? Huh? Don't you want someone sticking up for you?"

Jerrett was mesmerized by the discussion, so much so that he jumped when Caroline appeared beside him again, in her quiet way. She held out a glass of lemonade which Jerrett gratefully accepted. Glancing at Dean, he saw he already had a glass. Caroline was about to leave when Jerrett seized the opportunity to gain some information.

He dropped his voice to a stage whisper. "Hey, Caroline, who is that big guy? And the one he's arguing with?" He pointed to the black man and the banker.

Caroline nodded towards the black man first. "Oh, that's Ely Monroe. He used to be a Marine. I think he's getting tired of all the talk and wants to fight back somehow." She shrugged as if she couldn't perceive how that would be accomplished. "The one arguing with him is Andy Howland. He's very conservative, won't even meet on Sundays because of church." She gave another little shrug.

"How about Mr. Tattoo?" Jerrett whispered.

"That's a friend of Ely's. He just started coming a couple of months ago. His name's Jude Kinsey."

As they watched, Ely and Jude continued to argue with Andy Howland, who was joined by another man whom Caroline identified as Alonzo Ramirez.

The two sides couldn't be further apart on what to do about the current situation.

"We have to fight back! Now!" Ely raged, "We've already waited too long. The government is taking more and more of our rights away and we stand here doing nothing. We should have stood up when they started the curfew, but no, we let that one slide by. And when they made all the travel restrictions and checkpoints, we could have protested, but we didn't. And then the spy drones? Now they're arresting people for no reason and holding them as long as they want. We can't let this go on." Ely was fired up now, pacing the room and ranting loudly. "How bad are things going to get before we do something? Huh, Ramirez? Are you gonna still be law-abiding when they take your father because he goes out at night? Or your wife because she buys a book that's blacklisted?"

Alonzo Ramirez spoke up. "The blacklist is a rumor, Ely. No one can prove they're making one. Let's stick to the facts here, not speculations." Alonzo had stepped up toe to toe with Ely, even though he was several inches shorter. He stood with Andy Howland, the conservative churchgoer, and continued, "Look, we've always been a law-abiding group. If we change that now, then we are giving the government a perfect excuse to silence us. If we work within the system, then maybe we can make some changes. Once you step outside the system, there's no turning back. You'll be branded a criminal. Maybe even treasonous. What can you possibly do from inside a jail cell?"

Ely and Jude argued back that it was time to fight, time to make a stand. They were tired of the Guards pushing them around and the authorities taking more and more of their rights away.

Jerrett and Dean just stood, gaping at the turmoil in the room and unsure what to make of it. Others in the room added comments here and there to the argument, but none were as vehement about their positions as Andy and Alonzo versus Ely and Jude. Mitch was trying desperately to keep things civil as they threatened to spiral out of control.

It was then that the front door suddenly slammed open with a crash. The arguing ceased immediately as they all fell silent, frozen in place.

Had the Guards somehow found out about the meeting?

Fear gripped Jerrett. His heart pounded in his chest. He could feel Dean tense beside him, ready to spring into action. He dropped a hand on his brother's arm to still him.

Seconds later, a young woman strutted into the room. The crowd reacted with sighs of relief and the tension instantly drained away.

"Evie! What the hell are you doing, storming in here like that? Don't you know how bad you scared us?" Mitch scolded the late arrival.

The woman was pretty, in a natural, down-to-earth sort of way. She wore little makeup and dressed in a western-style button-down, jeans, and boots. Her long mane of fiery red hair flowed halfway down her back in an unkempt mane. Green eyes blazed with passion – that or anger. Jerrett wasn't sure which.

"Yeah, you got something against knocking?" Jude asked, resentment flashing across his face.

"Shut up, Jude." She marched over to Mitch and brushed his cheek with a quick kiss.

"Who… is… that?" Dean whispered, under his breath, to Caroline.

"Our niece, Evania. Evie to most. She's fired up about something. Well, that's pretty normal for Evie, I suppose. She's always been a hothead." Caroline went on to tell a few of her niece's exploits. She was proving to be a valuable source of information. Apparently, Caroline liked to gossip.

Jerrett glanced over at Dean and did a double take. Dean was barely looking at Caroline, his eyes glued to the scene in the middle of the room. His mouth gaped open as he stared at Evie, who had quickly joined the renewed debate.

A wide grin burst out across Jerrett's face. Dean had been somewhat of a recluse the last two years or so, after his girlfriend, Lydia, had dumped him. He'd been ready to propose when she told him it was over and had broken his heart. Jerrett had been there with him to pick up the pieces, staying with him through the rage, the denial, and eventually the breakdown. In the years since then, Jerrett had tried to get him to date again, but to no avail. Seeing him go gaga over this girl was a refreshing sight.

As Caroline finished her story and headed back to the kitchen, Jerrett moved in closer, not being able to resist a bit of needling. He said with a chuckle, "Close your mouth, brother, you're drooling all over the floor."

Dean's mouth snapped shut like a trap and he looked abashedly at Jerrett, having been caught in the act of staring. He returned the grin and sheepishly looked at his feet and then back at Jerrett. "She really is something, though, isn't she?"

Smiling, Jerrett answered, "Yeah, she's something all right."

Their attention was pulled back to the heated discussion in the middle of the room.

"Andy, enough already! You too, Ramirez!" Ely was shouting, jabbing his finger in Andy's chest. "I am sick to death of hearing how we need to be 'law-abiding'! That might have been true before, but everything's different now. Now is the time to revolt! How long are we going to wait? Huh? Until they storm in here and arrest us all? It'll be too late, then. If we wait and they manage to shut down all the militia groups, what hope is there?"

Jude was nodding his assent, as well as several other members who had remained silent during the confrontation.

"That's right! We need to strike against them *now*. And make them hear us!" Evie chimed in, green eyes flashing. "Before it's too late."

Mitch finally stepped up and in a booming voice, called out, "Now hold on everybody. Simmer down a little. We can't get too carried away. Both sides have valid points, but I do think things are changing rapidly around here for the worse. New laws *are* being enacted every day. More and more people *are* being arrested. I hear the blacklist on books is due out next month. But, remember guys, the rally is coming up in a few weeks. Let's not make any decisions until after that. Let's see how things go there. You all know our goal is for a peaceful gathering of like-minded people, with so many of us in attendance that the government can't ignore it. The media will have to cover it if we make it big enough. And if the media covers it, then we can get other militia groups to rally to the cause. It will be a way to send a message to our brothers –" Evie shot him a glare, "– and sisters," he added, putting his hands up in surrender, "that if we all stand together, we can make the government listen to us. But if they won't, then Ely, you may be right. We may need to consider more revolutionary actions."

There were nods of agreement around the room. Most of the group seemed to agree that they needed to do something more. Something to stop this mess.

Jerrett wondered idly where he and Dean fit in. What exactly did they think about all this, and which side were they on? He wasn't sure what he felt, just that he needed time to digest it all. He wondered what the rally was all about and what they hoped to accomplish there.

His attention was drawn back to Mitch, who was still speaking, "Look now. We need to finish up some details tonight for the rally. Let's break into committee groups and work on that, OK?"

The group dispersed, meandering into different rooms, murmurs of conversation drifting along with them. Jerrett turned to Dean, just in time to see him walk away, heading towards the redhead. Jerrett watched as Dean introduced himself, shaking her hand. He was definitely over the moon for that one.

Jerrett spotted Mitch making his way over, looking a bit frazzled and distracted.

"Hey, Jerrett, glad you could make it tonight. So, what'd you think? I know it got a little heated there for a while."

"Yeah, but I can understand why. There's a lot of truth on both sides."

Mitch scratched his chin, "So, which side do you think you stand on?"

Jerrett crossed his arms over his chest, shrugging his shoulders. "You know, I'm really not sure. I need time to think about all this. I can tell you this, though; it's killing me to see what's happening to our country. I want to see things get better, especially for my kids, you know?"

Mitch nodded in agreement, "You're in the right place then. It's the same desire that drives us all. Just takes us in different directions. Back before the martial law and the Elite Guard, we never talked about bucking the system. Well, maybe a little, but overall, it was about preparation for anything Mother Nature could throw at us. Discussions about the government were pretty much just theories, you know? No one thought things would come to this. Now some're talking about striking back, maybe with violence." He rubbed a hand through his buzzed hair as he stood to move on. "I don't know." He shrugged, "Maybe it is time."

Jerrett felt a chill go through him as he watched Mitch circulate through the room. What exactly did he mean? Jerrett didn't like the sound of that, but if he were honest, a part of him agreed. Maybe the time *had* come to strike back. But could he actually go out and hurt somebody? And if he couldn't, would it be right to expect others too? It was hard to think about and yet he was tired of sticking his head in the sand, ignoring what was happening, and doing nothing. Martial law was wrong; arresting innocent people was wrong; denying Americans their freedom was wrong, but what could they do to fix it? It didn't seem to Jerrett like the PPM knew either.

The rest of the evening, Jerrett wandered from group to group, observing and listening to all that was going on.

The rally sounded like it was going to be a huge event. It would be held near Philadelphia, in a park on the outskirts of the city. Many militia groups were invited. Hundreds, even thousands were expected to attend. Speeches and music were planned with some from the local governing bodies agreeing to be present. Many private citizens would be recording the events and posting the videos online.

Mitch reckoned the videos would be taken down by authorities eventually, but if they could get anything out to the rest of the states, it would be progress. Some of their affiliates had boasted of hacking skills that would allow them to post things in a way that would make it very difficult for authorities to stop, at least for a little while. Eventually, the footage of the rally would spread and hopefully ignite the rest of the country.

People were coming from as far away as the West Coast, Mitch bragged. Government officials would have to take note of how upset the citizens had become. Maybe that would be enough to repeal martial law. Jerrett certainly hoped so, but he was afraid of the militant stance of some of the members.

As the evening wore on, the numbers dwindled as members began to leave.

Jerrett went to search out his brother; it was time to head home. He found him on the back patio, sitting on a low stone wall with Evie, the militant redhead, deep in conversation. As much as he hated to break it up, he needed to get going.

He called to his brother, "We've gotta go, dude."

Dean jerked up, startled. "Oh, hi." He gestured towards Evie, "This is Evie. Evie, meet my brother, Jerrett." Evie smiled and gave Jerrett a wave.

"Hi, brother Jerrett."

She was cute; Jerrett had to admit, as he smiled at her. "Sorry to break things up, but we gotta get going. I have to get up early, my wife works the early morning shift and I have to get the kids off to school."

Evie, turning to Dean, offered brightly, "I can take you home. Maybe we can go for a drive or something?"

Dean smiled at her and then turned to Jerrett, "You heard the lady, bro. Here's the keys." He tossed the jeep keys to Jerrett. "See you later."

"Well, have fun, you guys. Nice meeting you, Evie."

"You too, brother Jerrett."

"See you around," Jerrett called.

Out in the driveway, he hopped into Dean's jeep and started for home.

The events of the evening swirled around in his head. He was just as confused as before the meeting. Here was a group that had the potential to make a difference, but could they do it through peaceful means, or would they need to resort to violence to make their point known? Did he want to be a part of that? But could he stand to ignore what was going on any longer?

Nothing was clear, and he didn't know what to do. His thoughts were troubled as he drove home.

CHAPTER 6

Change in the Air

"I can't believe you're even considering this!" Gwennie stormed around the kitchen, fury evident in her actions, as she slammed lunch boxes onto the counter and roughly tossed in the contents. "The Guards will find out about this! You know they will. You'll be arrested! Dean too. Did you ever think of that? Did you? This will not only ruin your life and ours, but your brothers' too! You can't do this!" she shouted at him.

He'd known she was going to be upset when he told her about the rally, but Jerrett hadn't foreseen the intensity.

Their dog Jasper paced around Jerrett's legs. He was unsettled by the loud voices and was panting and whimpering. The kids and Trevor had drifted away from their video games and were lingering in the kitchen doorway, listening intently. Cami looked close to tears.

Jerrett felt his anger rising in him. "You aren't going to tell me what I can or can't do, Gwennie. I *am* going to that rally! And don't tell me about all the things that could go wrong, either! I already know all about it. I'm not stupid. There'll be thousands of people at that rally, they can't arrest us all. I *need* to go. Don't you get that? I can't just sit here with my head buried in the sand anymore."

"You don't even care what I say! You already made your decision, didn't you Jerrett? What am I – just a spectator in this relationship? Doesn't what I think even matter?"

48

"Not when you're being unreasonable it doesn't!"

"Unreasonable!" Gwennie whirled to face him, "That's it! You do what you want. Get arrested for all I care!" Gwennie threw the dish she'd been holding into the sink, so fiercely that it shattered. Without a second glance at the remains, she stormed from the room.

Jerrett was left standing in the middle of the kitchen. He knew he shouldn't let her go, but he didn't have the energy to prolong this debate. Later, he told himself, I'll talk to her more later, once we've had a chance to calm down. His attention was drawn to the kids still glued to the doorway. Trevor looked shell-shocked, no doubt the argument taking him back to the fights he'd had with their dad. His sons just looked on, frozen in the moment. Cami was sniffling, tears welling up in her eyes. It was unbearable to Jerrett to see her so upset, especially when it was his fault.

"Come 'ere, Cami." He held his arms open wide to her and she ran to him. He gathered her up and held her, murmuring, "Shh, it's OK, baby. Mommy and I were just talking, it's OK now." When Cami had calmed somewhat, he turned to the boys.

Dalton pulled away from the doorway where he'd been leaning and approached his dad. "I want to go with you, dad. To the rally."

Jerrett was shaking his head before Dalton even finished talking. "Absolutely not. No way."

"Why not? Why can you go and not me?" Dalton's voice rose, his brows furrowed.

"Because you're a kid. You're too young to get involved."

Dalton's fists clenched, and a red glow quickly spread across his face. He burst out, "That's not fair! I'll be 16 soon! I'm old enough to decide for myself!" He paced the kitchen as he ranted. "How can this be OK for you and not for me? It's my future you're so worried about here. Why don't I get a say in helping make it better? I'm going, and you can't stop me!"

Jerrett shifted Cami to one hip and pointed a finger at Dalton. "You aren't going, and that's final. And shut up about it in front of your mom. I don't need another fight."

"This sucks!" Dalton growled as he stormed past Jerrett and out of the door.

Jerrett stood watching him go, overtaken by a sense of defeat. The energy went out of him like a balloon, leaving him hollow and flat. He sank into the stool and set Cami down. Jasper sank his big head onto Jerrett's lap, whimpering. "Shh, Jasper." He rubbed the dog's ears absentmindedly as he brought his gaze up to Trevor and Troy, who was watching him intently.

Trevor spoke, though hesitantly. "Ya know … he's right. It *is* his future at stake here. Maybe he should have some say in it." He shrugged his shoulders uncertainly.

Jerrett was surprised at Trevor's boldness. "What about you? How do you feel?"

Trevor shrugged again. "I don't know. I don't want to get arrested or in trouble, but I'd like to see what it's all about." Jerrett nodded.

Troy stood by Trevor's side, watching and taking everything in. "You OK, dad?" the ten-year-old asked worriedly.

"Yeah, bud. I'm fine. Don't you worry about all this. It'll get worked out." Wracking his brain for a distraction, he picked the kids' favorite video game, "Let's go play that racing game of yours, OK?"

Troy grinned and nodded; anything involving motocross was right up his alley. Trevor mumbled something about checking on Dalton and slipped quietly out the door.

Sighing, Jerrett escorted the kids to the living room. His anger drained away like water down a pipe, leaving him exhausted and depressed. He hated fighting with Gwennie and wished they'd been able to sort out their differences. And Dalton would be mad at him forever if he couldn't go to the rally. But Jerrett saw no way out of this one. He needed to go, but he absolutely could not take his son. It just wasn't safe enough. There was no way to make everyone happy in this situation and that saddened him even more.

● ● ●

Later that night, as the sun sunk lower on the horizon, two figures cast shadows across the patio behind Jerrett's house.

Jerrett took a long draught of his beer and tilted his metal chair back on two legs. Dean sat across from him, staring him down, but Jerrett turned to avoid his brother's steely green eyes boring into him. He knew Dean had to be wondering why he'd called him to come over.

Dean picked at the label on his beer bottle absently and asked, "So, did you fix Troy's bike?"

"Yeah. Fork seals were out."

"Anything else wrong?"

"Nah, the rest was good. He's ready to rock again." Jerrett answered. "He even came up to the shop to help me do the job. Good little mechanic in the making, that one."

"Yeah, he'll be the one that follows your footsteps. He's the motorhead, that's for sure."

"Remember when dad helped me tear down that old Ninja I had?" Jerrett's mind drifted back to their teen years and the sport bike he'd had. There had been *some* good memories back then, with their dad, though they were few and far between.

"Yeah, I do. You wouldn't let me anywhere near that bike!" Dean chuckled, then added, "Mom nearly had a heart attack when you rode it over to her house for one of our visits."

"I remember. She hated motorcycles, still does. She called dad and railed at him, yelling and screaming at him for letting me get one. It turned into a huge fight," Jerrett reminisced. "Just par for the course with those two."

Their parents, Peter and Teresa, had divorced after years of fighting. Afterward, Jerrett and Dean split their time between two equally dysfunctional households. When they were teenagers they'd gone to live with their dad, and Teresa seemed to forget she had two kids. Their get-togethers became increasingly rare. The fight over the motorcycle had been more about stirring up drama than actual concern for her son.

But that was all ancient history, as Dean liked to say. The two brothers tried not to dwell on their miserable childhood and rarely talked about it.

Jerrett pushed the memories back and focused on more recent events.

"So, Dean, tell me what happened the other night with Evie?" Jerrett pried. When Dean smirked and took a chug of his beer without answering, Jerrett added, "You know, the chick from the militia meeting?"

"I remember her, Jerrett," Dean answered sarcastically. He shrugged non-committally, his smile vanishing. It had ripped Dean up something awful when his girlfriend, Lydia, had said no to his marriage proposal. It haunted him to this day. Jerrett knew it had to be hard for Dean to even think about venturing into a new relationship, but he was hoping the interest his brother had in Evie was a step towards his healing.

"Well, spill! What'd you guys do after I left?"

Dean's mouth quirked up slightly. "We talked, hung out. It was nice." Now a fully-fledged grin spread across his face. "It was *really* nice."

Jerrett laughed at his brother's obvious pleasure. "Do tell, little brother, do tell!"

"You aren't getting any more details than that, you old pervert."

"Old pervert? Me?" Jerrett feigned innocence, hand over his heart. "Are you at least seeing her again?"

Dean spun his beer around, then answered, "Yeah. We're going jogging tomorrow morning and hiking on the weekend."

"Health nut."

"Beer gut." It was their old standby exchange.

Jerrett continued, "I don't have a beer gut."

Dean countered the familiar routine. "You will if you keep drinking like that."

They fell into a companionable silence after that, until Dean finally spoke up and asked, "So, big brother, what did you call me over for anyway? What's on your mind?"

"Can't I just want to hang out with my brother?"

"No. Now spill."

Jerrett sighed and before he knew it, he was telling the whole story of the fight with Gwennie and then with Dalton. "I don't know what to do. But I feel like I've got to do something! It seemed so right to join up with the militia and finally accomplish something. But Gwennie's scared, Dean. Really scared. How can I do this to her?"

Dean was thoughtful, "Well, Gwennie has a point, ya know. I can see why she's freaked." He held his hand up to his brother's protest. "But I can see why this is important to you, too. I don't know what to tell you to do, bro, but I got your back. If you decide to go to the rally, I'll be right there with you, OK? We can check it out together. But if you decide not to, that's OK with me, too."

"And Dalton? The kid's pissed at me for sure, but I can't let him go along. He's too young. And Gwennie'd kill me if I did."

"I agree. You're a dead man if you bring him. Maybe when he's older."

"Yeah."

It felt better to get it all off his chest, but Jerrett was still in a dilemma. Gwennie was scared, Dalton was mad, the kids didn't understand, and he didn't know where Trevor stood on things. There were no easy answers.

CHAPTER 7

True Intentions

Jerrett propped his feet up on the stained surface of the old desk in his office at the shop, as he sorted through work orders. It was a bit of a stretch to call it an office. The ratty desk stood in the corner of a dark, dusty storage room. The walls were lined with metal racks full of parts, engines, and bins of assorted odds and ends. A dented old fridge hummed in the corner, and a cast-off microwave sat on an old toolbox next to it. A giant decorative handlebar pad made of Styrofoam hung crookedly beside a banner advertising Valvoline. It was an eclectic sort of mishmash, but Jerrett liked it. It felt homey.

His thoughts drifted back to the last few days. After he and Gwennie had fought, they'd virtually ignored each other for the next day and a half. Finally, when neither of them could stand it any longer, they'd begun talking again, though the subject of the rally had been avoided.

Last night, Dean and Evie had stopped by on their way to the movies. Gwennie had heard of the blossoming romance and had been badgering Dean to introduce her to Evie. Sipping glasses of wine, the women had hit it off immediately, laughing and sharing stories about Jerrett and Dean, and chatting about work. The kids, especially little Cami, enjoyed the energy and fun Evie brought with her. Cami had found herself a new hero in Evie; the two being much alike in personality – all spunk and fire. Gwennie and Evie had enjoyed each other's company so much that Evie and Dean ended up staying all evening, never making it to the movies.

Gwennie's mood had improved dramatically after meeting Evie. The women had had a lengthy discussion about the militia and the rally as the evening wore on. Something about the intense redhead had reassured Gwen. Maybe it was Evie's 'take-on-anything' personality or her knowledge of the militias that had won her over. Either way, while Gwennie didn't expressly give Jerrett her blessing to attend, she'd become more accepting of the idea.

Jerrett was relieved; he had hated the tension between him and his wife.

Dalton was still mad at him, and as much as Jerrett wanted to straighten that out, there didn't seem to be anything, other than attending the rally, which would assuage the boy's fury. He'd just have to wait it out; once Dalton got his mind on something else, the rally would be old news. He just hoped it would happen soon.

The shop phone rang, its screech bringing Jerrett back into the present.

Friends had been calling the last few days, wanting to share with him about the rally. Though the mainstream news hadn't been covering it, several fringe outfits had.

After Jerrett hung up the phone, he called out to his younger brother. "Hey, Trevor! Come 'ere." Trevor was helping at the shop, making some extra money on the side. Barry was off today since his daughter, Caitlyn, had a dentist appointment.

Trevor appeared in the doorway, his light brown hair tousled and messy, sticking out from under a cap with the shop's name, JN Cycles, on it. "What?"

"Did you change the oil in that Honda 250?"

"Yeah, it's done." Trevor nodded. "You want me to call them to come get it?"

Jerrett looked the work order over. "Yeah, that was the last thing we needed to do to it on it. Go ahead." He passed over the paperwork to Trevor, who took it and scurried off. Jerrett turned back to the pile at hand. If he could just get a half-hour uninterrupted, he should be able to finish.

Barely was the thought out of his head when Dean popped into the office. "Hey, dude, how's it going?"

Jerrett looked up briefly before going back to his paperwork. "What is this? Take your brothers to work day?"

Dean's laugh rang through the room. "Oh, you're a comedian, aren't you? As if I don't stop by here almost every day." He plunked himself on the corner of Jerrett's desk. "What'cha doing?"

"Hang gliding," Jerrett deadpanned, not looking up from the paperwork.

"Haha, Mr. Funny Man." Dean picked up a model dirt bike from the desk and turned it over absently in his hands. "So, you get many more calls about the rally? You had, what, twenty yesterday?"

Jerrett rolled his eyes and took the model from Dean, returning it to its spot. "Five, Dean. Five calls, not twenty. And five is bad enough. I had more today. I thought this rally was more of a secret, ya know?"

Dean nodded in agreement, "Yeah, me too. It seemed that way at the meeting. But I think it's become bigger than they planned, and the word's gotten out. There are a lot of fed-up people out there, wanting to do something to make a change. Trevor's mom had even heard about it. She called to grill him and make sure he wasn't going."

"Really? Michelle actually gave a damn about her kid?" Jerrett referred to their stepmother, who had hardly bothered with her son since Jerrett had taken him in.

Dean nodded in affirmation, shrugging his shoulders.

Trevor suddenly popped his head in the office, calling out, "Hey, Jerrett, that Mitch guy from the militia is here."

Jerrett sat up straighter, concerned. "What's he doing here?"

His brother shrugged his shoulders and turned away indifferently, as a voice called from the showroom. Jerrett heard Trevor telling Mitch to come into the office. Trevor pushed open the office door for Mitch and followed the man into the room.

Mitch wore a camouflage t-shirt, with jeans and boots, his familiar buzzed haircut unchanged. He held his shoulders and back straight, his posture stiff. His close-set, beady eyes watched Trevor warily.

Trevor moved behind Jerrett, who still sat at the desk. Dean roosted on his perch on the corner of the desk.

"Hiya, Mitch," Jerrett called out, rising slightly from his chair to extend a hand to him. Mitch took it and shook it firmly, sparing Jerrett a small smile. He shook Dean's hand as well and then turned a suspicious gaze onto Trevor.

Jerrett followed his stare and then realized Mitch had never met his youngest brother. "Oh, Mitch, this is our other brother, Trevor. He knows about the militia as well."

The brothers watched as Mitch's face relaxed. "Oh, good, that's OK then. Nice to meet you." He extended his hand to Trevor and nodded. Glancing around briefly, he noticed a vacant stool in the corner and pulled it up to the desk, making himself comfortable.

"What's up with the rally, Mitch?" Jerrett asked. "I thought it was pretty hush-hush stuff, but my phone's been ringing off the hook."

A proud grin burst out across Mitch's face. "Word's gotten around! I've been on the phone all day, too. It's going to be huge, Jerrett, huge! This is gonna make the authorities stand up and listen to us, they'll have to end martial law after this." Jerrett quirked an eyebrow at the suggestion and he wondered if it were really possible.

"We'll show 'em! They can't ignore us anymore!" He rubbed his hands together gleefully, like a little boy. "This could be it, the start of something big! Jerrett, it could even be a revolution. I think even the president realizes it." His voice fell into a secretive hush. "A friend of mine in the government sector said they're really nervous about this rally and what it could mean. They'll be sending soldiers and Elites there in droves. We have some of our own media guys coming, too. They've figured out how to link up with some websites around the country and are going to be broadcasting it all over the states. Everyone will be able to see it, even all the way out in California. There won't be any hiding this. Everyone is gonna know!"

Jerrett shifted in his chair, resting his elbows on his desk and his chin on his fists. Mitch's words left him feeling unnerved. "Mitch, this sounds like a bigger deal than I thought it would be. Elite Guards and soldiers are going to be there? What's to stop them from arresting people?"

"Or hurting them?" Dean added. "All those soldiers; one wrong move and they could start firing."

"I'm guessing they will," Mitch stated flatly.

Jerrett looked at Mitch warily, sure he hadn't heard him correctly. "Did you just say you think they will start shooting?"

"It's a strong possibility."

Jerrett stood up abruptly, sending his chair wheeling away. "What're you talking about?" He could feel the anger rising in him. A rally was one thing, but a plan to start something – something violent? That was quite another. "You can't mean that! It wasn't supposed to go like that. It was supposed to be a peaceful protest." He was aware that Dean had risen from his perch as well and could see his brother's fists clenched in rage. Trevor hadn't moved.

"It started out that way, Jerrett, but now…I don't know, things have taken a different turn." Mitch shrugged indifferently. "The Guards have issued threats against anyone who attends the rally; they're gunning for us. If the Guards start shooting, the militia will shoot back. They want us to back down, but we won't. Not this time! They never intended to lift martial law! Unless we make something big happen, they never will." Mitch placed both hands on the desk and leaned in close to Jerrett. "Jerrett, don't you see – this is what our country needs! Our people have got to wake up and face the truth! Nothing will change if we don't take a stand. The people must rise up against them! Don't you see? This is it! This is our chance!"

"You're crazy; it sounds like you want to start a war!" Jerrett shouted.

Mitch nodded grimly. "I do. It's the only way to stop martial law and change things." He lowered his voice ominously. "We need a revolution."

Jerrett leaned his hands on the desk. "People are going to get hurt, Mitch. They're going to this rally, thinking it's a peaceful event, not a catalyst to some war!"

Mitch moved in so that he was only inches away from Jerrett. "Yes, it started out that way, but it's become so much more. If we get others to finally fight back, then it'll all be worth it!"

Jerrett grabbed Mitch, bunching his t-shirt up in his fists. "It's not worth it! Not if people get killed! The ones at this rally, they aren't soldiers, they aren't there to fight! You're just using them! You're planning to kill innocents!"

Mitch pulled away from Jerrett's grip, the anger flaring. "Get your hands off me!" Mitch snarled, spittle flying from his mouth. "The people are choosing to go of their own free will. I'm not making them! What happens, happens! Is it my fault if it can be used for something good?"

Dean, never one for controlling his temper, finally snapped. He moved towards Mitch. "Get out!" he snarled.

Jerrett gripped Dean's arm to restrain him. He didn't need him to start swinging, but Dean was right, Mitch needed to leave.

"You heard him. Get the hell out of my shop and don't come back!"

"Lines are being drawn, Jerrett, and you don't want to be on the wrong side," Mitch growled out ominously. He turned and stormed out of the shop, slamming the door behind him.

Dean spat out, "That asshole! I'd like to smash my fist in his face! He's going to get people killed and he doesn't even care!" Dean's entire body was stiff with rage. Jerrett, still gripping Dean's arm, squeezed it before releasing him.

"I know, Dean. I know … I'd like to hit him, too." He drew in a steadying breath. "I can't believe what he's planning!" Jerrett slammed a fist into his desk. He took a deep, shuddering breath. "At least we know what's really going on now."

Dean nodded at Jerrett. "Yeah, so we stay away from that rally."

Jerrett sighed. They'd come so close to being a part of a battle, a revolution even, and getting innocent people hurt. At least they knew the truth now.

Behind them stood Trevor, forgotten for the moment, but watching and absorbing everything, still and silent.

DONT TREAD ON ME

CHAPTER 8

Violence Brewing

On the day of the rally, the shop was dead calm. It was almost eerie, especially with the energy that had been flowing through the place in the last few weeks.

Even with the spooky silence, Dean was glad he'd come today. There was nowhere else he wanted to be on a day like today.

He often came on Saturdays to help Jerrett out. It was his day off, but working on the bikes was fun, mostly, and he liked hanging out with his brother. As he knelt to retrieve a bolt that had rolled off the workbench, he wondered how the rally was going. How big was the turnout? What were they saying, doing? He wondered at the mood: was it calm or tense? Had the military shown up in large numbers?

Most importantly – had someone fired the first shot yet? He was gripped with a sense of foreboding; what would this day bring?

Dean pushed that thought from his mind. This was only a rally, he told himself, and it's not going to start a revolution, no matter what Mitch hoped.

Jerrett sauntered by, holding a wrench.

"Hey, bro, ready for a lunch break yet?" called Dean, straightening up, the escaped bolt in hand.

"Yeah, soon. But none of that healthy crap you made me eat last week."

"It was hummus," Dean retorted.

Jerrett made a face, "Health nut."

"Beer gut."

"Think it's too early for a beer?" Jerrett quipped.

Dean came back with, "It's five o'clock somewhere."

Jerrett cracked a smile at that and ruffled his brother's hair.

Dean rolled his eyes, shook his head, and turned back to his work. He was quickly engrossed in the job of replacing a sprocket. Fighting with another bolt, he barely registered the phone ringing.

The sudden intensity of Jerrett's voice startled him.

"What? When did this happen?"

Dean stood up, the wrench forgotten in his hand. Jerrett paced by the counter, phone in hand, raking his fingers nervously through his hair, his voice frantic. Dean maneuvered around the bikes, dropping the wrench, to move closer to his brother's side.

"Troy! Calm down." He softened his voice, "Stop crying for a sec. Tell me exactly when they left." Jerrett's eyes were wide, fearful as he talked.

Dean interrupted, "What is it? What's wrong?"

Jerrett shook his head at Dean in a silent message to wait. After listening a bit longer, he told Troy, "OK, bud, it's going to be OK. Dean and I will take care of it. We'll get them. I need you to be calm now. You've got to take care of Cami and Jasper till we get back. Can you do that?" Jerrett paused, listening while still pacing. "Good. I knew you could. I love you, buddy. We'll take care of it."

Jerrett threw the phone down on the desk where it bounced and landed on the floor. He dropped his elbows onto the counter, his head falling into his hands. He rummaged through his hair again, and then pushed off the counter, turning one way, then the next, like a child's toy robot.

"We gotta go, we gotta go now," he mumbled, turning suddenly and running to the door.

"Wait, Jerrett! What's going on?" Dean was scared and worried. He'd never seen Jerrett act this way before. His brother had burst out of the shop and grabbed the nearest motorcycle that was parked outside.

"Open the garage door! Help me get these bikes inside," he ordered Dean. Jerrett often pushed bikes out into the parking lot during the day, so they'd have more room to work.

Dean grabbed the nearest one and followed his brother inside. He parked it haphazardly and then blocked his brother, grabbing him by the shoulders.

"Stop, Jerrett! Tell me what's happened?"

Jerrett's gaze wandered from one side to another, focusing on nothing, while his body moved with frantic energy. Dean hung onto him, reaching up and cupping the back of Jerrett's neck. With a firm squeeze and in a stern voice he said, "Tell me."

Jerrett froze, the sound of Dean's voice getting through to him at last. "Trevor and Dalton, they … they took your jeep … they went to the rally…" Fear was evident in Jerrett's eyes.

Dean felt cold fingers of dread creep around his heart. His stomach churned with fear. All day he'd had the premonition that something terrible was going to happen at the rally. And now his little brother and nephew were smack dab in the middle of it.

"OK then," Dean said, trying to stay calm while his mind spun in several directions, "Gwennie is at work, right?" Jerrett looked confused but nodded. Dean continued, "Call her, she's closer to them, she could get to them faster than we could."

"No," Jerrett answered, shaking his head, "I don't want her there. It's too dangerous."

Dean nodded, "Right, OK then. We don't tell Gwennie until we have them. She would go after the boys for sure. Let's throw these bikes inside and take your truck."

Dean and Jerrett were in the pickup truck in record time. Dean drove, as there was no way he trusted his brother behind the wheel. Jerrett seemed to be in a state of shock, staring out through the windshield, his body rigid and his face pale.

Dean sped down the highway as fast as he dared; he didn't need to be pulled over for speeding – especially not tonight. It would take about an hour and a half to get to Philly. Dean just hoped the boys would be safe until they reached them.

"Try Trevor's phone, Jerrett!" ordered Dean.

That shook Jerrett out of his stupor. He fumbled in his pocket to retrieve the phone, and then punched in the number. Dean watched as Jerrett waited for a few tense seconds, eventually hanging up in frustration. Then he tried Dalton's.

"Nothing?"

Jerrett shook his head without answering, brow furrowing with tension.

They drove on in silence for a while. Suddenly a shrill noise broke the quiet. Jerrett's phone. He grabbed it and put it up to his ear.

"Gwennie," he answered. He listened briefly, and then interrupted her. "No, Gwennie! No! We're on our way, let Dean and I handle it. Stay out of there!" He paused, "Gwennie! No! Gwennie!"

Jerrett hung up and threw the phone to the floor.

"She's going after them, isn't she?"

Jerrett nodded grimly.

"How'd she even find out?"

"Troy called her after talking to me. I can't believe she'd even try this! She's heading into – God knows what!"

Rounding a corner, Dean's blood went cold as he spotted a roadblock ahead. Armed Guards stood on the roadway, rifles slung over their shoulders. The Guardhouse with its red stripe around the middle sat off to the side, a black bar reaching across the road. Dean felt a feeling of dread rise within, something that he always felt when he encountered one of these mandatory stops. He swung the truck into the line of vehicles. His stomach clenched. If the Guards didn't like what they saw, they could restrain him and Jerrett for as long as they liked. He inched along behind a silver Audi. He watched as the Guards strode up to the window and took the papers from the driver. He wondered if it was going to be waved through, or told to pull over to the side for further investigation.

The Audi was sent through. It was Dean's turn now. He pulled up and put the truck into park. Jerrett silently handed Dean their documents. Dean met his eyes briefly, seeing the same fear reflected in his brother's face. He gave Jerrett a brief nod and they both turned back to the window. The Guard was there, his dark skin glistening under his helmet, his steely eyes glaring at Dean.

"Papers." He ordered, his emotionless gaze never wavering.

Dean handed them over. His palms were sweaty, and his heart pounded. He gripped the steering wheel, trying not to let his anxiety show. If he gave the Guard any reason to think he wasn't on the up and up, they would take them into custody. He and Jerrett could be held for hours or even arrested. He glanced at Jerrett. His brother's face was white and he was sweating. He was staring at the Guard, tension radiating from him. If the Guard noticed, he would think they were up to something.

Dean held his breath.

Finally, the Guard handed back their documents and waved them on.

Dean eased out onto the road, breathing deep to calm down. "We're OK, bro. We made it through." He looked at Jerrett. His brother hadn't changed position at all. He stared, blankly, his face as white as ever. Dean reached over and squeezed his neck reassuringly, but he didn't know what to say. Concentrating on driving, he sped off as fast as he dared.

CHAPTER 9

The Rally

After many tense miles and two more heart-attack-inducing checkpoints, they reached the park where the rally was held.

The sight that greeted them was unbelievable.

Faces filled with terror pushed past them. Screams rang out. Soldiers and civilians were everywhere, running in all directions. There seemed to be no rhyme or reason for where they were trying to go, as if they didn't know, either. A sea of cars filled the lawn in front of them. Dean threw the truck into the first empty patch of grass he could find. They jumped out, scanning the area, trying to get their bearings.

The acrid smell of smoke filled the air, billowing past them, choking them, and making them cough. They couldn't see the source of the smoke, but it seemed to fill the space all around them. Dean and Jerrett froze, coughing and squinting, not sure where to go.

"How are we going to find them in all this?" Dean choked out. He glanced over at Jerrett who had his shirt pulled over his nose.

"I'll try Dalton's cell again. Maybe he'll answer this time," Jerrett shouted over the din. The two of them moved to a more sheltered spot next to a shed. Jerrett pulled out his cell and punched in the number. No one answered. "Damn it!"

"Now what?" Dean asked. "Try Gwennie's phone?" As Jerrett searched for the number, Dean's phone rang.

Dean snatched it up. "Hello?"

"Dean?" There came a tentative, shaky voice. "It's m-me, Dalton. We ... we need help." His voice sped up, rambling now, and panicky sounding. "I tried dad, but his phone was busy, I couldn't get through. I don't know what to do. Mom, mom ... I ... where are you guys? I don't know what to do..."

"Dalton! We're here, at the park. Your dad and me. We came looking for you." Dean tried to get Dalton's attention and focus. "Where are you?"

"Where is he? Give me the phone," Jerrett demanded, trying to grab the cell, but Dean deftly dodged him and waved him off.

Dalton's shaky voice answered. "By the ... um ... the pavilion. Mom's here. She's ... hurt ... I don't know how bad ... and Trevor, too. There's blood. Lots of ... blood. Blood is everywhere..." His voice trailed off, leaving Dean's heart frozen in his chest. What had happened? My God, how bad was Gwennie hurt? Or Trevor?

"OK, Dalton. Just stay right there. Don't move. We're coming. Do you hear me? Stay there! We'll be right there. Just hang on," Dean commanded the boy before he broke the connection.

"Where are they? What happened?" Jerrett demanded frantically.

Dean took in a steadying breath and broke the news to his brother. "He says Gwennie is with them, but she's hurt."

He watched as his brother froze, the color draining from his face. "How bad? What's wrong?" Jerrett grabbed Dean's arms.

"I don't know, but Dalton said there was a lot of blood." He watched as Jerrett sucked in a hard breath. Dean gripped his arm. "Let's go, brother. They're over this way."

They took off at a sprint, dodging soldiers and civilians as they ran. No one seemed to notice or care about them and they were able to continue unhindered. Suddenly, a sharp crack was heard bursting through the air. Dean stopped, confused, wondering what it was he'd heard. Before he could process it entirely, he felt himself being thrown to the ground and Jerrett landing on top of him. He struggled to get up until he heard Jerrett's voice hiss in his ear.

"Gunshots! Stay down." They waited until the sounds had stopped, then cautiously stood up.

"Let's go, but stay low," Jerrett reminded Dean. They hurried off, stooped over. More gunshots rang out, but they were further away, in another part of the park. Dean couldn't help but wonder what exactly was going on. Who was firing at who? Had the militia, in their frenzy, started it, or the Guards? It didn't really matter though; bullets were bullets, no matter who was shooting them. Dean's heart was pounding in his chest, fear and adrenaline coursing through him. They had to find the kids and Gwennie, but he was scared. More gunshots burst over their heads, sending them diving into a gully running through the grass.

They waited a bit, then jumped up and resumed their run. As they crested the gully, the pavilion's roof was visible just across a clearing. Dean stopped, head whipping from side to side, taking in the scene. Where were they? He saw groups of people huddled in clumps here and there, crouching low to the ground. As he looked closer, he could see many were injured, blood pooling on the ground beneath them. It looked like a battlefield, except these people had no weapons.

"Where are they, Dean?" Jerrett's voice was frantic as he scanned the area for his family. Dean didn't answer but just looked on in horror. From the corner of his eye, he saw Jerrett suddenly lurch into motion. Dean stood still, frozen, watching his brother's desperate run towards a small group huddled under a tree, just to the right side of the pavilion. In a split second, his brain registered what Jerrett had seen – two boys, crouching and sobbing, and a still figure lying on the ground at their feet.

Dean took off at a dead sprint after his brother. He watched as Jerrett fell to his knees next to his wife's lifeless form. Sobbing, his breath coming in quick gasps, Jerrett pulled her limp body into his lap.

"No! No, no, no!" Jerrett moaned, cradling her. His face was buried in her hair, his arms rocking Gwennie back and forth. Her blood coated his shirt, turning it red instantly. "Gwennie!" His scream was primal and grief-filled. Dean knelt at his brother's side and felt Gwennie's neck for a pulse. There was none. He saw then the blood coating her face, the blue lips, the hole in her forehead.

He felt nausea well up in his stomach and willed it away as he turned his head from the sight.

Only then did he remember the others. Dean tore his focus away from Jerrett and Gwennie to the boys. They were dirty, bloodied and crying, but OK.

"Trevor, Dalton!" He grabbed onto them both at once, drawing them to him. Clutching them tightly, he could feel them both shaking. "It's OK, now. We've got you. We're here."

When Dean finally released them, Dalton fell to the ground and curled into a ball, but at least he looked unhurt. Trevor rocked back on his knees, clutching his right arm with his hand, blood seeping between his fingers and down his sleeve. "Oh my God, kid, what happened?" Dean grabbed the boy's shoulders. Trevor flinched as Dean touched his wounded arm.

Dalton lurched out of his ball, grabbing Dean's arm, his voice tinged with hysteria. "They ... they shot him!" Dalton burst out. "We were just standing there ... and they started shooting! Shooting everybody! I don't know ... we couldn't get away. And then Mom – " He stopped, unable to continue. The boy dropped his head to his knees, misery pouring out of him as he sobbed uncontrollably.

Dean hesitated, not sure what to do next, his brain seemingly frozen in shock. Had all this really happened? He couldn't wrap his head around it and stared at the ground, chest heaving and the world spinning around him.

And then he felt a hand on his shoulder. Looking up he found himself staring into the pain-laced eyes of his silent kid brother. Trevor said nothing, just waited, blood pouring down his arm. The sight finally shook Dean awake. He needed to tend to Trevor and get that bleeding stopped. But what could he use for a bandage? There was nothing. He whipped off the t-shirt he wore and tied it over his brother's wound, pressing down hard, even though he could hear Trevor gasp in pain. When the blood finally seemed to slow, Dean placed Trevor's free hand over the improvised bandage.

Rocking back on his heels, he looked down at his hands resting on his thighs and saw bloody handprints all over his jeans. It looked like a macabre version of a child's finger-painting. What a strange thing to notice amidst all this, he thought to himself.

He turned reluctantly to Jerrett and Gwennie. Her blood still flowed, pooling on the dirt under her, coating her clothes and Jerrett's. This was her life draining away in the grass. Dean watched, mesmerized by the gory sight of the grass and dirt turning dark red beneath them. There was so much blood and he wondered how it could all fit inside one body.

She was gone. Nothing would ever be the same again.

Another burst of gunfire jarred Dean out of his daze. He ducked low, covering his head. He heard Dalton's terrified scream. *We need to move …* now! He thought to himself as he came to his senses. When the shots stopped, he raised his head and assessed the situation.

"Jerrett!" He grabbed his brother's arms, "Jerrett! She's gone. You have to let her go. There's nothing we can do for her." When he didn't respond, Dean resorted to shaking him, the panic rising. "Jerrett, we have to get out of here! Jerrett! Jerrett!"

CHAPTER 10

The End of the World As We Know It

From beyond the fog clouding his brain, Jerrett could hear Dean's voice. It was frantic, imploring him to do something, but the words floated by without comprehension.

Gwennie, oh Gwennie …

He pulled her tighter to his chest, his hands fisting in her clothes. They were stiff, wet and sticky. Jerrett could hear someone moaning, and then wailing. His world had narrowed to an impenetrable bubble, his vision graying and sounds fading into meaningless noise.

Gwennie …

He had come to rescue her, to save her, and now he'd done it, she was in his arms, safe at last. He had gotten to her in time. Hadn't he? Images pressed into his brain.

He saw her white sweater, blood spreading across it … her body … lying lifeless in the dirt. He heard the screaming, the panic-stricken voices, the gunshots …

No. No. She's here, in my arms. She's safe!

Someone was pulling at his arm, tugging. They wouldn't stop. He fought them off, pulling away and cradling Gwennie, rocking her back and forth.

A sudden pain exploded across his cheek and Jerrett's head whipped up. In that one instant, the artfully constructed shell around him disintegrated.

He saw Dean, inches away from him, his hand still upraised and red. *He slapped me*, Jerrett realized.

"Jerrett ... have to move ... Jerrett!" The words were fading in and out along with the gunfire and the screaming. "We have to move ... get out of here!" Dean was shaking him.

Jerrett's gaze dropped to the body in his lap. Gwennie was still, unmoving. He gasped as the reality rocked him to his core.

"No, no!" He moaned as he pulled Gwennie up to his shoulder.

"Jerrett, we've got to get out of here!" Dean shouted. Jerrett's head rose to look at his brother. It was as if Dean were in high definition, every freckle and wrinkle suddenly becoming crystal clear. An explosive noise burst from somewhere nearby.

"Trevor's hurt. We have to get him out of here!" Dean pleaded. "Jerrett, please, snap out of it. They need you." Dean pointed behind him at Dalton and Trevor.

Jerrett followed where he pointed. Dalton was huddled in a ball, keening in grief. Trevor cradled his arm, blood saturating his sleeve.

Jerrett took one final look at the body in his arms. She was gone. He looked up again, at his son and his brothers. She was gone, but they were still here, and they needed him.

Dean seemed to read the change in awareness in his big brother. His voice softened, "Come on, Jerrett. We've got to go, gotta help Trevor. We've got to get home to Troy and Cami. They need us, Jerrett."

Jerrett's voice, rougher than usual, ground out, "Troy? Cami?"

"Yeah. They need you. They need their daddy."

Jerrett looked down once more at his wife, and back up to Dean. "I'm not leaving her here."

"Of course not," Dean soothed.

"Help me get her up," Jerrett implored. Together, the brothers hoisted Gwennie up, her lifeless body draped across Jerrett's arms.

"I got her."

Dean turned to the others. Jerrett heard him ask Trevor, "Can you walk?" Trevor looked back up at him, his face ashen. He nodded grimly.

Dean reached down and hauled Dalton to his feet, murmuring to him quietly. Dalton staggered, but Dean hung on, wrapping his arm around the boy.

Jerrett choked back his tears, sucked in a quivering breath, steeled himself and started off. Dean and Dalton followed with Trevor staggering behind.

The journey back to the truck was slow and arduous. With the heavy burden Jerrett carried, and the two shell-shocked teens to guide, their pace was slow. Gunfire rang out in frequent bursts, sending them ducking for cover. Several bodies lay motionless on the ground. People ran in every direction.

When they finally reached the truck, Jerrett was gasping for breath. Trevor's face was a mask of pain, and Dalton seemed lost somewhere inside himself. Jerrett watched as Dean reached in the truck and pulled out a blanket. Wordlessly he spread it out on the ground.

"Jerrett, put her down." Grateful, Jerrett laid Gwennie tenderly down on the blanket. His arms ached, but that was nothing compared to the ache in his heart. He straightened, looking around for a minute. It seemed a little calmer here; the crowds were thinner, and the gunfire was off in the distance. They had a little time to sort themselves out.

When Jerrett looked back, Dean was wrapping the blanket over Gwennie. "No!" he gasped. It was wrong; it felt wrong to cover her up like that. Like she was gone. Dean paused and looked at him.

"Shouldn't we call someone, like the police or 911 or ..." Jerrett's voice trailed off, the words stuck behind a lump in his throat. He wasn't sure what to do. "Who do you call when, when ..." Unable to finish, he gestured to the body, the tears flowing.

Dean looked at him, pity in his eyes. He rested his hand on his brother's shoulder. "Jerrett, who would we call?" He spoke softly. "No one is going to come help us. This is about survival now, brother. We gotta get out of here, quickly. We'll have to figure out what to do about Gwennie's ... body, later."

Jerrett realized what needed to be done, but there was no way he could bring himself to pull that blanket over her face; it was too final. "Go ahead," he told his brother, turning away. Jerrett absently rubbed a hand over the stubble on his face. He heard a grunt from Dean, as he lifted her, and the groan of the truck as something heavy was placed in the bed. It was hard to imagine her precious body being put in the bed of the truck like cargo, not like a person.

Jerrett felt as though his legs were going to collapse under him. Tears ran down his face continuously and he pictured her the last time he saw her. His mind whirled around, images of his wife coming unbidden to him. He let them come, powerless to stop them. Sagging against the truck, he sank to the ground, legs like jelly. He was dimly aware of others around him, moving, talking, but it was all a blur of sound and color, nothing distinct. His mind could grasp nothing, nothing made sense, so he gave up trying and did nothing but cry and remember.

How long he stayed that way, he didn't know, but when he finally he raised his head, he looked owlishly around him.

Trevor sat in the front passenger seat, with the door hanging open. Dean was finishing up bandaging Trevor's arm, an open first aid kit on the floor of the truck, with ointment tubes and wrappings scattered about. Jerrett took in Trevor's ghostly white, tear-streaked face, but noticed that Dean seemed to have things in hand. As Dean tied off the bandage, Jerrett could hear quiet words of comfort spoken to Trevor.

Hearing a noise, he turned his head. Dalton was huddled on the ground, leaning sideways against the truck, curled in on himself. Something paternal arose in Jerrett, shaking him out of his stupor. He crawled on hands and knees to his son, pulling him into his arms.

"Shh, shh," he soothed. Dalton grabbed him in a death grip, his arms wrapped tightly around his dad's neck, the boy's tears soaking his shirt.

Soon Dean crouched down in front of them. He had an old t-shirt in his hand and extended it to Jerrett. "Get rid of that shirt, Jerr, and put this on." Jerrett took the shirt wordlessly and robotically changed, dropping the old one on the ground. "We've got to go," Dean said, his voice soft and gentle.

Jerrett nodded in agreement and together, he and Dean pulled Dalton up off the ground. Jerrett steered Dalton into the back seat of the truck, climbing in beside him and closing the door. Dean hopped into the driver's seat, as Trevor reclined beside him with his eyes closed.

"You OK, Trevor?" Jerrett didn't like the way his brother looked. Trevor halfway turned and nodded without speaking. The boy looked terrible, but seemed stable.

The truck lurched as Dean shifted into gear and pulled out.

Jerrett settled back and let his thoughts drift, the vibrations of the vehicle lulling him into a stupor. Dalton had fallen silent now, his head resting on his dad's shoulder. Questions swirled around in Jerrett's head. Was this really happening? What did it mean for tomorrow? For their future? Where would they go from here?

Gwennie. She wasn't really gone, was she? She was just here this morning, packing lunches, managing the chaos, planning for dinner. He'd taken it all for granted, never giving a thought to how fragile it all was. How had life changed so irrevocably?

He turned towards the window, watching the landscape flying by as they headed down the highway.

Dean suddenly shouted, "Hold on!"

The truck swerved, throwing its occupants into each other. Trevor moaned in pain. The traffic in front of them had slowed to almost a stop.

Jerrett felt like he had stepped into an alternate universe. Cars were being pulled over all along the roadside. Government vehicles were parked on the shoulder, with Elite Guardsmen swarming like ants over the civilian cars. Passengers had been ordered out of their vehicles and were standing about. As he watched, a Guard forcefully yanked a middle-aged woman out of her car by her hair. Troop transports passed them on the other side of the highway, heading into the city.

It looked like a scene from a war movie.

Dean maneuvered into the passing lane, around the stopped traffic. They drove along as fast as they dared.

"What's going on?"

"I don't know," Dean answered, as he flicked on the radio. They all knew that the stations were government controlled, and therefore often counterfactual, but it was the only source of information they had at their disposal. The radio crackled as Dean dialed in a station. He finally found a news station which was giving an emergency announcement.

"Expanded martial law has been decreed in the greater Philadelphia and surrounding areas," stated a nervous-sounding broadcaster. "All residents are ordered to stay in their homes; travelers must pull over at roadblocks and be granted a pass to continue. Curfew will be enacted at dusk. Military personnel are to report immediately ... ," the announcer continued, listing further restrictions.

Another commentator came on, reading an official government report regarding the disturbance in Philly. It blatantly accused the militia of having had the intention of starting an uprising from the start. The report went on to announce the arrest and deportation of anyone associated with the militia groups. Wanted lists of specific organizations were read aloud. Soldiers and Guardsmen had been called in to quell the uprising.

Those in the truck listened with terror.

Another convoy of military vehicles passed them on the opposite side of the highway. They were silhouetted against the fading light of the sunset.

"How'd they get all the soldiers here so fast?" Trevor asked his voice tight with pain.

Jerrett shook his head, "I... don't know ... unless –"

"Mitch said this would happen." ," Dean cut in, as he reached to turn on the headlights. "They must have been ready for the fighting to break out, so they could move in. They're going to use this as an excuse, you know, to do whatever they want to do to us. They can arrest anyone they want now, under the expanded martial law."

"What ... what will they do with the people they arrest?" Trevor rasped out. Dean shrugged in response.

"What about the camps?" Dalton spoke up softly.

Jerrett realized that was the first he'd heard Dalton talk since they got in the truck. "What camps, buddy?"

Dalton, who still looked a little lost, answered meekly, his voice so quiet it could barely be heard. "The ones Luke told us about, the last time we were at the track," Dalton shrugged and continued. "He said the military were building these huge fenced-in camps, but no one knew what for."

"Could be a place to hold all the dissidents they'll be rounding up." Dean speculated.

Jerrett had no answer for that. Could it be true?

An uneasy silence crept up on them, weighted with tension. What was going to happen to them? If the military decided to flag them over, they were finished.

"We need to get out of here. Back roads would be best, Dean."

Dean nodded in agreement, and looked for an off ramp.

They passed another group of Elite Guards, with work lights blazing over a designated area along the road. As Dean passed the ruckus on the shoulder, they could see civilians, kneeling on the ground in a row, hands on their heads.

They had a front row view to the horror that unfolded next. As they inched slowly past, the Guardsmen drew their weapons, aimed, and fired on the unarmed civilians. Horrified, they watched as the victims toppled to the ground.

"Get us out of here, Dean!" Jerrett commanded, frantically. "Now!"

Dean nodded and jerked the wheel to the left, into the grassy medium, passing several cars. He scooted back up onto the roadway. He counted on the traffic impeding any Guards that might try to chase them. Dodging in between a van and a pickup, he changed lanes, looking for a way out of the traffic mess. The vehicles slowed to a crawl, both lanes blocked, but they were past the checkpoint now.

The pickup truck was hemmed in from behind and in front.

"Try the shoulder," Jerrett prompted.

Veering off to the right, Dean raced along the edge of the highway, narrowly missing road signs. Other civilian vehicles followed him, desperate to escape the inevitable appearance of the Guards. The truck lurched from side to side as they raced along.

Finally seeing on off ramp, Dean jerked sharply to the right, and without slowing, raced down the cloverleaf. The abrupt movement elicited a grunt of pain from Trevor.

Jerrett reached up and rested a hand on his brother's shoulder to steady him.

Once off the highway, Dean made several quick turns to throw off anyone who might try to follow. They soon found themselves speeding along a dark and deserted back road. Fortunately, there were no roadblocks here and little traffic, as people obeyed the decree and stayed home.

Silence fell upon those in the truck as the adrenaline left them, settling their feelings down into a numb, empty grief.

CHAPTER 11

Saying Goodbye

Jerrett leaned back against the seat, exhausted, as Dean drove on. His mind constantly drifted back to Gwennie. He found himself replaying the last time he'd seen her, how he'd kissed her goodbye and she'd hugged him, how they'd teased each other over something silly.

It wasn't really over, was it? In an instant of time, his entire world had shifted.

Troy and Cami were at home, waiting for them. How did someone tell their kids that their mother was gone? There wasn't a handbook for things like this; no one had taught him how to handle something this horrible. What was he going to do? He dropped his head in his hands.

When he finally raised his head, he looked around at his family. Dalton was staring out the window, silent and haunted. In the front seat, Trevor had finally passed out; the blood loss and shock having taken their toll. Dean was gripping the steering wheel with white knuckles, shoulders rigid with tension.

Jerrett leaned forward to talk to him, "Do you think Trevor's OK?" He asked Dean softly, pressing himself into the space between the seats so Dean could hear him.

Dean glanced over at Trevor. "I don't know. I'm not exactly well versed in treating bullet wounds. Should we take him to the hospital?"

Jerrett was shaking his head before Dean was even finished. "No. Too dangerous. They have to report gunshot wounds and we don't need any Guards involved. We'd better just try to treat it at home. Right now we need to get out of here."

"I know, I'm going."

"No. We need to clear out completely. It's too dangerous to stay. Once the chaos at the rally is over, both sides will be organizing themselves. That's when the real fighting will start. The militias aren't going to back down after this, it's what they've been waiting for – it's the catalyst they need to start a full-on revolution." Jerrett paused, running a hand through his hair. "Dean, we were at one of the meetings, and we talked to Mitch all the time. Who's to say the Guards haven't already linked us to them? They could've bugged the phones. They may even know Trevor and Dalton were at the rally. We could be taken in for questioning." Jerrett grabbed his brother's shoulder. "Dean, do you understand what I'm saying? We have to run; we need to find somewhere to hide. Clear out for a while at least and wait for the dust to settle. See what's going to happen."

Dean's eyes were wide in shock as he glanced back at Jerrett, digesting what his brother had said. He sucked in a ragged breath laced with a sob and blew it out slowly. He finally nodded in agreement. "OK. You're right. But where can we go? It's too bad we don't have a hunting cabin in the mountains. That would be a perfect hiding spot."

Jerrett racked his brain. Where could they go? They needed a remote place where they could hide, and they needed to get there fast.

"Starlight," said Dalton, suddenly pulling himself out of his paralyzed state.

Starlight was a motocross track hidden in a remote valley in the Allegheny Mountains. The owners, Saul and Markie Carrigan, had spent many nights around the campfire with the Nolan tribe. They lived on the property with their three daughters, all of whom raced motocross. The friendship between their families went back many years. Jerrett's mind flashed back to Markie Carrigan shaking Dalton's hand before handing him his first trophy.

It would be good to be up there with the Carrigans, to be with loved ones right now.

Jerrett squeezed Dalton's shoulder. "That's a good idea, son."

Turning back to Dean, Jerrett said, "Starlight's the perfect place. The track is hidden up there in the mountains, remote enough, but not too far."

"Yeah," Dean agreed. "That would work."

"I'll call Saul and Markie when we get home. See if it's OK to come up there. And safe."

It felt good to have something else to focus on and his mind spun through the logistics of the journey. "We can pack up the truck tomorrow, grab supplies, and be on the road, oh ... maybe by late afternoon –"

His voice cut off suddenly. Gwennie. What would they do about her? They would have to bury her, have a funeral. The thought chilled him, and he collapsed back into his seat. A funeral. How did one plan a funeral? Didn't that usually take a few days to organize? Did they even have a few days? His thoughts flew in a million directions, never landing in one place for long.

"Jerr?" Dean called, concerned by the silence. "You OK, man?"

Jerrett couldn't answer, couldn't get his tongue to form the words. His throat tightened, a lump forming that was hard to get past, "What ... ah ... what do we do ... about Gwennie? We have to ... bury her."

Dalton made a gasping sound and covered his face.

After sparing his son a glance, Jerrett closed his eyes and reluctantly continued. "Do we call the ... funeral parlor? We ... we have to wait to leave town until we can have the ... funeral. We can't leave until after that."

Dean fidgeted in his seat, not wanting to answer, but finally said softly, "Jerr, I don't think we can risk a funeral."

Jerrett leaned forward to protest, but Dean continued. "Look, we moved the body. I'm pretty sure that's against the law. If we take her to the funeral home, they'll have to notify the police and they'll find out she died at the rally. There's no way we'll stay out of jail or a camp then. The kids could even be at risk, especially Trevor and Dalton. We have to protect them, Jerr."

Jerrett reeled in shock. No funeral? He needed to say goodbye. What about her parents and brother? They were out of state, but surely they would want to come. His mind swirled with thoughts, but he couldn't seem to grasp onto any of them. Jerrett didn't know what to do.

As if reading his mind, Dean spoke up. "Look Jerrett, we need to get out of town – the sooner the better. Tomorrow, if we can, like you said. That means we have to take care of Gwennie ourselves." He paused, not wanting to say what he had to next. "We have to bury her ourselves."

Jerrett could not hold in the groan that escaped his lips or the tears staining his cheeks. He was suddenly aware of Dalton sidling up to him. Jerrett grabbed his boy, wrapping his arms around his son. He was shaking, and his tears soaked Jerrett's shirt. They held each other for the rest of the ride.

By the time they got home, Jerrett had reluctantly accepted the inevitable. Dean was right, they had to bury her themselves and get out of town immediately.

As they pulled into the driveway, Jerrett steeled himself for what had to come next.

Troy appeared at the doorway, his tall, lean body silhouetted in the light. Jasper, tail wagging, slipped past him to greet the arrivals. Cami pushed in beside her brother.

Jerrett had never dreaded coming home as much as he did right then. Dragging himself out of the truck, he swept a hand over his face and tried to get his emotions under control. He had to be strong now, for them. He was their daddy and the only one who could do this. Putting his own grief aside as best he could, he braced himself for the agony that was coming.

He met Troy on the porch. Cami hung back in the doorway.

"What is it, dad? Did you find them?" Troy asked.

Jerrett nodded and answered grimly, "Yeah, Troy. Dalton and Trevor are safe, though Trevor's been shot."

"Shot! Is he OK?"

"Yes, he's OK. But something else happened. Let's go in and talk." He led the children into the living room where he sat them on the couch and crouched in front of them. Bowing his head, he took a deep breath, dimly aware of the sounds of the others in the kitchen and Jasper's tags rattling as he darted among them. Jerrett looked up, seeing the innocent faces before him. He was about to change their lives forever; nothing would be the same for them after he spoke. The trust in their faces struck him; their daddy could always fix things, keep anything truly bad at bay. He was about to destroy that trust. He didn't know if he could do it.

"Dad?" Troy inquired, his face belying the creeping realization that something terrible was coming. Cami's puzzled face darted back and forth between her brother and her daddy.

Jerrett knew he had to say it. There was no more putting it off. "Guys, something bad happened. Mommy found Dalton and Trevor at the rally. She was going to get them and bring them home … but she got hurt."

"Hurt? Mommy's hurt?" Cami gasped, her eyes filling with tears.

"Yes, honey, she got hurt really bad. Someone shot her … and she … she … died." Jerrett watched as Troy's face crumbled and Cami shook her head.

"No! Not mommy!" She screamed, tears falling. "Where is she? I want mommy!" The child's screams ripped through Jerrett's heart and soul. Hysteria set in as she lurched up, trying to escape.

"Baby, come here! Come here, Cami!" Jerrett grabbed her and picked her up in his arms. "Shh, shh, baby, it's going to be OK." How could he say that? Nothing was going to be OK again. She stopped fighting though and melted into his arms, crying and shaking and begging for her mommy.

"Mommy! I want mommy!"

Jerrett held onto her as he eased down next to Troy, who was still and frozen, and wrapped an arm around him.

"I'm still here, and I'm going to take care of you. I'll keep you safe, I promise you. I'm always here for you. I love you … I love you …" He didn't know what else to say as the tears, the grief and horror choked him. All he could do was hold them and keep murmuring the same words to them over and over. *I love you,*

I'm here, I'll take care of you... What good words would do, he didn't know, but words were all he had now. The three of them cried in each other's arms.

Eventually exhaustion took over and Cami's sobs quieted, though the tears still fell. Troy's face was red and swollen.

The others had long since joined them in the living room, faces grim. Trevor sagged in the recliner, obviously still in tremendous pain. Dalton sat on the floor, hugging Jasper who seemed to sense the sadness in the room, as he let Dalton cry into his fur. Dean perched on the edge of the chair, hands clasped.

Clearing his throat, Dean rasped out, "We'll need to bury her before the sun comes up. We can't take the chance of anyone seeing us." He paused, then added, "I'm sorry. I wish we could wait."

"Why can't we?" Troy asked softly.

"Because a lot happened tonight. Not just to our family. There's a lot of fighting going on and so we're going to go away for a little while. To Starlight, where it's safe," Jerrett tried to explain. He went on to answer their questions as best he could while shielding them from any more fear or pain.

"We're going to bury mommy in her favorite place, out in the flower garden, so the pretty flowers will be all around her when they bloom."

"Mommy'd like that," Cami stated, sniffling and swiping a hand across her nose.

Jerrett hugged her to him. "Yes, I thought so too." His heart was breaking, and he didn't know how much longer he could be strong.

Dean sensed it, as usual, and stepped in, moving closer. "Can you two stay in here with Uncle Trevor and take care of him while we get everything ready?"

The two children nodded solemnly as they moved to Trevor's side. Dean pulled Jerrett up off the couch and headed for the door. Remembering at the last minute, Jerrett pulled away and said, "Dalton, you stay with them. We'll come back when we're ready." The boy would carry the guilt the rest of his life, knowing it was him his mother had died trying to save; Jerrett refused to burden him with any part of digging his own mother's grave. That would fall to Jerrett's shoulders to bear.

● ● ●

Jerrett and Dean had found the perfect spot, among Gwennie's flowers and under the sagging branch of a pine tree which nearly touched the ground. The garden and tree limb should hide any evidence of a recently dug grave.

After they'd finished digging, they retrieved the others. They stood, by lantern light, saying goodbye. Gwennie had been laid in the hole, wrapped snugly in a blanket. Before lowering her, they had pulled back the cover for one final look at her face, peaceful and still. After each had said goodbye, Jerrett and Dean gently placed her on the ground.

Jerrett didn't even know how to describe what he felt. It was surreal. The pain in his heart was not physical, but hurt just as bad; the tears washing over him in a never-ending cascade. The children were by his side; Cami sobbing, Troy on his knees, keening, and Dalton still and silent. Dean leaned on the shovel, blank-faced and exhausted. Trevor, though sitting on a chair, still looked pale and sickly. They remained for a while, no one sure what to do next.

Jerrett knew it was time to pull them together. He had to be strong for the family; it was all on him now, to get them out of here and up to the mountains safely.

"C'mon, guys. Let's go inside." He helped Trevor to his feet and guided him along. The rest mutely followed, lanterns swaying.

Once in the house, Jerrett could see they were all dead on their feet. Even though there was much to do and probably a short time to do it in, they desperately needed to sleep.

"Let's bed down for a few hours and then we'll get started in the morning. OK, Dean?" His brother nodded mutely.

Craving solidarity they decided to all crash in the living room. Trevor was given the couch, Cami commandeered the recliner, and the rest scattered about the floor. Jasper piled on top of Dalton, his touch comforting. Despite the horrors of the day, Jerrett managed to fall asleep from sheer exhaustion.

● ● ●

Early the next morning, Jerrett was the first to wake and, in his grogginess, he forgot for a moment what had transpired the day before. But in a sudden rush, coherence returned, leaving him gasping with shock. He bit his fist to keep from crying out, as he stumbled out of the tangle of blankets and bodies, and dragged himself out to the porch.

No longer able to choke back the wave of sorrow, he sank down against the wall and let the sobs break out. Giving in to the grief, he allowed himself to be consumed by it, absorbed in the horror of what had happened.

He sat there for a long time, head bent in sorrow, only rising when he felt the sun's rays peeking above the horizon. He watched the pinks and oranges shooting across the sky.

Gwennie loved sunrises. She'd tried to photograph or paint them many times, but was often frustrated that the images were so hard to capture.

Jerrett felt the tears drying on his face as he watched the colors waver and shift, eventually drifting away. As the last wisp of pink vanished from the sky, it was as if Gwennie's spirit slipped away with it.

Jerrett leaned back against the wall. Gwennie was in a better place now, safe and happy. He knew what she'd say if she were here; she'd tell him to get up, to move on, and to take care of the family. He could do that for her. She wouldn't be disappointed in him. "I'll take care of them, Gwennie. I promise to keep them safe." He nodded to himself, took one last look at the pink strands fading into the blue sky, and picked himself up. He had work to do.

CHAPTER 12

The First Day of the Rest of Their Lives

The ringing phone broke the silence, as Jerrett made his way back into the kitchen. A sense of dread filled him. Anyone calling this early and under these circumstances could not have good news. He picked it up reluctantly.

Matt Kepler was on the other end. They hadn't seen each other since the last race, but that wasn't uncommon since the Keplers lived an hour away, near Philly.

A brief hello was all Jerrett got before Matt launched into his news. "Jerrett, it's bad. I don't know what's going on, but there's fighting everywhere. I got a call from a friend in the city and his neighbor's house was raided because of its strategic position. The family was told to get out, and when his oldest son refused ... they shot him – right in front of his parents, Jerrett."

"Oh, God."

"We have to get out of here. We're packing up the RV right now ... but I don't even know where to go."

"Starlight, Matt. That's where we're going. It's only a couple of hours away, tucked up there in the mountains. It should be out of the way of any fighting. I know Saul and Markie won't mind us staying there. Get out of there, Matt! You guys are way closer than we are to the fighting. Get out while you can."

Matt agreed readily. Then he asked, "When will you and Gwennie get there?"

Jerrett choked back the lump that had suddenly formed in his throat and closed his eyes. He couldn't speak.

"Jerrett? Are you there?"

Pulling in a shaky breath, he forced himself to tell Matt about Gwennie. The shock and disbelief were evident in Matt's voice when he offered his condolences.

Jerrett cut the call short, knowing he was going to break down if he kept talking. That was something he couldn't afford to do just now. There was too much to take care of. Matt promised to call Luke Bradford and tell him about Starlight.

After he hung up the phone, Jerrett ventured into the living room. Dean lay snoring on the floor, next to Trevor's couch. The children were still asleep as well: Cami stretched out on the recliner and the boys curled around Jasper.

"Hey, guys, wake up." Jerrett knelt between his brothers, shaking Dean's shoulder. He watched as Trevor stirred, a grimace on the boy's face as he woke to pain.

"You OK, Trev?"

His brother cracked open an eye and grumbled, "Go 'way …"

Jerrett allowed a ghost of a smile to dance across his face, then persisted, "Come on guys, we've got to pack up the camper truck and clear out of here – the sooner the better." Trevor moaned, groggy but awake. Dean reluctantly sat up, looking shell-shocked and zoned out.

Jerrett filled them in on Matt's news about the fighting in Philly. As he talked, Troy sat up, followed by Dalton and Cami. Jasper stretched, pranced around, and made for the door. Troy took the dog outside.

Trevor, holding his arm to his side and wincing, made his way into the kitchen and turned on the radio.

"Maybe we can get some news." The others filed into the room, quiet and numb, too exhausted for tears. As they scrounged for something that resembled breakfast, Jerrett dug through the medicines Gwennie had stashed in a basket. He found what he'd been hoping for – some leftover antibiotics. He passed the bottle and some pain medicine over to Trevor. As if on cue, Dean handed Trevor a glass of juice a second later.

Trevor chugged down the pills, his face pinched with pain as he continued to fiddle with the dial on the radio.

They all moved about as if in a fog, the new reality of their situation beginning to sink in. The absence of Gwennie was felt all around them. No one was bustling about, packing lunches and reminding them of appointments; no one was checking last-minute homework or helping finish a report; no gentle hugs or kisses were dropping on recipients without notice. The energy and vibrancy of the household was entirely different. It was an uncomfortable feeling – of home not being home anymore. It was as if a gigantic hole had opened in their lives, one that could not be closed again. To the children it was scary and uncertain; to the adults, gut wrenching and mind-numbing. Would they ever feel *right* again?

Though his heart ached, Jerrett was determined not to let his grief get in his way. He needed to take care of the family and get them somewhere safe. He'd promised Gwennie.

The sudden voice of a newscaster out of Philly brought all their focus on the radio. Quietly, they gathered close, and even the children were still.

The man's voice rose as he told the story of the day before. It was filtered news, of course, censored by the government. People had long since learned to take the information on the news with a grain of salt. The announcer touted the rally as a peaceful gathering to promote citizens working together with the Elite Guards. The story spun was that the militia had turned the affair into a violent attack. It claimed that the government's armed forces were maliciously provoked, forcing them to protect themselves. Apparently, fighting was still going on around the Philadelphia area and spreading out from there. The radio warned people to stay inside, mind their own business, and answer any questions officials had for them.

Anger swelled up in Jerrett. How could the media twist things around like that? People had died! He had seen the firing squads along the highway. How could it say the Guards were innocent?

Dean slammed his fist into the counter. "What the hell are they talking about? The Guards were pulling people out of their cars and shooting them! They were innocent!"

"Yeah, and at the rally, the Guards just started firing into the crowd. As soon as the first shot was fired, they aimed right at the audience," Trevor added. "Didn't even look to see who they were killing."

"Is that when they killed mommy?" Cami's teary voice interrupted.

"Oh, sweetie," Jerrett scooped up his little girl. "Shh ... it's OK." She wrapped her arms around him in a death grip.

"Well, is it...?" Troy persisted. Jerrett hesitated then nodded reluctantly. Troy sniffed and rubbed his nose. Dean appeared by the boy's side and wrapped an arm around Troy's shoulders.

"It's all my fault," Dalton started to say. "If I hadn't gone, mom wouldn't be ..." he stopped, trying to control his feelings. Hugging his arms around himself, he continued. "It's my fault. I'm so sorry ..."

"No, son, no," Jerrett interrupted, passing Cami to Dean and coming to stand in front of his eldest. He brought Dalton's head up to look at him. "Don't you go blaming yourself. It's not your fault. Your mom wouldn't let anything stop her from getting to any one of her kids if they were in trouble. A whole army couldn't have kept her away. You didn't get her killed. The Guards did. Put the blame where it belongs, bud. On them, not you." He gathered Dalton into his arms and then turned to Trevor. "Same for you, Trev. You guys didn't know what you were getting into."

"But we should've listened to you," Trevor admitted softly, eyes downcast. "You said not to go."

Jerrett sighed, turning towards Trevor while keeping his arm around Dalton. "OK, you're right. I did say that, and you went anyway. But there was no way you could have known what would happen. You aren't to blame for what happened. However, from now on, you've got to listen to my instructions exactly, understand? This is a whole new world we're in. The country's at war. We might run into other dangerous situations and I need to know you'll do just as I say. All of you."

The kids looked at him with wide, scared eyes. Heads nodded.

"So, dad ...," Troy began his expression thoughtfully.

"Yes?"

"Does that mean mom was a hero? 'Cause she went there to save Dalton and Trevor?"

Jerrett eyes filled with tears, a smile spreading across his face at the same time. "Yeah, bud. Absolutely. She was the ultimate hero. She would've done anything to save her family. She's the best kind of hero there is."

Troy nodded affirmatively, a proud smile on his face, cheeks wet with tears.

Jerrett hoped he would always think of his mom that way. A true hero.

● ● ●

After they'd finished talking and eaten a quick breakfast, Jerrett assigned the family tasks. A sense of urgency filled him. It was time to get out of here.

Trevor would pack the food from the pantry, which he could do using just one arm. Dalton would carry the boxes to the truck afterwards. They had found an old sling for Trevor, which eased his pain somewhat, but he was still too pale for Jerrett's liking. He ordered him to rest after he was done.

Troy and Cami were filling laundry baskets with clothes. Dalton was packing coolers with food from the refrigerator.

Dean had gathered up whatever guns and ammo they had at the house; it wasn't much – just an old hunting rifle and a handgun. Jerrett slipped the handgun into a shoulder holster and strapped it on, sliding his jacket over it. It was weird, a bit uncomfortable, but reassuring, too,

The dog, Jasper, roamed around underfoot, getting in everyone's way until Cami remembered that no one had fed him. The seven-year-old took care of that task diligently.

Jerrett took stock of the camping gear that was already stowed in the camper truck for their stays at the track. There was the propane stove, with canisters of gas, sleeping bags and old quilts, lanterns, and flashlights. Other assorted gear filled the cabinets and bench seats.

In the trailer, a big, yellow generator stood in the corner, next to jugs of gas. A toolbox and the family's four dirt bikes were always stored in the trailer. Jerrett thought about taking them out but instead left them. It would give the kids something to do, maybe to distract them from their grief for a while.

After inventorying all the contents of the truck, Jerrett headed into the house. Trevor was still working on the pantry, slowly, because of his arm.

"Need some more painkillers, Trev?" His brother looked up at him and nodded, agony evident in his eyes. He wanted to have Trevor lay down, but they needed his help to get out of here. Jerrett patted his brother's shoulder and headed upstairs.

Rummaging through the bathroom cabinet to select what to bring, he heard a noise that caught his attention and stopped him in his tracks. Someone was crying. He swept his arm across the shelf, knocking everything into the bag. Grabbing up the duffle he headed down the hall.

In Cami's room, he found his little girl lying face down on her bed, surrounded by clothes and stuffed animals, crying into her pillow.

"Cami, honey, come here." Sitting on the bed, he held his arms out to her. She flung herself onto him, her little body shaking.

"I miss mommy," came her tiny voice. Choking back his own tears, he just squeezed harder, not trusting his voice and having no idea how to comfort her. He couldn't fix what was wrong this time. Gwennie would have known how to help Cami, what to say to soothe her, but Jerrett had no idea how to get her through this; he didn't know how to get himself through it.

Making shushing noises, he rocked her, feeling her body gradually relax and hearing the sobs slow. He breathed in Cami's scent, a mixture of children's shampoo and sweat. Eventually, her breathing evened out, broken only by an occasional hiccup. Easing her back, Jerrett saw she was asleep in his arms. Poor thing, she was working on only three hours of sleep and facing the biggest tragedy of her life. Maybe he was expecting too much of her, maybe of all of them. But what else could he do? They needed to get out of here and quickly.

He lowered her down onto the bed and carefully covered her with her flowered comforter. Kissing her tenderly on the forehead, he left the room on tiptoe and closed the door carefully behind him. She could sleep until they were ready to go.

Leaning against the wall in the hallway, he breathed deep, rubbing over his head. A sob broke loose, but he choked it back. Pushing himself off the wall, he moved on to the next task. There was much to do.

The scene in the living room was one of organized chaos. Bags, boxes, and baskets sat everywhere, with the guys bustling around, packing, moving, and sorting. Jasper was into everything. Jerrett passed Trevor a couple of painkillers. "OK, guys, we need to move this stuff out to the truck, get it all loaded. Trevor, not you." He pointed at his invalid brother. "You stay in here and make sure no box gets left behind. And guys, Cami is sleeping, so let her rest awhile. I need to run out to the shop for some tools and to get all the cash out of the register. Then I need to go to the store for propane, gallons of water, and whatever else we might need. The bank, too, if I can."

Dean spoke up, "The bank should be open soon, but it'll be packed. Everybody's going to be looking to have cash on hand right now. You better go there first. But then again, the store will be overrun, too. Maybe I should go to the store, while you do the bank and the shop?"

Jerrett thought about it. "I'd rather not leave them alone here." He pointed to Trevor, Dalton, and Troy.

Trevor was already shaking his head, and Dalton rose. "We'll be fine, dad. Trevor can supervise the packing. Me and Troy will carry the stuff out to the truck. You guys go."

"Yeah, Jerrett, it's fine," Trevor added.

Not liking it, but not seeing much of a choice, Jerrett agreed.

"Stay close to the house, and get everything ready so we can leave when we get back. If you hear or see anything strange, stay inside, lock the doors. Don't forget about Cami. Trevor, can you call Barry and tell him where we are going?" Trevor nodded.

"Shit, Jerr, I just realized we only have one vehicle. My jeep's still in Philly with the SUV. What can I use?"

Trevor and Dalton looked chagrined at that. Their escapades had lost the family two vehicles.

Jerrett pondered the issue briefly, "How 'bout I drop you off at the store and meet you back there later? It's not ideal, but I don't know what else to do."

Dean looked uncomfortable with the idea but agreed, as there was no other choice. "OK, I guess, but I'm worried about crowds and rioting."

"Let's just drive over and see how bad the store looks, OK? Then we'll decide." Dean agreed.

They said goodbye to the boys and headed off.

DON'T TREAD ON ME

CHAPTER 13

Rioting

Jerrett dropped Dean off at the nearest store. People were streaming into it, but it looked peaceful enough.

Dean opened the door and started to climb out of the truck. "Hey, be careful," Jerrett halted him with a hand on his arm. "We need the supplies, but we need you more."

Dean flashed him a slight grin and hopped out of the truck, then joined the throng heading into the store.

Jerrett watched him go, wondering if he was making the right decision. He didn't like the idea of leaving Dean there, not with all that was going on. What a strange turn of events, being afraid of leaving his grown brother at the store alone? When had that ever entered his mind before all this? Now he didn't like the idea of being separated at all. Being away from the children bothered him even more. What if something happened to them while he was gone? He'd never forgive himself.

It'll just be an hour, Jerrett told himself. We should be home in an hour. He made himself drive away from the store and down the road to the bank.

At the bank, the ATM was closed, forcing him to go inside. In the lobby, he was dismayed to find himself in a line seven people deep at the nearest teller. The other tellers were just as busy. The lines snaked through the waiting area like a serpent. Jerrett surveyed the folks around him. They were fidgeting, glancing all around them, checking watches; the tension in the air was almost palatable. It made the hair stand up on the back of his head, and Jerrett almost left. But he needed the cash. Breathing deeply, he forced himself to wait calmly.

As he waited, his thoughts drifted. Yesterday's happenings swirled through his mind as if he were watching a movie.

Gwennie was gone.

Standing here, doing something he did all the time, he could almost pretend nothing *had* happened. It seemed like any other day. But it wasn't. So much had changed that Jerrett feared life would never seem normal again. He felt as though everyone standing around him should be able to see it written all over him; it seemed inconceivable that they didn't know about Gwennie. The whole world should know just by looking at him. Surely he didn't look the same as he did yesterday, did he? Not when he felt so completely ripped apart inside. How was it possible that they didn't know?

Lost in his thoughts, he was oblivious to the crowds around him until they suddenly began pushing against him. The sudden pressure yanked him away from yesterday and back into the present. Looking around, he noticed three large men pushing their way through the crowd to get to the counter.

"Move it!"

"Get outta my way!"

"Sirs, you will have to wait your turn," a clerk called out, noticing the disturbance.

"Yeah, wait your turn!" someone yelled.

"We all want our money!" another voice added.

"We want our money, now! You can't stop us from getting our own money," one of the men answered, as they continued to push against the line. Shouting rose from among the crowd, but it pressed in tighter, a blind need consuming people's common sense.

"Lady, I ain't waiting in this line just to find out you ran out of cash before we got up there. I want my money right now!" another of the men called out.

"I want my money, too!" another added.

The press of the crowd got even tighter. "Get me out of here! I'm being crushed!" someone yelled.

Shouting broke out all around Jerrett as bodies pressed into him. Sweat poured down his back and his heart pounded. What should he do? He needed all the cash he could get, but the situation was rapidly going south. Pressed in on all sides, he wasn't even sure he could get out anymore.

The clerks had gone from frazzled and overworked to panicked. One was on her phone, frantically calling 911. The people in the lobby continued shouting and pushing each other.

Jerrett had to get out; he would be crushed if he didn't. But how? He scanned around him, looking for a way. His eye landed on the table where the customer slips were held in tiny sections. If he could get up on it, maybe he could get past the crowd that way? But there were several rows of angry, frightened people shoving each other between him and the table. Glancing around the room, he came up with an idea. Riding along with the tide, he allowed himself to be pushed towards the counter. A few well-placed elbows got him to where he needed to be, tightly pressed against the wooden barrier separating him from the tellers. Nudging the man next to him gave him just enough space to propel himself up onto the counter. One of the tellers shouted for him to get down, but Jerrett ignored her as he made his way across the space, dodging barriers and hands as he went. It took him almost to the door, but not quite. He would need to drop back into the crowd, to get to the table by the door. Once over the table, it was only a step or two to the door. Glancing behind him, he saw that two other people had followed his idea and were now on top of the counter as well.

"Come on!" he motioned them along. Not bothering to see if they were still following him, he propelled himself off the ledge into the crowd, giving people no choice but to shift out of his way or be landed on. Pushing his way through, he found himself at the table. He hauled himself up but was stopped by a child's cry. Glancing about, he soon found himself face to face with a young mother, holding a toddler in her arms. Tears streamed down the woman's face as she desperately clung to her child.

Without further thought, he reached down to her, grabbing her under the arms and pulling both of them up. Another man and woman reached the table and joined him in hoisting the young mother up to safety.

"This way!" Jerrett said to the others. They scrambled across the table, leaped off the other side, and found themselves at the door. Bursting out, they ran away from the entrance. The young mother thanked Jerrett and then ran for her car. Jerrett did the same.

As quickly as he could, he sped away from the chaos. He needed the cash, but there was nothing to be done about it now.

Heading down the road, he hurried around slower cars in his quest to get to his garage.

At the shop, Jerrett cleared out the cash register, pocketing the meager supply of cash. Checking the hidden stash in his toolbox, he found another $500. That would hold them for a little while. It was supposed to be for the mortgage, but Jerrett figured that was something that could be dealt with later.

Jerrett pocketed the money. He grabbed a plastic crate, upended the contents, and turning to the toolbox, he began filling it with the tools he thought he might need.

Repeating the procedure with several other boxes, Jerrett stood back to take one final look around. He took in the sight of the neat rows of oils, the stacks of t-shirts, shelves of helmets, and toolboxes of equipment. Several customers' vehicles were lined up in the bays, waiting to be worked on. When would he be back? A cold shiver ran through him at the thought, and he suddenly feared he might never see this place again. He didn't want to lose yet another piece of his life. Choking back the lump in this throat, he grabbed the nearest crate and hurried out to the truck.

Just as he was turning off the lights, his phone rang.

"Hey, Dean – " he started to answer.

"Jerr! Get over here, man. It's turning ugly. People just started pouring into the store, they're grabbing up everything in sight!" Dean's voice sounded tight and scared.

"I'll be right there. Hang tight."

"OK. I'm hiding outside, at the rear of the store. Go around to the left of the building, I'll watch for you."

After Jerrett had left him at the store, Dean had stood for a moment, scanning the scene before him. It was only a little after 9 am, but the place was filled with people. Dean grabbed a cart and hurried away. If all these people were here preparing for a crackdown, they'd all be after the same supplies. He raced down the aisle towards the camping section. They needed propane canisters, and lots of them, to fuel the camping stove or they'd be eating a lot of peanut butter and jelly sandwiches. No thanks.

He passed several people on the way to the camping section, which thankfully was empty. Apparently, no one had thought about these supplies yet. Dean imagined the canned goods aisle was probably packed. He hurried down the aisle, grabbing propane, of course, along with a selection of freeze-dried foods and waterproof matches.

Finishing up, he fast-walked his way towards the food section. He could hear more voices as he neared. Heading down the bottled water aisle, he was dismayed to see the shelves nearly picked clean. He grabbed whatever was left and threw it in the cart. Racing up and down the aisles, he grabbed whatever he could find. Most of the aisles were filled with people; he avoided the busiest ones completely.

As his cart filled, so did the store. People were pouring in and they were running through the store. He watched helplessly as a thin woman was bowled over by a larger man and nearly trampled. Passing by another aisle, he heard a woman shriek, then saw a young thug grabbing items out of her cart and running away. The teen headed right for Dean.

His blood boiling with outrage, Dean stuck out a foot and sent the youth flying. The boy sprawled onto the floor, and Dean pounced on him.

"Give it back!" he snarled, teeth bared.

The youth put his hands up, pleading, "OK, OK!" Cautiously Dean stood and watched as the young man handed over the women's items.

The rumble of the crowd was getting louder, more agitated, accompanied by screams and angry voices. It flashed Dean back to the only time he'd gone Black Friday shopping with his ex-girlfriend, Lydia. At a preset time, a large group of items went on sale and the crowd went completely nuts – the roar that filled the air, the screaming, pushing, and trampling was the same thing that was happening right now.

Dean felt the same red-hot sensation burning inside him. There was plenty here for everyone if people would just calm down and take a reasonable share. But looking around him, he knew that wasn't likely.

The situation was quickly getting out of control and he needed to leave now. Racing for the nearest cashier, he paid for his items and high tailed out of the door and around the back of the store to hide.

● ● ●

It took longer than usual for Jerrett to get to the store; the roads were clogged with traffic. As he neared the store front, he could see the crowds pushing their way inside, desperate for supplies. Jerrett whipped the truck around the building, narrowly missing people recklessly racing across the lot.

Rounding the back of the building, he didn't see anyone at first, but Dean had been watching for him and sprung out from behind a dumpster, towing a shopping cart behind him.

"You made it!" The relief was evident on Dean's face. He smiled at his brother, then turned to the cart, scooping up the first bag.

Jerrett jumped out to help. In short order, they had the truck loaded and jumped in. "Ready?"

Dean nodded in affirmation as his brother peeled through the parking lot. At the front of the building, people dodged the truck as it careened through the area. Jerrett gave it all the speed he could, trying to prevent anyone from bothering with them or their loot. Back to the house they sped, sticking to side roads. Encountering no further trouble, they were soon home.

Troy burst out of the door to meet them as they parked the truck. Dalton followed.

"Any problems here?" Jerrett asked.

Dalton shook his head and answered softly. "No, dad, we've got the truck all loaded."

"Were you able to get propane and stuff?" Troy wondered.

"Yeah. But it got crazy at the end, a nasty crowd was gathering so we beat it out of there," Jerrett answered. He craned his neck to see past the boys. "Where are Trevor and Cami?"

"Inside. Sleeping," Troy answered.

"Good, let's transfer all this stuff into the campertruck and then we'll wake them. Let them rest as long as possible." The boys nodded in agreement and silently went about their work. Jerrett took a moment to watch, impressed at their ability to keep going. They had to be exhausted and reeling from their mother's death, but they soldiered on. He was proud of them, and he needed to find some time soon to tell them that. Filing that thought away for another time, he grabbed up a box and hauled it into the camper truck.

Before long they had the rest of the supplies loaded and were ready to go. Jerrett stood for a moment, taking in the sight before him. Gwennie's honeysuckle bush was blooming, and the sweet smell filled the air. Toys littered the porch, cast off and abandoned. The house, with its peeling paint and sagging wood, looked depressed and empty.

The grief he felt was so deep, so permeating, that he was afraid he'd never get rid of it. He was empty, sad, and numb.

They piled in the truck and were soon pulling out of the driveway, the 20-foot trailer following along behind.

Jerrett kept his eyes on the road, refusing to look back. Someday, somehow, they'd return.

CHAPTER 14

Help Along the Way

With an hour of travel behind him, Jerrett's mind had begun to wander. Gripping the steering wheel, he fought against the dark thoughts threatening to consume him. Even in a truck full of people, he was filled with loneliness. He missed Gwennie. Her absence was like a gaping wound inside him and he feared he would never be complete again.

Jerrett tried to stuff his misery down inside. If he didn't, he wouldn't be able to function. And he had to – this was no time to give in to the sorrow – he had to get his family away from the danger. Blinking back the tears, he forced himself to breathe deeply.

A hand landed heavily on his shoulder and squeezed. He knew without looking that it was Dean.

"Hey, bro, how're you doing?"

Jerrett swallowed and tried to reply but couldn't get past the lump in his throat.

In a soft voice, Dean asked, "You want me to drive?" Jerrett answered by shaking his head. He wanted the distraction; he needed something to keep himself from falling to pieces. The heavy traffic they found themselves in demanded his attention as it slowed to a crawl.

"What's that up there?"

Jerrett's eyes were drawn to where Dean pointed: the sawhorses placed across the road and the Guards standing nearby.

They were motioned to stop by a dark-skinned man with a bald head and squinty eyes. Jerrett slowed the truck down and stopped, his heart pounding in his chest. What would the Guards do? Would they let them go on, or place them in custody? His mind flashed back to those reeducation camps Luke had told them about.

"OK everybody, just stay cool. Don't say anything," Jerrett ordered.

The squinty-eyed Guard strode up to the window. "Papers," he demanded crisply.

Trying to steady his trembling hand, Jerrett held the documents out. With a steely glare, the Guard accepted the identity papers and stepping back, looked them over. Jerrett nervously wiped his sweaty palms up and down his jeans, trying to look nonchalant. The weight of the gun strapped under his coat pressed against him like an anchor.

What would he be forced to do if the Guard wouldn't let them pass?

"What are they doing, daddy?" A tiny voice interrupted his ominous thoughts.

"Shh!" Dalton hissed at her. Jerrett turned in time to see Cami stick her tongue out at Dalton. Jasper, sensing the tension, began to growl. Cami continued to question.

"Troy, hang onto Jasper. Try to keep him quiet." Jerrett whispered. "Cami, hush. I'll explain later." Scowling, she crossed her arms over her chest but fell silent. Troy knelt on the floor next to Jasper.

The Guard returned to the window and narrowed his eyes impossibly tighter, matching the scowl on his face. "Where are your travel papers?"

Jerrett cleared his throat nervously. "We didn't have time to file them, the fighting was getting close and we had to get out of there. I'm sure your supervisor will understand under the circumstances."

The man offered no sympathy in words or expression as he walked back to the Guard shack with the identity papers still in his hand.

"These assholes better let us through," Dean scowled.

They watched anxiously as the two Guards conferred briefly, then the one inside picked up his rifle and followed Squinty Eyes out of the Guard shack. The look on their faces and the raising of the rifle told Jerrett and Dean everything they needed to know.

"He's got a gun! Jerrett! Go, go!" Dean shouted. Jerrett made a split-second decision and throwing the truck in gear, he burst past the roadblock.

"Get down everybody!" Jerrett shouted. Cami screamed, which set Jasper to barking. Jerrett glanced back to see Dalton throw his sister down to the floor. Trevor, one arm in the sling, had the other around Troy, as they hunched under the table.

Looking back to the road, Jerrett gunned the engine as fast as it could handle. The old truck whined in protest. He glanced down at Dean on the floor beside him and shouted, "Find a way off this road, quick!"

Dean pulled out his phone, looking for the GPS.

Cringing, they heard the sudden popping of gunfire behind them. Ducking involuntarily, Jerrett hoped they were out of range or that the heavy metal sides of the truck would prevent any bullets from reaching his family.

The racket inside the truck was deafening: the dog was barking, Cami was crying, and someone was screaming. Jerrett careened around a corner, the heavy trailer dragging along behind him like an anchor, swaying from side to side. He wished he could cut it loose.

"Up ahead, turn right!" Dean yelled over the din. "Then another quick right after that!"

Jerrett didn't answer; all his focus was on the winding road ahead of him.

"Are they following us?" Trevor yelled.

Jerrett glanced at his mirror. "There's a jeep back there, but it's pretty far behind." It must have taken the Guards a while to start the pursuit. He whipped the truck around the first right turn, and then the next. "What now, Dean? That won't stop them for long."

"Gun it, bro. Then take the second left turn up ahead." Dean's voice was strained and tense. Jerrett followed his brother's directions. After several more quick turns, it became evident they had lost their pursuers. As they straightened back up, they breathed a collective sigh of relief.

"Everyone OK?" Jerrett called out. Affirmative replies came from all.

"How the heck did we just do that?" Dean wondered aloud.

"There was no way we could have outrun them in this rig. They should have had us way back there," Trevor added.

Jerrett had been thinking those same thoughts all along. "I'm guessing they got called off the pursuit. Someone bigger than us needed their attention."

"You realize our identity papers are back there, right? What are we going to do without them?"

"Avoid any more roadblocks," Jerrett deadpanned, his heart still threatening to beat its way out of his chest.

He fell silent, deep in thought for a time. Identity papers were everything nowadays. You were supposed to always have them with you: without them, you could be arrested. What would they do now that the Guards had theirs?

After thinking it through, Jerrett answered his brother. "We have to go underground for a while. Stay up in the mountains until this whole thing blows over. Hide out. We'll park the rig and won't move it again until everything clears up." A thought struck him. "I'm sure we can get our papers replaced after things settle down. We can't be the only ones to lose theirs." He glanced at Dean to gauge his reaction. His brother looked doubtful but kept his thoughts to himself.

As they drove along they found themselves heading into traffic again, even though the road was not a major highway. It seemed everyone was heading west, as they were, except for the military vehicles they passed. They were going the opposite way, towards the fighting.

Jerrett felt a sense of unease with each vehicle that passed. He hoped their friends and neighbors had gotten away.

He thought of his father for the first time in a while. Even though he hated the man for a lifetime of torment and the beating he'd given Trevor, he found himself torn on whether he should've called him and given him a warning about all this, or hoping he'd gotten what he deserved.

Jerrett's thoughts were brought back into the present by the sight of hikers along the side of the road. As he drove along, the foot traffic got even heavier. Some were equipped with heavy camping backpacks, others a mishmash of backpacks and luggage, and still others had nothing but the clothes on their backs. Some even had children with them. Jerrett couldn't imagine fleeing home like that, especially with children. Occasionally they saw someone with a wagon, or wheelbarrow, hauling an invalid or a stack of belongings. A bicycle passed through, then a motorcycle. Jerrett couldn't take his eyes off the waves of humanity they passed. What was he seeing? Refugees in America?

"Daddy, where are they going?" Cami's small voice spoke up.

"I don't know, baby. Running away from the fighting, I guess."

"But that girl doesn't even have any shoes."

Jerrett glanced back at her and followed her gaze. A little girl, about Cami's age, was walking along with a woman beside the road. Entranced, Jerrett slowed the vehicle down to a crawl to get a good look at her. The girl's bare feet and legs were splattered in mud, her dress torn and her hair disheveled.

Jerrett's heart stopped. What was this? It was like witnessing refugees in some third-world country, not America. His mind spun, and he felt disoriented.

"Stop the truck, Jerr. We have to help them." Dean's voice was full of pain. Looking at these poor people was more than he could bear.

"OK, Dean, but only the woman and girl. Get them on quick. We can't take all these people and we don't want to get mobbed." It broke Jerrett's heart to have to say that, but he knew they would need their supplies once they got to the mountains. He had to care for his own first. Dean climbed down the steps and slid the door open.

Jerrett kept a close eye on the side view mirror, watching the crowd.

It didn't take long to convince the girl's mother to join them, for which Jerrett was grateful. He had just noticed a group of rough-looking men coming up behind them on the driver's side of the truck. "Hurry up, Dean! We got trouble coming!" He called out of the door. The woman and girl scrambled into the truck, just as the group of men neared the driver's side door. Slamming down the door lock, Jerrett peeled out in a flurry of gravel, speeding as fast as he dared with people walking all around. Pedestrians scrambled out of his way. "Lock the door, Dean. There are some angry-looking guys out there."

Dean obeyed as the women and girl took seats at the table with Troy, Cami, and Trevor. Dalton had moved to sit on the plastic cooler to give them room on the benches. Dean took his place beside Jerrett.

Jerrett chanced a glance back as he drove. The woman sat, clutching her daughter tightly, looking terrified. "Hi," he smiled, trying to be friendly. "I'm Jerrett Nolan. These are my kids and brothers." He paused, and then added, "Are you OK?"

The woman nodded her head and took in a deep breath. "Yes, thank you. Thank you for picking us up. I'm Mary and this is Tori," she nodded to the little girl.

Dean offered her a water bottle from the cooler, which she took and shared with her daughter.

"What happened to you?" Troy blurted out. Dalton nudged him hard while Jerrett scolded his son's nosiness.

"No, that's OK," Mary assured him. She went on to explain that they'd gotten a ride with a friend, trying to get away from the battle. They'd left quickly, taking very little along. A short way down the road, Mary and her friend had gotten into an argument over which way to go. In a rage, her friend had pulled over and shoved her out of the car, then unbuckled her little girl and deposited her beside Mary. By the time Mary had gotten her feet under her, the friend had sped away in a cloud of dust, leaving them beside the road. They hadn't even had the chance to gather their things or Tori's shoes, which the child had kicked off. With no other choice, they started walking. They were headed to Mary's mother's house, another hour and a half down the road by car.

When she finished, there was silence in the truck. Jerrett couldn't believe how someone could do that to their friend. He set his mouth in a grim line, forcing himself to concentrate on navigating through the throng of people instead.

A little voice broke through his thoughts. "Do you want my flip-flops? They're kinda small for me anyway," Cami asked the little girl. The child smiled and nodded, and Cami went to retrieve them. Jerrett burst into a grin. The next thing he knew, the boys were falling all over themselves offering things to Mary and Tori. Food, water, clothes, toys. He saw Mary beaming as she accepted a hoody offered her. Jerrett laughed out loud, the scene a balm to his soul.

They were finally able to help someone, and it felt wonderful.

Mary's mother's house was only a half-hour out of the way. It was a jolly atmosphere the entire way. The family shared sandwiches, chips, and cookies with Mary and Tori. The visitors were each sporting a hooded sweatshirt now, and Tori's washed feet swung back and forth in Cami's cast-off flip-flops. Jerrett knew they all needed some relief from the stress and fear and grief, and the two rescuees were the perfect distraction. Mary was gracious and appreciative, while little Tori was as sweet as could be. In no time at all, they'd arrived at their destination. They deposited their passengers at the end of a short driveway and a slim, gray-haired woman rushed out the door of the house to greet them.

With a sense of satisfaction, Jerrett pulled back out onto the road.

CHAPTER 15
Danger on the Road

It took some time, but they eventually found themselves back on track. Their route had taken them off the highway and onto a narrow, desolate road up into the mountains. Jerrett was glad they'd left the crowds behind; he was relieved not to be faced with that sea of humanity.

The sun had sunk below the horizon, leaving them deep in the shadows. The lane they traveled was riddled with potholes. The weeds along the roadside were nearly as high as Cami.

The seclusion of the area made Jerrett feel safer now, he could almost forget what was going on and pretend they were just headed to the mountains for a vacation.

His illusions were shattered, though, when a loud backfire burst out like a gunshot. The truck's engine began breaking up with a 'pop, pop, pop' sound. Cami screamed, which made Jasper start barking again.

"What was that?" Someone yelled. With a groan, Jerrett swung the truck to the side of the road, tramping down the weeds shooting up beside the pavement.

"Great, now what?" Dean rolled his eyes in frustration. Troy, the junior motorhead that he was, clambered to the front, curious to see what the problem was.

"Come on, let's check it out."

"And hope it's nothing." Dean quipped. The whole family climbed out. Jerrett heaved open the hood, leaning over to examine the engine. Dean and Troy crowded in.

Between the three of them, they checked everything they could think of that would cause the engine to act up the way it had. Then they did it all over again. But even after two hours had passed, they still hadn't reached any conclusions. The frustration had been mounting steadily until even Jerrett was ready to explode; Dean had already lost his cool some time ago.

Trevor and Dalton had set up a few chairs when they had finally gotten tired of standing around. Trevor was dozing in one. He still looked pale and sickly, Jerrett noted, his gunshot wound giving him discomfort. Troy, who had finally gotten bored staring into the engine compartment, gathered sticks for a fire while Cami sat in the doorway of the truck, playing with some toy cars she'd found.

Jerrett was chugging back a beer when his brother called out, "Here it is! The distributor cap is cracked!" Dean pointed at the offending part. Jerrett rushed over to look, the kids following. Everyone crowded around, trying to see the crack. It was the first excitement they'd had in hours and they all wanted in on it.

"What do we do, dad? How do you fix that?" Troy wanted to know.

Jerrett looked thoughtful for a moment. "JB Weld or an epoxy might work."

"Do we have that?" Dean wanted to know.

"Nope."

Dean growled in frustration. "Then why bring it up? What can we use that we do have?"

"Nothing. We need a new cap."

"Know any place around here that might have parts?" Dean asked.

Trevor, who had woken from the noise, spoke up from his chair. "How are you going to get to a garage or store anyhow?" He nodded towards the broken-down truck.

Jerrett pondered for a second and pulled out his phone to look up a map of the area. Luckily he found a signal.

"Hey! I know! You could take the dirt bikes!" Cami said, excitedly.

Troy chuffed at that, "No, dummy, they can't take them on the road!" Cami shoved him, and he shoved her back.

"Knock it off you two," Jerrett mumbled robotically, not even bothering to take his eyes off the screen. "Look here," he nudged Dean and pointed to the map on his phone. "There's a garage just a few miles down the road. We *could* probably take the bikes. This road isn't exactly hopping with traffic. Doubt anyone would even care with all that's going on."

"Haha, I told you dirt bikes would work!" Cami teased.

Troy stuck out his tongue at her, "Shut up, Cami."

Dean ignored them as he headed for the trailer. In minutes he had two bikes pulled out. In a low voice he asked his brother, "Should you *and* me go? Or just one of us?" He raised his eyebrows and tilted his head towards the rest of the family. He wasn't sure it was safe to leave them here alone.

Jerrett followed his glance back to the others. "I think at least two of us should go, for back-up. Who knows what we'll find out there." He thought about it for a minute and then added, "I don't like the idea of taking Dalton. He's too young. Trev can't ride, of course, with that arm. Do you think between them they can handle anything that comes up here?"

Dean looked thoughtful for a minute, and then answered, "I guess they'll have to. I don't want you out there alone. Someone's got to keep you out of trouble."

Jerrett grinned at him. "Should we take the gun or leave it?" He was uneasy about leaving his kids, especially along the side of an abandoned road at night and in these circumstances.

Dean shrugged. "Take it, I guess." Jerrett agreed and tucked the gun in his waistband, under his jacket. Jerrett got a quick kiss from Cami and then hopped on his bike. Dean revved his engine impatiently.

The road they drove down was cracked and riddled with potholes, making for a dangerous ride. No streetlights were here to light their way, only the moonlight. A few sparse farmhouses dotted the landscape, most well back from the road.

Jerrett followed Dean down the road. He hated driving off and leaving the others behind. What if something were to happen?

They soon passed a tiny cafe, a post office, and some houses beside the road. Finally, they spotted the garage. It was a ramshackle old building, its sign worn by age and weather.

Jerrett and Dean pulled their dirt bikes into the parking lot and shut them off. Leaning them against the building, they cautiously made their way to the door. Jerrett peered in the dirty window, trying to see if anyone was inside.

"Should we go in?" Dean wondered aloud.

Jerrett shuddered as a wave of fear came over him. Something wasn't right here; it felt off. But they needed the part. Warily, he pushed open the door and stepped over the threshold.

He was barely inside when a voice called out, "Stop right there!" A thin, dirty man stepped out from behind a shelf. He held a double-barreled shotgun and it was aimed at Jerrett. "What do ya want?"

"Ah … we … ah," Jerrett stumbled over his words, heart thudding in his chest, "We need a part for our truck. That's all. A distributor cap. We can pay." Jerrett raised his hands over his head, the hidden handgun pressing against his side. He didn't want to have to use it.

Dean rattled off the specific make, model, and year of the truck.

The man lowered the shotgun. "OK. Sorry about the gun. You can't be too careful these days. I've got caps. Hold on a sec." He made his way over to the long shelves of parts behind his counter. Jerrett dropped his arms and tried to still the thudding in his chest. The man rummaged around awhile, his back turned, but the shotgun still resting over his arm. He finally came out with the part and held it up for inspection.

"100 bucks."

Jerrett wasn't sure he'd heard him right. "Excuse me? What?"

"100." It was more than double the normal price. "Take it or leave it."

"Jerr, we need it," Dean whispered. Jerrett knew he had no choice. He reached into his pocket and pulled out his wallet. The man took the money and gave him the part.

"Now go on outta here." His steely eyes watched their every step.

Jerrett and Dean cautiously backed out of the garage.

At the door, Dean, unable to control himself any longer, spat out, "Hope you can sleep tonight, after ripping us off, nice job taking advantage –"

"Dean, come on, let's get out of here." Jerrett pulled him away, cutting off the rest of his brother's comments. He didn't want Dean to start a fight; he just wanted to get back to the kids. Angrily, Dean followed him to the bikes.

They soon found themselves back on the lonely, deserted road. Wishing his dirt bike had a headlight, Jerrett carefully steered his way around a large pothole. Pennsylvania roads were known for their killer potholes. The truck was soon in sight and not a moment too soon by Jerrett's reckoning. He breathed out a sigh of relief.

Pulling their dirt bikes up to the driver's side, they dismounted and rested the bikes against the vehicle. As they were rounding the front of the truck, Dean, apparently still reeling with anger, spoke up. "That jerk mechanic … I'm still pissed off! We ought to go back and –"

His voice cut suddenly as he rounded the front of the camp and came in sight of the campfire. He froze.

Jerrett nearly ran into him. "Dean, what the hell?"

When his brother didn't answer, Jerrett followed his gaze to the campsite in front of them.

What he saw took his breath away and made his stomach drop.

Two Elite Guards stood in the firelight, guns drawn. One Guard, head shaved and portly, held a gun pressed up to Trevor's head as Trevor squatted on the ground. Blood trickled from a gash on his forehead. Dalton stood behind the fire, his arms around Cami and Troy, keeping them close. Another Guard, dark-skinned and curly-haired, stood by them, his gun pointed straight at Jerrett. Cami's soft cries could be heard as tears streamed down her face. Jasper's barks echoed from inside the truck where he'd been stowed.

Dean's hands went up instantly, the forgotten distributor cap still clutched in his hand. Jerrett followed suit.

"What's going on here? What have you done to my brother?" Jerrett asked, anger and fear combating within him. He took a step forward but froze as the bald Guard pressed the muzzle of his gun harder into Trevor's head. Trevor trembled visibly, fear and pain evident in his eyes. Jerrett felt Dean go still by his side. "OK, OK. What do you want?" Jerrett tried to remain calm. Cold fingers of fear curled around Jerrett's heart.

"You're under arrest. This one," the bald, chubby Guard jabbed Trevor again with his gun, "Says you have no travel papers. You will need to come with us," he ordered.

"Travel papers? We were running for our lives! What are you talking about?" Dean raged.

The man's robotic voice continued, "You may be helping the enemy. You will be taken in and questioned."

"What? This is crazy! We have little kids with us. We're just trying to get away from the fighting, that's all," Dean argued vehemently. Jerrett nudged Dean, silently, willing his brother to keep his cool.

"Look, can you at least let him up?" Dean indicated towards Trevor. "You're hurting him. He's not going to do anything."

The bald Guard nodded and straightened up, backing off just slightly and indicating with a nod for Jerrett to help his brother.

Jerrett rushed to Trevor's side and gently hauled him to his feet. "Are you OK?" He peered into Trevor's pale, bloody face. His brother nodded grimly. Still supporting Trevor, who seemed a bit wobbly, he looked over at his kids. "You guys OK, too?"

Troy nodded while Dalton answered, "Yeah." Cami's sobs continued. Dean scooped her up, holding her close.

"Let's go. Oscar, get them in the van," the bald guy said, pointing to the police vehicle, parked down the road, in the shadows beyond the trailer.

The family, herded together a few paces ahead of the Guards, were close enough to whisper. "Dalton, take Trevor." He thrust Trevor into Dalton's grasp. "Troy! Hold onto Cami and keep going. Dean, be ready." Jerrett hurriedly ordered. Jerrett slowed down, trying to put some distance between the rest of the family and himself. Without a word, Dean followed his lead.

"Move it," the Guard ordered. When the rest of the family safely behind the protection of the trailer, Jerrett stopped.

"What about the dog?" Jerrett turned and faced the Guards, hands upraised. "We can't just leave him there. He'll die."

The bald Guard paused, looking thoughtful. "Yes, no need for the animal to suffer. We'll put him down." Baldy turned to look back toward the truck. Oscar too, turned his head to watch his partner. In that second, Jerrett whipped out his handgun, clicked off the safety, and fired at the bald man, intending to hit him in the arm. At the last second, the man moved, and the bullet caught him square in the chest. He dropped like a rock.

At the same time Dean tackled Oscar, and they crashed to the ground in a heap. Oscar's gun went spinning away. He smashed a fist into Dean's face and jumped up and sprinted off into the underbrush.

Jerrett held his gun pointed at the bald man on the ground. Why wasn't he getting up? He willed the man to twitch, or groan … anything.

Dean rose beside him and called to the others. "Dalton! Keep them back there a second. We need to take care of something."

Jerrett felt Dean's eyes on him, but he couldn't move. "Jerr, put the gun down," Dean's hand closed around his and pushed down. "Safety, Jerr," he reminded his brother. Jerrett absentmindedly clicked the safety on the gun and slipped it into his waistband.

"Dean … is … is he …?"

Dean glanced at him and went over to the Guard. Through a fog, Jerrett watched as Dean checked the man's pulse. His brother turned to face him and shook his head.

Jerrett turned away, fist over his mouth. He'd just killed that man. Killed him!

A noise made him look up and he saw Dalton and Trevor peering around the back of the trailer.

His family was safe. He'd done it to protect them. He raised his chin defiantly in the air. He'd done what he had to, and he'd do it again. Suddenly coming to his senses, he scooped up the Guard's gun and handed it to Dean, who pocketed it. He motioned for the teens to go back to the children, then turned to the unpleasant task at hand.

Without a word, they both knew what they needed to do.

Together they dragged the Guard's body into the scrub. Dean kicked some dirt over the blood on the ground, so Cami wouldn't see it. Not knowing what to do about the Guards' van, they left it where it was, hoping they'd be gone before anyone came to investigate it.

Jerrett called the family over to the fire and gave them all a quick once over. Tilting up Trevor's face, he eyed the gash. Luckily it didn't appear too deep; the blood was already clotting.

"You OK?"

Trevor nodded as Dean brought over the first aid kit.

Leaving Trevor in Dean's capable hands, Jerrett headed for the hood of the truck. Ever mindful of the remaining Guard who had fled, he assigned Dalton to stand guard. Reluctantly handing over his gun to the boy, Jerrett went to work switching out the part. He saw Troy and Cami gather around Dean to stare at Trevor's head.

Jerrett's insides felt hollowed out, emotions numb. He still couldn't believe what had just happened. Had he actually killed a man? He wished Gwennie were here. Jerrett's hands shook as he worked, but he couldn't let himself dwell on it. They had to get out of here. Time was of the essence.

"Dad, do you think that Guard will come back?" Dalton called, his voice shaking. He pointed the flashlight into the woods, pistol ready in the other hand.

"No, son, he's unarmed and outnumbered. He's hiding, waiting for us to leave so he can get to the van."

"Won't he just radio for help?" Dalton wondered aloud.

"Good thinking, kiddo. We'll have to do something about that." He called out, "Dean, can you take care of the radio in the van when you're done there?"

"Yeah."

Minutes later, Dean came to him, Troy in tow.

"I'll go take care of the radio now and dig around the van for anything we can use. Troy's going to help," Dean informed his brother. Jerrett nodded and went back to work.

An hour later, the truck was finally repaired and everyone was loaded and ready to roll. Added to their firearm collection was a new rifle and ammo scored from the Guards' van.

Just as he was about to shut the truck rear door, Jerrett stopped. What had he just heard? He froze, straining to hear.

"Dean, what's that?"

A faint pop popping noise could be heard in the distance.

"Is that gunfire?"

Suddenly an earsplitting explosion rocked the air, and both brothers could see flames shooting into the sky, only a mile or so behind them. They ducked instinctively.

"Let's get out of here!"

Jumping in the truck, they tore off down the empty road, gunning the vehicle as fast as they dared.

"Dad! What was that?"

Jerrett gritted his teeth. He knew but couldn't bring himself to answer.

It was the front lines of the war, just behind them. As they sped off down the road, Jerrett and Dean watched the battle and explosions behind them in their mirrors. The rest of the family peered out the rear window.

Eventually, the sounds faded in the distance and Jerrett finally felt as if he could breathe. They were on their way again, but would they ever be safe?

CHAPTER 16

Home, Sweet ... Home?

Two hours later they left the pavement behind as they turned onto a remote dirt road. The winding path was hard to navigate in the dark, forcing Jerrett to concentrate fully on what he was doing. He welcomed the distraction. Coming here was like coming home; the sight of the track and the sharp, refreshing, outdoorsy smell of the pine trees always brought a swell of excitement.

But something was missing tonight. Gwennie's absence was felt like a punch in the gut, leaving them all hurting and breathless. Even the soothing balm of the lumbering trees and fresh piney air couldn't do away with the ache and hurt.

Jerrett knew Dalton and Trevor must be plagued with guilt. His love for the boys battled with an overwhelming load of blame. They *were* the reason Gwennie had gone there and been killed; he couldn't deny that. And yet, he wouldn't ever say that to them. Even in his overwhelming despair, he knew voicing his blame would be more than they could take. If he wanted them to be able to move on at some point, they could never know how he felt. He was afraid those feelings would surface if they talked about it, and so he vowed to be silent on the matter for the time being.

He cleared his throat, finding it thick with unshed tears, and called to his family.

"Hey, guys," he turned to look at them. "We made it." Trevor lay reclining on the bench seat, gray-faced with pain, his temple swollen and discolored, and his arm in the sling. Troy had his head on the table but raised it when he heard his dad. His eyes looked hollowed out, dark circles from the lack of sleep. Dalton didn't look any better. Cami was dozing on the floor, using Jasper as a pillow. Dean, who had set up a lawn chair inside the truck, stretched his arms and sat up straighter.

"Finally," Dean commented, his face grim.

As they pulled off the road, they bounced along the rough, pothole-lined dirt driveway. The trees were thick on each side, obscuring the view beyond them even in the daylight. The underbrush, along the sides of the lane, was a wild tangle. Here and there random trails cut through the growth.

Jerrett bumped along at a crawl, trying to avoid the potholes where possible, but failing on the narrow lane. It was barely wide enough for two vehicles to pass each other and enormous tree trunks rose up on both sides, reminding the drivers to stay alert. As they drove on, they soon came into a clearing and the road widened. To his left, Jerrett saw the long sweeping hill, bare of trees, which led down to the motocross track nestled in the valley. Generally, that was where they would park and camp for the weekend when they came here to race. He could see the small sign-up shed, sitting smack dab in the middle of the hill, where Saul Carrigan and his wife, Markie, the owners of the track, ran the races. Their house was down in the valley, out of sight, to the right of the track.

Jerrett pulled into the upper lot. The level space, about as long as two football fields, was surrounded by the trees with a large, cleared space in the middle for RVs to park. Jerrett could see many vehicles already there, though none were parked in the middle of the lot, rather they were snuggled up under the trees, along the edges. Lanterns and campfires lit up the area and people milled about.

Dean spoke up. "Why are they all parked over there? It looks as if the motor homes are sitting in the brush." Troy and Dalton crowded upfront to see.

Jerrett didn't answer but instead pulled over when he spied Matt Kepler, their faithful friend, jogging towards him, lantern in hand.

Jerrett was filled with relief that their friends had made it. He hopped out of the truck.

Matt grabbed him in a tight hug. "Jerrett, I'm so sorry. I'm so sorry about Gwennie." His voice trailed off. There were tears in his friend's eyes. Jerrett could only nod, not trusting his voice.

The rest of the family clambered out behind him then, giving both men an excuse to change the subject.

Dean, easing up behind his brother, squeezed Jerrett's neck gently as he took over the conversation. "Hey, Matt. Glad you made it. Everyone OK?" Matt nodded.

"Why is everyone parked under the trees?"

Matt glanced behind him. "Oh, yeah, that. Well, Saul and Markie thought it might be good to hide the vehicles, just in case any drones fly over. I don't know," he shrugged, "Maybe it's silly, but it made sense to err on the side of caution."

Jerrett nodded, not trusting his voice. Others were making their way over now, ready to greet the new arrivals.

Laura Kepler, Matt's wife, gave out hugs all around, tears in her eyes. Laura and Gwennie had always been friends. The Kepler kids huddled near, welcoming their friends, but unsure what to say. Jennica Bradford, her long prairie skirt flowing out behind her, followed Laura and the kids. Her own four children followed, the youngest, Marlowe, clinging to her hand.

Jerrett was grateful to see no one else had lost a family member, but also a bit jealous.

Matt, sensing how close his friends were to breaking down, quickly steered things in another direction.

"Why don't we show you around? Let you see where everyone is and what we've set up." Matt slung an arm around Jerrett's shoulders and steered him toward the encampment. Jerrett glanced back to see the rest of the family. Laura and Jennica were fussing over Trevor and his injuries, and Terra and Thalassa Bradford, the twins, had Cami between them, holding her hands. Troy and Dalton were surrounded by their friends.

Jerrett allowed himself to be led as they moved around the parking area. Dean followed along.

Passing by a trail worn through the brush and lit up by tiki torches, Matt explained how it led to the creek. Saul had shown them the path and offered to let them refill their water tanks there. As they neared a medium-size red tent parked next to a matching red car, two young Italian men that Jerrett didn't recognize came over to greet them.

"Jerrett, this is Salvatore Caruso and his brother, Paulo. Salvatore went to college with Saul and Markie's oldest daughter, Fiona." Jerrett reached out to shake hands with the brothers while Matt went on, "Salvatore is a paramedic in Philly, studying to be a doctor. His brother goes to Temple."

Salvatore chuckled at Matt's description, "Well," he clarified, "Not quite. I want to go to med school, but I'm not there yet." He flashed a wide grin and arched his bushy eyebrows. "Gotta save up some dough." Salvatore had chin-length curly hair and eyes so dark they looked black. Paulo, resembling his brother only as a fellow Italian, was short and wore his hair close cut.

"Would you mind looking at my brother?" Jerrett was inspired to ask. "He was shot two days ago in the riots. Then a few Guards roughed him up earlier this evening."

Salvatore's face took on a look of concern, "Absolutely. Where is he?"

Jerrett looked around, surprised that Trevor wasn't among the group. How had he missed that?

"He's with the ladies," Matt informed him, pointed to the Kepler RV. "They took him over there to 'mother' him." Jerrett thanked Matt and he and Salvatore hurried off, the rest of the family and friends trailing after.

Inside the Keplers' RV they found Trevor, slumped over, Laura and Jennica hovering over him.

Jerrett dropped a hand on Trevor's shoulder. "Trev." He waited until the young man looked up. He was as pale as a specter. "This is Salvatore Caruso. He's an EMT."

Salvatore was the picture of professionalism as he bent to examine the wounds. He gently removed the bandages on Trevor's arm, eliciting a gasp from the boy.

"It looks like it went right through. You're lucky it didn't break a bone."

"I don't feel lucky," Trevor intoned softly. He was a pitiful sight indeed, with a hole in his arm and the ugly bruise swelling on his forehead.

Salvatore checked over the gunshot wound carefully and then tilted Trevor's head toward the light to look at the wound there. After asking a series of questions to assess his patient, he turned to Jerrett.

"Could you tell my brother to get my red backpack? I stuffed it with meds and supplies before we left. I think I have a bottle of antibiotics in there. Trevor's got a slight fever, which may be a sign of infection starting. Just in case, he ought to start on the medicine."

"I got this," Matt answered, exiting the RV, and grabbed the nearest kid to act as a messenger to Paulo.

"We cleaned it out the best we could," Jerrett explained. "Put a bunch of antibiotic cream on it, too, but that's all we could do. The fighting …," his voice trailed off as a feeling of failure came over him. He should have gotten Trevor to a hospital somehow. If he lost another member of the family, he didn't think he could survive it. His throat tightened with emotion, and he had to cough to clear it before he could speak again. "Is he going to be OK?"

"Well, he will be in pain for a few more days, but he should be fine eventually."

Paulo burst in just then, handing over his brother's red bag.

Salvatore fished around his backpack and pulled out an orange bottle. "Here they are! It's the only antibiotics I grabbed, so let's hope they do the trick. I'll clean this and rewrap it." Salvatore got to work on Trevor's arm. After it was cleaned and rebandaged, he helped the boy get the sling back on. He cleaned the cut on Trevor's head next. Jerrett was amazed at the tenderness in his touch. Rising from a crouch, Salvatore patted his patient's shoulder and reminded him to rest and take it easy. Handing off a bottle of pain pills and the antibiotics to Jerrett, he called to the ladies, "Can someone get Trevor some water, so he can take the pain pills right away?" Laura was quick to comply.

Salvatore stood and moved away from his patient, motioning for Jerrett to follow. In a low voice, he continued, "As for the head, he's not vomiting, but he probably has a mild concussion anyhow. He says he has a headache and feels a little dizzy. He seems a little out of it, kind of confused and tired. Keep an eye on him and I'll check on him again tomorrow. He needs rest and time to recoup, OK? No strenuous work for the next week or more. Let me know if he gets worse, but I think he'll be OK." Salvatore patted Jerrett's arm in reassurance.

"Stay here for a sec, Trev," Jerrett commanded, though it was unnecessary as his brother didn't look inclined to go anywhere. Jerrett ducked his head out the door, looking for Matt. He found him, and the rest of his family, seated on lawn chairs around the campfire. The littlest kids were toasting marshmallows.

He could almost believe it was just another night at the track.

"Matt, where should I park the truck? I need to get everything set up, so Trevor can lie down and sleep."

Matt and Luke Bradford stood to join Jerrett. Luke came over to greet his friend with a hug and a sad smile. The three of them, followed by Dean, headed over to the truck and trailer to get it moved.

Across the clearing from Luke and Matt's RVs, the group maneuvered the trailer as deep into the trees as they could, and then unhitched it. Moving the truck into position beside it, Jerrett rammed the rear of the truck into the brush. The trees overhead shadowed the vehicle, providing camouflage.

Once settled, Dean and Jerrett turned on the interior lights and began the process of getting the beds set up for the night. It would be a little tight with all of them, but they settled on the kids sleeping in the three bunks stacked along the wall, Dean on an air mattress on the floor, and Trevor would take the most comfortable bed, the fold-down table bed, and share it with Jerrett. Jerrett felt strange sharing a bed with someone other than Gwennie, though an empty spot beside him would be even worse. If there were any other choice, Jerrett would gladly have given Trevor the whole bed so he could be more comfortable, but they were out of options.

Back in the motor home, Matt offered to let Trevor stay the night with them. Trevor threw his brother a look of desperation and a sight shake of the head. Trevor, always was a little shy around other people and especially in his current state of health, was not up to being a polite house guest. The boy had been through a lot in the last two days and Jerrett knew he just wanted to be with family.

"That's OK, Matt. We've got everything all set up." Jerrett liked the idea of them staying together too. They thanked Matt and Laura and headed to their truck.

Sleep did not come easy that night for most of the Nolan clan, but one by one, pure exhaustion eventually claimed them.

CHAPTER 17
A New Way of Life

Over the course of the next week, the temporary village took shape. An odd cluster of vehicles and shelters materialized around the edges of the wide, grassy area. Thick woods surrounded the cleared area. A cluster of trees sat in the middle, creating a cozy area for evening campfires. Trails sprouted through the woods in many directions, leading through Saul and Markie Carrigan's expansive land. They owned several hundred acres in all.

Saul and Markie's house was completely hidden, down in a dry ravine some distance away from the track. Jerrett and Gwennie had always loved visiting Saul and Markie at their house. Chatting over coffee and snacks, they relaxed in the large, rustic cabin, the cool mountain breezes drifting through open windows. Gwennie had loved learning about the birds and wildlife that came to visit the many feeders outside the cabin. Saul would regale them with stories about the bear and deer that would visit. Once he shared how a bear wound up on their deck, nosing about a feeder until he set his dogs after it. The hounds had raised such a ruckus that they chased the predator away and tree'd it.

Jerrett and Gwennie had shared many happy hours in that house with Saul and Markie. Saul, with his bushy, reddish beard and hair, trapped under a stained baseball cap, still looked fit and trim at 54. Smile lines crinkled his friendly, weathered face. He was a hands-on guy, who could fix almost anything. He loved the peacefulness of the woods. Dean often hiked with him.

Markie had wild brown hair and eyes and was most comfortable in rugged boots and muddy jeans. Markie was tough, but kind, and always said exactly what she meant. She was usually seen whipping around the property on her four-wheeler, juggling the many jobs of a race day.

Together they made a wonderful couple and were known for their generosity, warmth, and compassion. They were free spirits who wanted to give up life in the city for a simpler, more peaceful one. They had raised three daughters up here, teaching them to hunt, track, fish, and ride. All three girls rode motocross, though the middle daughter, Felicia, was the true star on the track.

Starlight was a home away from home to the entire Nolan family, and the only place that felt like the right place to go considering the circumstances. The aura surrounding the woods and its people was relaxed and calm. Just what they needed.

In the week since they'd arrived, it was clear to all that Dean had made it his mission to keep a watchful eye on his family.

Trevor and Dalton were both wracked with guilt. Trevor hardly spoke, retreating into the same silent shell he'd been in when they had first gotten him away from his abusive parents. It saddened Dean to see him revert. He longed to break through Trevor's silence and hear him laugh again.

Dalton had been given to fits of sobbing; it was gut-wrenching to witness. He missed his mother terribly and insisted it was his fault she was dead. No amount of comfort seemed to help him, though Jerrett and Dean had both tried to reason with him. The boy knew the truth; if he hadn't gone to the rally, his mother would still be alive. Dalton had begun taking long, solitary walks in the woods, and Dean often followed at a distance, just to be sure he was OK.

Jerrett was deeply grieving, but Dean had never heard him utter a word of blame to either his older son or their kid brother. Even away from the boys, he never gave voice to those thoughts. If someone outside the family tried to bring it up, Jerrett would either walk away or avoid the subject. It had made for some awkward conversations, but Jerrett didn't even seem to notice. In fact, Jerrett didn't notice much. Dean's big brother was living in a fog.

Most of the household chores had fallen on Dean. He was the one who made sure the kids ate, that Trevor's wounds were looked after, the dog fed and water collected. Jerrett alternated between wandering the area, sleeping, or just sitting around, zombie-like. At times he would seem lucid and converse with the family, but then something would trigger a memory of Gwennie and he would just fade away. He rose early every morning to watch the sunrise, something he and Gwennie had often done. When he returned, his eyes would be red-rimmed and swollen. But he didn't cry in front of the kids; Dean knew he was trying to be strong for them.

Cami had woken up crying again last night, like she had so many times this week. The thoughts of her mother permeated her dreams. She'd crawled in bed with her daddy, who had been lucid enough to comfort her before they'd both fallen back to sleep together. Dean had allowed himself a smile at the sight of them curled up together on the bed, drawing comfort from one another. By morning, Troy had joined them, and they resembled a litter of puppies, with their limbs all tangled together.

At times Dean felt as if he were going to explode from the pressure of holding things together and the ever-present sadness. It weighed over the family like a thick, black cloud with no escape. He wondered if this would be their new normal. If it was, he didn't know if he could survive it. Dean longed for the laughter that used to fill their times together. He didn't know when he'd last heard Cami's giggle or one of Troy's corny jokes. Would they ever act like kids again?

Dean missed Evie. He longed to talk to her, to have someone to listen to how he felt and just be there for him. He wanted her company, and to know she was alright. He knew she was with her uncle, Mitch, and his militia, who were right in the thick of the battle back home. It kept him awake at night, wondering and hoping that she was OK.

In the middle of the week, Barry Forrester, Jerrett's mechanic, had joined them, along with his twelve-year-old daughter, Caitlyn. It was a relief to see they'd made it safely and felt good to have Barry with them. They were bunking in a pickup truck with a capper, tucked among the trees like all the rest. Saul's brother, George, and his family showed the day after. Saul had teared up upon seeing them finally safe. They bunked in the house with Saul and Markie.

Each new arrival was grilled for any tiny morsel of information. The internet and TV channels were blacked out, so gossip, though unreliable, had become the only news source they had. Unfortunately, the stories were always colored with the tellers' point of view and opinions.

Most nights, everyone would gather at a communal campfire and dissect the latest tale.

Dean found himself starting to go stir crazy, needing desperately to know what was really going on. And even more than that, he needed to talk to Evie. He'd tried her phone over and over this last week, but to no avail. It went straight to voicemail. He was worried sick.

He spent the day absentmindedly going about his chores, his mind on Evie. Somehow, someway, he needed to get ahold of her.

But before he could figure out a way to do that, Mitch called Jerrett. The tension was palatable between Jerrett and Mitch after their last encounter at Jerrett's shop. Dean pranced around Jerrett, motioning for the phone. After a brief conversation, Jerrett handed it over, obviously glad to be rid of Mitch.

"Mitch, have you heard from Evie? Is she OK? I haven't been able to get a hold of her." He tried not to sound too frantic, but knew he wasn't successful.

Mitch answered, "She's right here with me, Dean. She's fine. Her phone was damaged, but she's fine. You want to talk to her?"

Dean fumbled for an answer, the words tumbling all together in his eagerness to connect with her.

"Dean? Are you there? It's me."

Listening to Evie's voice, Dean felt a wave of peace settle over him; it was like a balm soothing his rough edges. A smile spread across his face and his eyes pricked with tears. He barely choked out an answer.

Evie filled him in on what had been happening with the militia. They talked for some time, sharing the chaos and horror they'd both encountered. Somehow, it was more tolerable when shared with another.

Dean longed to hold her in his arms; just speaking to her felt like a heavy weight had been lifted off his shoulders. He could only imagine how wonderful it would be to hold her again.

He wanted the conversation to go on forever, but all too soon they were cut short, the phone's battery dying.

"Oh, Dean, I don't want this to end. It's been so good to talk to you again."

"Me neither." Something had happened to both of them, some kind of connection, and neither wanted to let the other go.

"I miss you, Dean. I want to see you again."

"I dream about you, Evie. I dream about holding you, having you near … of sharing my day with you. You've got to find a way to come up here. It's safe. I want you to be safe. I can't stand the thought … the thought of something happening to you." The sentiments welling up inside Dean were impossible to explain. It was ridiculous, wasn't it, to feel this way so quickly and so strongly? Dean wondered if he were going crazy.

"I'll try to come. But it's so hard right now. There are battles all over and they need me here. I do miss you, Dean. I want to see you again. Please know that if I could, I would be there with you." The longing was evident in Evie's voice.

The battery died, and the call ended without a goodbye.

Dean felt as if he were on cloud nine. The rational side of him knew it was too soon to be feeling the way he was about Evie; they'd only known each other a short time. But with the world turned upside-down like it was, they both needed something to hold onto. He'd learned his lesson – life was short: he wasn't about to waste any more time pining away for Lydia. It was time to take a chance and put himself out there again. Evie was the one worth taking that risk for. There had to be something good to come out of this mess.

● ● ●

Later that evening, Dean wandered over to the communal campfire. It was built in the center of the clump of trees, and the high branches, hanging thickly overhead, blocked the view of the fire from above.

Tonight, Dean was pleased to see Jerrett had joined them, even though he was staring vacantly off into the fire. Barry sat beside him, with the Caruso brothers next to him. Salvatore Caruso, the resident EMT, had just looked at Trevor again today and declared him to be healing nicely. Dean settled into a lawn chair. If he let himself, he could almost be convinced it was just another night at the track after a race. He wished Evie were here with him.

Across from them sat Luke and Jennica Bradford, Jennica wearing a long prairie skirt as usual and Luke in his favorite torn flannel. Their youngest, eight-year-old Marlowe, sat on his dad's lap, his long legs stretching out to the fire. Matt and Laura were there, and Laura cradled their youngest daughter asleep in her arms. Saul and Markie's three daughters were there too, though Dean always had trouble remembering which one was which, so he avoided calling them by name whenever possible.

In the dark, they could hear the other children calling to one another. Devoid of TV and video games, they'd resorted to the age-old custom of playing games like tag and hide and seek. Tonight, Troy had told Dean, they were playing Manhunt, a variation of hide and seek.

When they were tired of the game, they joined the adults.

The group had fallen into one of those silences that always seem to appear around a campfire, everyone off in their own thoughts and watching as the flames crackled and swirled.

"What's this war called?" Marlowe Bradford, the young intellectual, spoke out, breaking the silence.

"What do mean, horey?" his mother asked.

"This war we're in now. I learned about a lot of wars in school. What's this one?"

Laura spoke up, "This isn't exactly a war, Marlowe. It's a ... well ... I'm not sure what to call it."

"Aren't we revolting?" one of the Bradford teens asked. "Like, against the government?"

Her sister chimed in, "Yeah, just like in the first revolutionary war. This would kinda like be the second revolutionary war, wouldn't it?"

The adults were stunned into silence, history lessons flooding their minds and the shock of the similarities mind-boggling. Finally, Luke spoke, "I guess you're right, Marlowe, this is a war." He turned to his twin daughters, "The Second Revolutionary War."

"I never thought of it like that."

"Me neither."

"Can you tell us about the first one?" Troy asked, apparently not having studied the war in school yet, or not remembering that he did.

Laura began, with the others inserting tidbits as they remembered them. "Well, back then the British ruled over us here in America. We had no voice in government, no power –"

"And they were taxing the shit outta us."

"Geez, language!"

Laura hushed them and continued, "It was in 1775 that the Americans and British started fighting. It was a long, hard war, fought right here on American soil. The British were a strong force and the Americans were not very well trained or equipped ... but we wanted a victory more."

"Yeah, and we kicked their asses!" one of the teens chimed in, eliciting giggles from the younger crowd.

"Yes, we did," Laura agreed, trying to ignore the rabble-rousers. "Even though it looked as if we weren't going to be able to, we did win the war. That's why America is ours now, not England's."

Troy spoke up, brow wrinkled in concentration. "What's that flag with the snake on it? Didn't that have something to do with it? Dad, doesn't Trevor have one of those in his apartment?"

Trevor, usually silent of late, spoke up softly. "Yeah, Troy, I do. It says, 'Don't Tread On Me'. The snake was a symbol of the American colonies, coiled up and ready to strike."

"Cool!" Troy said. "Can we have one up here? We're ready to strike!"

A nervous titter floated through the group; no one here was ready to do battle.

Dean finally spoke to Troy, "Sure, we can make one for the camp. After all, we certainly don't want anyone treading on us!"

Troy beamed, and Marlowe and Cami immediately decided they wanted in on the action. The three began discussing where they could get what they needed for the project.

"Weren't the British called lobsters or something?" one of the teens questioned.

"Yeah, lobster backs, and redcoats, 'cause that was their uniform color."

Marlowe piped up, "We ought to have a nickname for the Guards like that." He looked thoughtful. "They don't wear red, they wear black. But they kinda have claws like a lobster – you know, when they grab people." Marlowe was silent for a while, deep in thought, then, like a light bulb flicking on, he called out, "I know, they're like black bears! Black is the color of the uniforms, and they have claws and can be vicious like a bear. And we're in the woods, where the bears are! We can call them the Black Bears!"

Laughter erupted around the campfire, with the adults congratulating Marlowe on his idea.

"I love it, buddy!" His dad beamed. "I'm calling them Marlowe's Black Bears from now on."

☻ ☻ ☻

After the children were corralled and herded off to bed, the discussion around the fire turned to other matters.

"I think we should build some log cabins. Make a more permanent situation here," Barry was saying.

One of Saul's daughters answered, "Dad was talking about that last night. He says that would be OK, if the cabins were kept small. You could use his sawmill."

"As long as everyone helps maintain the property," her sister interrupted, flinging her pale braid over her shoulder.

"Felicia! You don't have to say that. Everyone knows." Ah, Felicia. Dean made note of the name of the sister with the white-blond hair. Now if he could only figure out what her brown-haired sister was called.

"Cabins?"

Dean's head whipped around at the rusty-sounding voice of his brother. Jerrett had lifted his head and was looking around at the others, confusion in his eyes. "Why would we do that? We're going back home soon. Well .. .maybe not soon ... but we're going." He finished, blinking his eyes owlishly.

"What if we can't? Go home again, that is?" Luke Bradford interjected.

Dean watched his brother shake his head, his brow furrowed in confusion. "What are you talking about? Of course, we're going home." Jerrett's bewilderment was obvious. It seemed as if he were slowly awakening from his hazy week.

Salvatore Caruso spoke up then, "Well, some of us aren't well off up here, you know. A tent ain't exactly the best home away from home for any length of time. I think a cabin sounds great, even if it's just for a few weeks."

"We could share it for now. Just build the one," Barry offered. Barry, and his daughter, along with the Caruso brothers, were the worst off in terms of shelter.

"That sounds good," Salvatore's younger brother, Paulo added.

Dean watched his brother carefully. Jerrett was shaking his head incredulously like he couldn't believe what he was hearing. Matt reached over to Jerrett, laying a hand on his friend's shoulder to steady him.

"Look, Jerrett, it doesn't mean we aren't going home someday. I'm sure we'll all get back." Matt patted his friend's shoulder. "What I think we need most of all is information. It's driving me crazy not to know what's happening back home. My cell isn't even working most of the time anymore. I think the government has cut off some phone providers, unless it's just this mountain messing with the signal." He paused, waiting for everyone's attention. His serious expression drew everyone in. "We need to go on a scouting mission. I think some of us should head home, get the latest news and report back here. If we take the dirt bikes, we can go off-road quite a bit of the way."

"No, Matt! It's too dangerous!" His wife, Laura, grabbed his arm.

He patted her hand and said, "Laura, just hear me out. I've thought about this a lot. Don't you want to know if our family and friends back home are OK? C'mon, let's just talk about it, alright?" Reluctantly placated, Laura settled back to listen, but kept her hand on Matt's arm as if she was afraid he would jump up and go right now.

Dean picked up the conversation and steered it back in the needed direction. "Getting away from any Guards would be easier on the dirt bikes, too. They can't chase us off-road and the woods would be perfect hiding places. I, for one, want to see what's going on. I'd like to find Evie."

Jerrett perked up, sitting tall and looking awake. Finally.

"Yeah, we could check things out, find out where the fighting is and if it's safe to go back," Jerrett contributed. "But would we be able to stay off the roads the whole way? Does anyone have a map or a working GPS on their phone?" He looked more animated than Dean had seen him all week. That alone was enough to get Dean on board with this idea.

Someone produced an old-fashioned road map. A lantern was brought out and the map was spread out on a table. The group relocated around the map, plans and routes being discussed and argued about late into the night.

CHAPTER 18
MacGyvering

Once they decided the mission was on, the group began the massive undertaking of transforming the dirt bikes. By the nature of the sport, most riders or their parents knew something about maintaining dirt bikes or had experience in the mechanical trades. Having that many minds at work helped them come up with some creative solutions.

The dirt bikes were perfect for off-road travel and quick getaways, but they needed adjustments to improve their stealth and functionality. The first thing the group did was strip off the bright, colorful graphics and number plates. Race bikes were by nature flashy and bold, but scouting bikes needed to be dark, camouflaged, and unidentifiable. Most of the riders even painted the plastic and frame black. Troy and the other young riders cringed as the vivid, eye-catching graphics were destroyed. To Jerrett, it felt as if he was stripping away the old from himself, as well as the bike. He was no longer the rule-abiding garage owner who minded his own business. Now he felt like some kind of criminal, preparing to do wrong. His spirit felt dark; his true self hidden away. He wondered if he would ever feel normal again. Burying himself in the work, he was grateful for a distraction.

Saul's barn hosted heaps of assorted objects that could be used on the bikes, including a supply of half-filled cans of paint. He and Markie had thrown nothing away, it seemed, in all their years of living up here. Their barn was a treasure trove.

The group set the teens to work hunting and sorting for items they needed. Lanny, Saul's youngest daughter, led the other teens scavenging through the barn. Dalton, along with his friends, Woody and Owen, scaled the piles of scrap.

At times they found themselves balancing preciously over jagged holes in the worn floor of the barn.

At the end of the day, they had amassed several large piles of useful materials. Jerrett felt like a modern-day MacGyver as he rummaged through the heap. His thoughts ran in a thousand directions at all the possibilities. The guys gathered around him, surveying the objects.

"We'll need crash bars," someone suggested. "To protect the engine through the rough terrain."

That seemed like a good place to start. Over the next several days, metal fence poles were transformed into cages around the engines. Trevor turned out to be very good at welding, once Jerrett showed him how.

As they were digging through the piles for more bars, Dalton called out, "Dad, what's this for?" holding up the object in question.

"That's a light for deer spotting," Saul answered for Jerrett.

"Do we need lights on the bikes?" Dalton wondered.

Jerrett looked at the others and shrugged, "Yeah, that's a great idea, son." He smiled at the look of pride on his son's face. "You take Owen and Woody and see if you can scrounge up some more."

As the teens gathered the items, Jerrett, Dean, Saul, Luke Bradford, and Barry Forrester, began making adjustments to the vehicles.

"What about the noise?" Saul commented. "We'll need to silence the exhausts somehow."

Dean agreed, "Yeah, the Guards will be on us in seconds if we're this loud."

"You mean the Black Bears!" someone yelled, and the group burst into some much-needed laughter.

After some brainstorming, it was decided that tin cans, which were plentiful around the campsites, could be rigged with some welded-on washers and used as mufflers. Jerrett and Trevor took up the task of creating the silencers.

The group pulled together and worked hard, each contributing in their own way. Even the little kids had joined the act, painting small, twisted snakes on the bikes. 'Don't Tread On Me' was scrawled on the top of several tanks where the riders could see them.

A feeling of pride welled up in Jerrett. Starlight's residents made a good team.

Once done, the six dirt bikes were parked next to each other, little resembling their former glory. Stripped of flash, and rigged with an odd array of lights, batteries, crash bars, and the mufflers, they looked like something out of a Mad Max movie. Someone had even come up with a way to connect two backpacks that could be tied together and positioned under the seats to be used as saddlebags. Pieces of leather were sewed together as holsters for the rifles on three of the bikes. Other riders would wear handguns. Chicken wire had been stretched across the lights to deter stray branches from smashing them.

The six riders didn't resemble their former selves either. Dressed in dark riding gear, armed and angry, the garage owner, mechanics, realtor, student, and recent college graduate had transformed themselves along with their vehicles. They were now six nameless, anonymous spies. They felt brave, stupid, reckless, and determined. Wondering what they would encounter, they nevertheless were committed to the journey.

Their route had been carefully mapped out. The wooded areas of Pennsylvania were plentiful and would provide the necessary cover. And where the woods ended, fields often took up residence. Rural roads were in abundance, too, and would be used if all else failed. In plotting their routes, the riders avoided the cities and larger towns. Even with all these precautions, they knew they would be seen, but counted on their anonymity to protect them. Dirt bikes had no license plates and without number plates, there was very little to distinguish them from one another at a glance. Jerrett liked the feeling of being invisible; it helped him cope with the idea of spying, sneaking around, and exploring without travel papers.

It was decided to keep the scouting groups small to avoid being noticed. Jerrett and Dean would pair up with Barry, since they lived close to each other. It would be good to have someone as intimidating as Barry along.

As badly as Dean wanted to contact Evie, the idea was scrapped since they had no idea where she was and they hadn't made contact lately with her or her uncle, Mitch.

Matt Kepler would take Salvatore Caruso, who was hoping to check on his mother since they both knew the area around Philadelphia. Salvatore had ridden dirt bikes for years and used to own a street bike. He wasn't happy about being separated from his younger brother, but Paulo didn't have the necessary experience on motorcycles. He worried about leaving him behind.

"I'm not a child, Sal," Paulo protested. "I'll be fine here." In the end, it was Laura Kepler, Matt's wife, who was able to calm Salvatore down with the promise to look after his brother.

Fiona, Saul's eldest daughter, decided to come along, too. She and Salvatore had gone to college together and even dated briefly. That fling was over, but Fiona still had friends in the area she was concerned about. Salvatore welcomed her company, and Matt conceded that she probably rode better than all of them, having had a race track in her backyard.

The entire population of 33 people who resided at Starlight had gathered in the clearing to see the riders off. Jerrett was inspecting his bike one more time, when his younger son joined him.

"That's sad-looking, dad," Troy commented, shaking his head at his father's dirt bike. "You had such cool graphics on there. Now, nothing."

Jerrett grinned at the ten-year-old. "I'm incognito, kid. Can't have anybody figuring out who I really am."

"Like a spy?"

"Exactly."

"Cool." Troy nodded his approval.

Jerrett laughed, amazed that he still could. He fidgeted with his jacket zipper and then pulled on his gloves. Suddenly remembering, he said, "I can't seem to find my goggles. Maybe we left them at home. Can I borrow a pair of yours?" he asked Troy.

Troy nodded eagerly, "Of course, dad." The boy scurried off to find them. Cami drifted by, wearing a grungy motocross t-shirt two sizes too big, flowered leggings, and sparkly ballet shoes. Her hair had just been done by one of the other moms and was brushed and styled carefully in a neat bun.

"Hi, baby. I like your hair."

"Hi, daddy. Laura did it for me." She twirled a tendril around her grubby finger. "Are you leaving now?" she wondered aloud.

Jerrett knelt. "Yes, honey. But I'll be back in a few days. Dalton and Uncle Trevor will look after you."

Cami rolled her eyes. "Daddy, I don't need anyone looking after me. I look after me." Hands on her hips, she was clearly annoyed that her dad did not recognize her independence.

"Sorry, of course. Well, you look after them, then, OK?"

Cami nodded her approval. Wrapping her in a hug, Jerrett squeezed her tightly, not wanting to let go. When she finally squirmed away, he rose and looked around. Dalton was following Troy out from the truck, and Trevor joined them. Dean waltzed over to them, fastening a helmet strap as he went.

The family gathered close, awkwardly shuffling around, worried about how to try to say goodbye. Troy broke the silence by handing over his goggles to his dad, with a simple "Here you go," and then hugging him. Hearty slaps and hugs followed all around. When his family stepped back, Jerrett swung a leg over the bike seat and kicked over the engine.

He stopped then, taking in the scene before him, a lump suddenly rising in his throat. Trevor stood tall and silent, his good hand resting on Cami's shoulder, the other still in a sling. Dalton slouched next to him, hands stuffed in his pockets and shoulders sagging, eyes downcast. Troy stood off to the side, waving.

Pushing down the feeling that he might never see them again, Jerrett waved back. He couldn't let himself think that way, he chided, but the ominous feeling stayed even as he flashed a tiny smile, one last time, to his family.

CHAPTER 19

The Scouting Mission

Jerrett tilted his head to the sky and breathed in the sweet smell of pine. The wind blew against him and he enjoyed the feeling of freedom that always came with riding a motorcycle. For a brief moment, all his troubles were taken away with the wind.

The riders were headed down a narrow mountain road, with trees lining it on either side, obscuring the view from above almost entirely. They passed a ramshackle old cabin, built at the corner of Saul's property. Jerrett took notice of the rotting planks and disrepair. Skinny shoots of weedy growth wound their way up the supports, as nature fought to reclaim what once was hers. No other cabins were visible along the road.

It was not long, maybe a mile, until they came upon a paved road. Thick trees grew near the intersection and hung low over the road. Instead of trimming them, Saul had let them grow that way and had added some fallen, leafy branches over the lane entrance to hide it from prying eyes. The dirt was even swept clear of tire marks. To anyone not familiar with the area, they wouldn't realize a lane was even there. Or if they did, it was hoped they would assume it was an old logging road, now unused. Saul had taken down the wooden road sign pointing the way up to the track. Jerrett remembered a stop sign used to stand sentry here years ago, but it had been knocked over by a motorhome with an inexperienced driver one day and never replaced.

Although it was still light out, the canopy of trees created a dark, foreboding tunnel around them. Jerrett felt safe from prying eyes, but at the same time, the darkness seemed sinister and evil somehow, as if danger lurked just beyond the trees.

The ride home usually took around three hours by car; but by dirt bike, they would be forced to take slower, winding trails. The speeds wouldn't be as high and they would have to stop and rest.

For the first part of the journey, they would be able to stay in the state forests. There was a trail splitting the middle of the state, starting up north and stretching all the way to the Mason-Dixon Line. The riders would follow it as far as they could. After that, they would have to venture out on roads. Near the town of Pine Grove, the two groups would split up. The Philly group would head east, then south. Jerrett's group would go directly south.

A short time after the start of the trip they found themselves at the trail head. The group veered off the road and onto the path. Traveling up a hill they were soon rewarded with a sight that took their breath away. A beautiful vista stretched out before them, and they all stopped for a moment to take it in.

"Wow," Salvatore exhaled. "If this is what it looks like the whole way ..." His voice trailed off, amazement clear on his face.

"I wish it was," Barry answered. "C'mon, we got a lot of ground to cover."

As they drove along, they found themselves on a field of flat boulders, which obscured the path, but it looked level enough to travel on. Barry started first and seemed to be fine, when suddenly his front tire jammed into the ground and he flew over the bike's handlebars.

"Barry!" Propping his bike, Jerrett clambered over the uneven ground to his friend. Barry lay stunned on the rocks.

"You OK?" Jerrett gasped out, resting his hand on Barry's shoulder.

Barry nodded, sitting up. "Yeah, I think so. Just shook." As he sat, though, he rolled up his sleeve to examine a patch of raw skin where he'd scraped it on the rock.

"Ouch, that looks like it would hurt," Fiona said.

Barry was already rolling down the sleeve. "Nah, it's nothing. I'll be fine."

Matt and Salvatore were hauling Barry's bike out of the hole where it had lodged itself. Once it was upright, they examined it carefully. It seemed OK, the tire patch kits they'd packed wouldn't be needed yet – thank God. Pulling Barry to his feet, Jerrett and the rest remounted their bikes and took off, although a bit more carefully.

Once they had cleared the flat rocks, the ground leveled out for a while and so they were able to run at a high speed. Jerrett kept an eye on Dean as he rode just in front of him. His younger brother was not as experienced on a bike, but he seemed to be holding his own. A creek ran alongside the trail, occasionally crossing over it. They found themselves fording the creek more than once. It was quiet here, except for the sound of the dirt bikes.

Rounding the bend, they came up to a lookout where they could see for miles. Rolling hills were broken by a valley that ran between them. Trees covered the hillside. Jerrett paused a moment. It was breathtaking. He wished they could stay here forever, enjoying life and the beauty all around them. But Barry rode up behind him and nudged his way past, calling to Jerrett to catch up. Reluctantly, he rejoined the scouts.

He followed Barry onto the narrow trail. It looked barely wide enough for one person, with a long, sloping drop-off to one side and a cliff wall on the other. The ground was covered with tall weeds and a jumble of plants. Slowly they followed one another carefully down the skinny path. Eventually it widened, the cliff wall dwindling in height till it was just waist-high next to them. The trail led away from the drop-off on the other side, and they could breathe a sigh of relief. They rode for a while until they found themselves at the top of a steep hill, covered in giant rocks. The rocks jutted out every which way, just waiting to trap a dirt bike tire amongst them and send the rider head over heels.

"Can we make it?" Dean asked.

Fiona threw him a look of annoyance. "Of course, we can. Just go slowly and pick your way through. My sister and I ride through stuff like this in the mountains all the time." A few of the others looked doubtful, and Jerrett wondered if Fiona was just showing off. She seemed to read his mind and with an eye roll and exasperated breath, she said, "Look, I'll go first. Watch which way I take and follow me down, OK?"

Jerrett looked at the others. Barry nodded in agreement and Matt shrugged, while Dean and Salvatore studied the path. "OK, you lead," Jerrett told her.

Fiona began picking her way down the hillside, angling her bike between and over the obstacles. The others hung back, watching and waiting until there was enough distance between them for the next bike to start. Barry went next, followed by Salvatore and Dean. Matt and Jerrett hung back to make sure the others made it down. There were a few close calls, but they reached the bottom. Jerrett followed. The trail was steeply pitched, but he found he could work his way over the rocks easier than it looked from above, though a few spots did take his breath away. Once they were all down, they stopped for a break. Dean sprawled out on the ground, the others stretched out tired muscles.

"See, that wasn't so bad!" Fiona teased. Dean and Salvatore looked doubtful. "Well, if you think it was, wait till we have to go up it on the way back! That's the hard part."

"You aren't helping, Fie," Salvatore chided. Fiona just shrugged and chugged from her water bottle.

Soon enough they were back at it. One section of the trail was created when an old railway had been taken out, leaving a flat, grassy stretch where the trees formed a wall on either side. They could relax a bit there, and conserve some energy, which they needed when they reached the next surprise.

Coming to the end of the flat grass, they found themselves at the edge of a precipice that dropped off about 20 feet. In front of them ran an ancient railroad bridge composed of thick, rotting beams over a crisscross of braces. The rails and ties had been removed, and there was nothing along the edges. To compound that, between the beams ran a wide gap the entire length of the structure. One false move in either direction and they would plummet off the bridge or fall between the beams into the trestles.

"Whoa…!" Dean breathed out. Someone let out a whistle, and even Fiona seemed unsure.

"Is there another way around?"

Jerrett shrugged, "Not that I can tell. Anybody been this way before?" No one had.

"Well, let's walk out on the beams and check it out. See how sturdy it is," Matt suggested. They leaned the bikes against some trees and proceeded onto the structure. Each beam was about three-foot-wide, which a rider *on* a bike could navigate, but it was too narrow to push the bikes over safely. Even though vegetation had grown up around and on parts of the logs, it still felt solid beneath their feet. A few parts were rotting off, but the logs were almost as thick as they were wide, so the rot hadn't gone the entire way through.

Meeting back at the bikes, the group concluded that the bridge was the way to go. One at a time, slowly, they would ride over. They needed to be careful to maintain a perfectly straight path. Any deviation would send them over the edge.

Matt went first. He eased the dirt bike onto the beams, slowly creeping across. When he finally made it to the other side, he slipped off his helmet and called over, "It's not too bad, just go slow. Watch out for some of that moss – it's slippery. Stay on the right, I think it's a little better."

Fiona, Barry, and Salvatore followed Matt across in turn. Each one was successful.

"This looks easy. They had no trouble at all. I think we were worrying about nothing, big brother," Dean lifted his chin towards the obstacle.

"Don't think like that. Just because they got lucky…" Jerrett shook his head.

"I know." Dean fastened his helmet and started out on the log. Jerrett watched, his stomach clenched in anticipation.

Dean seemed to be doing fine, until suddenly his front tire hit the patch of moss Matt had warned them about. His front-end slid sideways. Dean dropped his feet to the ground and hit the brakes, stopping the bike just as the front wheel came to rest, teetering on the very edge of the log. He carefully, slowly maneuvered the bike backward.

"Careful, Dean, watch your back wheel!" Jerrett called out. His brother adjusted his steering to prevent the rear wheel from ending up over the other side. Once back on track, he paused for a moment and then continued to the other side.

Jerrett let out a breath he didn't even realize he'd been holding and hung his head. Now it was his turn. His heart thudded in his chest and he realized he was still rattled from seeing Dean almost fall. Giving himself a moment, he took a few deep breaths and then started across. Heart pounding, palms sweaty, and breathing heavily, he inched his way across. When he passed the slick spot where Dean slid, he felt a bit better. When he reached the far side, he felt a lot better. He slipped off his helmet, looked at his friends, and said, "That was a rush!" Relieved laughter rippled through the group as they congratulated each other.

● ● ●

After a lunch break, Jerrett was relieved to find the remainder of the trip was easier. When the woods gave way to civilization once again, the riders traveled across farmland and back roads. They stopped for a fuel fill-up at a motocross buddy of theirs. More than willing to help, he ran to the gas station for them and brought back several jugs of fuel. No one bothered them; it was thought that Marlowe's Black Bears were probably too busy with the fighting to patrol like they normally would. Near the small town of Pine Grove, they found an abandoned barn that would make a good stop for the night.

Rising the next morning to a chorus of stiff, aching muscles, they fixed a cold breakfast and got an early start.

Here the group would split.

Saying goodbye to Matt, Salvatore and Fiona was harder than Jerrett had thought it would be. These people were like family, even more so now that they were bound together as a community of sorts at Starlight.

Once Matt's group was gone, Barry, Dean, and Jerrett headed south, towards home. Jerrett was filled with a sense of anticipation. He was nervous at being away from his kids, but the need to know what was really happening was so overpowering. Would they be able to finally go back home? Was the fighting over, or had it at least moved out of their area? He wondered about his house and his shop. Thinking about home naturally made his thoughts go to Gwennie. How would he feel to walk through their home without her there? Everything in that house would remind him of her. Not to mention her grave. What would they do about that? It didn't seem right to leave her like that, buried in an unmarked grave in the backyard.

Jerrett shook the disturbing thoughts from his head and concentrated on the road. He had to get there first: one thing at a time. He glanced at the message scribbled across his tank: 'Don't Tread On Me'. The kids were waiting for him. It was time to see what had become of their home.

CHAPTER 20

Home Again

Jerrett, with Dean at his side, crept up the ridge overlooking his house. Barry had split off a way back, to check on his own house. They would meet up later.

Bellying their way up to the top of the ridge, the brothers peered through the tall grass which hid them from view. Pulling a pair of binoculars out of his pack, Jerrett scanned the street in front of him.

A chill crept over him.

Soldiers. Swarming all over the street, they were strolling in and out of his neighbors' houses at will. Their equipment and cars were parked haphazardly up and down the road, which was blocked off from traffic. The cornfield across the street had been razed and trampled down flat, with large military vehicles parked on it. They were using the whole street as some kind of staging area. Jerrett wondered briefly where all his neighbors had gone. Where they all captured?

Hands shaking with apprehension, he shifted the binoculars towards his own house.

Soldiers' camouflage laundry flapped on the line, an army jeep took up his space in the driveway and men milled about the property. As he watched, a bearded man, his thick belly hanging over his camouflage pants, wandered out the door and across the yard. He joined a group of soldiers lighting a campfire in the middle of his yard. One of the men called out to him "Hey, Wolff, come join us!" Jerrett seethed as they laughed at a joke, sipping beer and lounging on Jerrett's lawn chairs. Trash and beer cans littered the grass around them. The group was dangerously close to Gwen's unmarked grave, hidden among the flowers.

Jerrett watched as the bearded man turned, still laughing, and wandered over to the flower garden.

"What'd you see?" Dean asked, nudging his brother.

"There are soldiers in our yard and all over the street."

"Oh my God," Dean breathed out the words in a deep sigh. Jerrett didn't answer, eyes glued on the sight before him.

His home, his property – paid for with his blood, sweat, and tears – was being trod on. It was full of supplies they could use, full of memories and feelings and comfort. It was home. It was where Gwennie was. Jerrett could feel the hot, strong rage building inside him as his thoughts turned to his wife. What if the soldiers were tramping on her grave? Or parking their trucks over it? What if they decided to dig there for some reason?

Suddenly the bearded man caught his attention again. He'd stopped right beside her grave. What was he doing? Could he tell someone was buried there? As the man fumbled with his pants, it suddenly became apparent what he was about to do.

Fury exploded through Jerrett and without thinking, he sprang to his feet.

Rough hands grabbed him instantly as Dean pulled him to the ground, their momentum carrying them backward in a reckless slide down the hill, out of sight.

☻ ☻ ☻

Jerrett came to an abrupt stop, head slamming into a massive rock at the bottom of the hill.

Dean watched his brother tumble head over heels. He raced after him, the anger coursing through him. "What were you doing?" Dean hissed, his brow furrowed. He grabbed a fistful of Jerrett's shirt. "You'll get us caught!" With one last shake, Dean threw him back to the ground. He'd almost gotten them captured!

Jerrett lay in the grass, gasping for breath. He squeezed his eyes shut and punched the ground on either side of his body. His face was twisted in a grimace.

Dean was confused, what had happened? His flash of anger suddenly dissipated, replaced by worry. He rested his hand on Jerrett's arm gently. Jerrett barely seemed to register the touch, grinding his palms into his eyes.

"Gwennie … Gwen…"

"Hey, Jerr. Relax. Relax, man. It's OK." Dean patted his brother's arm, wondering at the sudden change.

"Oh God, Dean, he was going to … to …." Jerrett choked, shaking, unable to finish. "On Gwennie's grave … he was getting ready to … right on her grave!"

That was all Dean needed to hear, the awful picture painted in his head with only a few words.

"Oh Jerr …." He pulled his big brother up against his chest and held him tight as Jerrett's sobs ripped through him, muffled against Dean's shirt. His brother was falling apart in front of him. Dean gripped him tighter, wishing he could will away the pain. He moved his hand to cup the back of Jerrett's head but was startled when it felt wet. Blood.

What was going on?

Then it hit him. The rock that stopped his brother's fall down the hill: Jerrett must have hit his head! Dean pulled his brother forward to see his head. Pushing back his hair, he could see a gash leaking blood down the back of Jerrett's shirt. A sudden fear filled him. Scrambling for something, anything, to sop up the blood, Dean discovered an old glove in his pocket and pressed it to the wound. Jerrett's face was a mask of pain, with tears running in trails through the dirt on his cheeks. Eyes squeezed shut, hands gripping Dean's shirt, body shaking; Dean knew his brother was on the verge of snapping. He needed to get him away from here, now.

"C'mon. We gotta go." He pulled at Jerrett insistently. "There's nothing we can do here. Let's go." Jerrett allowed himself to be pulled along, Dean leading him by the arm.

Jerrett stumbled on the uneven ground. He found it hard to concentrate or to care what happened anymore. Tripping over a tree root, he crashed to his knees, and Dean dropped alongside him.

Jerrett oozed into the ground, jelly-like and liquid, all the fight gone out of him. If he couldn't even stop a man from pissing on his wife's grave, if he couldn't protect her in life or in death, what did it matter anymore what he did? Boneless, he lay immobile in a heap.

He wanted to curl up and stay here forever. He registered no sounds, no feelings, and no thoughts. It was as if he were suddenly in a vacuum and there was nothing anymore. He wanted to stay here, stay in this bubble and never think again. But Dean was in his face, and even though he couldn't hear what he was saying, his intense expression spoke volumes.

He could feel the shaking first, as Dean grabbed him; then he could hear his brother yelling, it seemed, but not quite that loud. He felt the grass itching him where his shirt had slid up in a bunch on his back, the hot sun blazing down on his face, and the breeze tickling his skin. The pain hammering in his head returned and all his senses suddenly crashed down on him. He heard, felt, saw, and smelled everything all at once. Dean was grabbing his shirt, pulling him, shouting at him and Jerrett allowed himself to be hauled up and dragged along. He stumbled behind his brother, tripping in the tall grass, but kept his footing. Dean released him to thread his way through the trees, yelling "Follow me!" Jerrett heard, he understood and obeyed, powerless to do anything else. As they crashed through the trees, all Jerrett knew to do was to follow Dean; he didn't remember where they were going or why, but he knew he had to stay with his brother.

● ● ●

The trees were stretched in a thin line along the edge of town, providing some cover as they made their way along. Jerrett followed, silent and senseless, with a sort of fog around him. Dean kept looking back, worriedly, keeping an eye on his wobbly sibling.

He grabbed for Jerrett whenever it seemed he was about to stumble or drift in the wrong direction. Was it the head wound, or was he just lost in his grief? Dean had no way to tell, but knew they needed to keep moving. They had to get back to the bikes.

The patch of trees gave way to a meadow, with grass as tall as their knees. They waded through to the bikes, hidden in the trees on the edge of the meadow. Dean looked about for soldiers, but even though they were stationed close by, there were none to be seen. The brothers moved out to meet up with Barry.

But looking at Jerrett, Dean was afraid to let him get on a bike. It was obvious his head wasn't in the right place to be riding. But what should he do? Ride double? Losing one of their machines, especially one that had all the conversions on it, would be a serious blow.

"Jerrett, we have to meet Barry. Can you ride?" Jerrett nodded mutely, eyes downcast, mind elsewhere. Dean yanked his brother's chin up. "Jerr, I need to know. Are you with me? Can you do this?" This time Jerrett met Dean's gaze and he could see reality kick in. Jerrett nodded firmly and took a deep breath. Dean handed Jerrett his helmet and turned to his own vehicle. Dean fastened his helmet strap and gathered up his goggles and gloves, all the while watching Jerrett furtively.

Mechanically, as if a robot had taken over, Dean saw Jerrett strap on his helmet, snap his goggles into place, and pull on the gloves. He kick-started the motor and slipped effortlessly into his seat. Dean had to hurry to fire up his own bike as he watched Jerrett zoom away, not noticing Dean still stationary behind him. In short order, Dean caught up to his brother and could see that even though Jerrett went through the motions, his riding style was distracted, slow, and wobbly. They called it 'goon riding' in racing, if someone rode sloppily beneath their ability, but this was no joke. Dean's palms were sweaty, and his heart raced as he followed behind his brother, sure that he was about to wash out, tip over, or careen off an edge. Thinking it might be better to lead and give Jerrett someone to follow, he passed his brother and pulled in front of him, forcing him to stop.

Once halted, Dean inched his bike back until he was beside Jerrett and grabbed the front of his helmet. He leaned in, inches from Jerrett's face and yelled, "I'll lead. You just follow where I go. Understand?"

Jerrett nodded again. Dean was getting sick of the head nods. Why wasn't he talking? He shook his head, but let go of Jerrett's helmet, his choices limited. Trusting Jerrett's riding instincts to take over, he headed off in the direction needed, glancing back every few minutes to see Jerrett not far behind.

When they finally arrived at the place where they were to meet Barry, it was empty. Dean was not surprised, as it would take Barry longer to travel back and forth. The trees overhead offered cover from drones and so they felt relatively safe for the moment. Jerrett parked his bike next to Dean's and wordlessly shed his helmet and goggles. Crumpling to the ground, Jerrett curled up in a ball on the soft grass. Dean quickly propped his bike against a tree and made his way to Jerrett's side. His brother's eyes were closed, and his face lined with fatigue, dirt dried and stained on his cheeks. Impossible as it seemed, Jerrett was asleep already. Seeing his brother's exhaustion, Dean let him be, knowing the rest would be good for him. He tried Evie's number, but it wouldn't go through … again. It would have been comforting to be able to talk to her.

Truth be told, Dean was scared to death. What was wrong with his brother? Was he just upset, or had he really hurt himself? What would he do if the Guards approached them? And how would they ever make it back to Starlight? Dean clenched his hands into fists, grim determination taking over. He would do whatever he had to, to protect his brother. No matter what that was. Pulling his handgun out of its holster, he checked the chamber. It was loaded and ready.

He squatted beside his brother's still form to wait. And watch.

DON'T TREAD ON ME

CHAPTER 21

Pushing On

It was nearly an hour later when Barry showed up, a heavily loaded pack on his back. Pulling off his helmet, he spied Jerrett groggily trying to pull himself up.

Brushing a hank of long, gray hair out of his face, Barry lifted his chin toward Jerrett, "What's wrong?" he asked.

"He hit his head," Dean answered. "Guards were crawling all over the house. It wasn't good." Not wanting to submit his brother to the agony of reliving the events again, Dean deflected the conversation back to Barry. "Did you find anything?"

Barry, taking the hint, swung his pack around and answered, "I was able to get into my place. I got whatever food and medicine I could find, some clothes for Caitlyn, a blanket..." He pulled out a box of crackers and tossed them to Jerrett, who dug in immediately.

"Should we head out, or do we need to stay here a while?"

Dean's eyes flickered to his brother. "Rest as long as you need, Barry. I think we'll be ready when you are."

Jerrett stood, brushing the crumbs off on his pants. "Let's go," he said, his voice rusty and hoarse. "We need to meet Matt and the others."

"You OK to ride, boss?" Barry asked.

Jerrett answered with a nod and moved past him to get his helmet. Barry let out a low whistle as Jerrett passed him, seeing the wound on his friend for the first time. "Whoa, sit down a minute." Grabbing a water bottle from his pack, and a rag, Barry sat Jerrett down and cleaned the wound.

"It hurts more now," Jerrett complained as he pushed away Barry's hands.

"Yeah, but at least it won't get infected," Barry admonished. "You gotta keep it clean."

"Let's go," Jerrett growled, and rose unsteadily to his feet, wobbling his way over to his dirt bike. Barry looked at Dean, who shrugged. There was no way of knowing how far Jerrett would be able to go.

"Look, I'll lead, Jerr, you just concentrate on following me, OK? If you need to stop, just let us know. Barry can bring up the rear," said Dean. Barry nodded and Jerrett agreed. Dean liked keeping Jerrett sandwiched between them.

They started off down a trail through the woods. It was just wide enough for one bike at a time, the grass worn down from foot traffic. Trees lined either side, their branches entwining overhead, forming a canopy that nearly blocked out the sun. The smell of honeysuckle filled the air.

The trailhead ended suddenly, thrusting the group out onto a small street. Glancing both ways, Dean pointed to the left, Barry nodded in agreement, and off they went.

They hadn't gone far when Dean heard Barry yelling.

Turning, he saw an Elite Guard, on a motorcycle, who had pulled out behind the trio. Dean's heart pounded in his chest. What should he do? Would Jerrett be able to keep up with them if he sped up? He had no choice. Gunning the engine, he glanced back to see Jerrett and Barry still close behind. Racing down the road, he quickly turned right, then left, Jerrett and Barry still following.

The Guard too. How were they going to get away? Realizing that the Guard had a street bike, Dean knew the only escape was offroad. Glancing back, he yelled, "Come on!" to the others and whipped the bike around to cut through a backyard. They wove around an obstacle course of lawn chairs, toys, and trees, narrowly missing a trampoline and a dog on a chain. At the end of the yard, Dean was surprised to find a narrow creek. Jumping at the last second, he almost didn't clear it. Landing roughly, he shimmied and wobbled, at last straightening himself out. Jerrett and Barry followed him more easily, as they were able to mimic his jump.

They found themselves in a park. Looking all around, Dean didn't see any sign of the Guard.

"Which way?" Barry asked, at the same moment that the Guard pulled into the driveway.

"Go! Go!" Dean shrieked. He took off through the park, avoiding a few picnickers and toddlers, who had braved going out. Taking a last-minute turn, he ended up in a church parking lot. Racing through, he saw Jerrett and Barry still behind him, though they'd drifted further back. Jerrett must be tiring. They needed to get under cover soon.

Dean took a second to get his bearing. Past some houses, there was a wooded area to his right, *that's where we need to go,* he thought. "This way!" he called, heading behind the houses, once more through the yards. The Guard was nowhere in sight, but Dean knew he would be on them in no time if they didn't keep moving.

They raced through four backyards and into the woods. Once under the cover of the trees, Dean found a skinny trail and led them further on. When he guessed they were far enough away from town, he stopped. Jerrett skidded to a stop and ripped off his helmet. Panting for air, he dropped his head down onto his arms, which were resting on the handlebars.

"Jerr! You OK?" Dean was worried.

His brother lifted his head, throwing him an annoyed look. *Of course not.* "Head's pounding…," he muttered.

Barry gave Jerrett some water and they stopped to rest. Soon, however, they had to continue. The chase had lost the Guard, but it put them on the wrong side of town from where they needed to be. They were to meet Matt and the others back near Pine Grove. Dean wondered if Jerrett would be able to ride all the way to Starlight today. There was a very real possibility they would need to camp somewhere tonight.

After a brief rest, Dean continued the trek, trying to pick out the easiest route. They worked their way around the town, sticking mostly to the woods, and found themselves finally back on the correct path. Traveling down the shaded trail, a sudden, niggling feeling overtook him, and he slowed, whipping his head around to check on the others behind him.

The trail was empty.

His blood ran cold and he spun the vehicle around, riding off the way he'd come. Quite some distance back, he spotted the bikes leaning on trees, two figures off to the side of the trail where there was a small pull-off area. Dean saw his brother hunched over. Ghostly white, one arm braced on a skinny tree trunk, Jerrett was leaning over and retching. Barry, still in his helmet, had an arm wrapped around Jerrett's middle, supporting him. Dean's heart went out to his brother, and he hastily dismounted and rushed over to lay an arm on Jerrett's shoulders.

"What happened? Did he fall or anything?"

Barry looked worriedly at him over Jerrett's back. "No, he just stopped suddenly and started throwing up."

After Jerrett was done, they helped him move away and lowered him to the ground. Barry passed him a bottle of water, which Jerrett accepted with a shaky hand.

"Sit and rest a while, Jerr."

Jerrett nodded in agreement, his face ashen, eyes glazed in pain.

Barry threw down his backpack. "Here, lay down." Jerrett complied without a word, using the pack as a pillow. The trees overhead created a false darkness, making it seem like it was evening already. Since this was the same trail Matt's group would be traveling, they decided to wait for them here instead of further north. Barry and Dean kept a close watch over Jerrett as the next two hours passed.

When they finally heard the tell-tale whine of the muffled dirt bike exhausts, both Dean and Barry hopped up to flag down their compatriots.

Salvatore slid to a stop, Matt and Fiona just behind him. After a brief explanation of events, Salvatore quickly followed Barry and Dean down to where Jerrett lay.

"Hey, Jerrett, wake up." Salvatore lightly tapped the man's face. "C'mon, sleeping beauty. Time to get up."

"Leave me 'lone!" Jerrett grumbled, as he swung at the hands hovering over him.

Dean pushed down his brother's hands. "Stop it, Jerr! ... Sorry, Salvatore."

"Ah, that's normal with head injuries. At least he's responding now," Salvatore quipped, continuing his examination, and peering into Jerrett's eyes while asking him questions.

"Well?" Barry asked impatiently.

Salvatore rocked back on his heels. "I'd say you got yourself one good concussion there."

"Thanks, genius. Could'a told ya that myself," the patient retorted, throwing his doctor an annoyed look, which was pointedly ignored.

"So, what's that mean? Can he travel?"

"I'm right here. Quit talking about me like I'm not," Jerrett scolded. "And yes, I can travel. Damn bike's too valuable to leave here, so forget about riding double."

"How do you feel?" the paramedic asked warily.

"Like shit. But I can ride." Dean wrinkled his face in doubt, but his brother continued. "I'm better than before. My head's still killing me, but I'm not seeing double or anything, and I can think straight."

There was some debate about the decision, but in the end, it was decided that they would let Jerrett ride. In a short time they were back on the trail heading north, Jerrett positioned in the middle of the pack of riders. The need for fuel was on all their minds. They knew they wouldn't have enough to make it back to the same friend's house who supplied them on the way down. Fiona, in the lead, eventually pulled over under a highway overpass and cut her engine.

When the others had joined her, she told them, "We need to get fuel. I'm almost out."

"Me too."

"Anybody have friends in the area?" No one did. Consulting the GPS, they found themselves not far from a small town. Hoping it would have a gas station, they decided to head towards it. Exposing themselves this way was not ideal, but they had little choice. They needed fuel.

Always the protector, Barry had moved to the point position, leading the way. Warily watching all around him, he would pull ahead of the group, scout the road, and wave them on if no Black Bears were in sight. In this manner, they traversed the small town. Just as they were about to give up, Fiona spotted a bright sign, advertising a popular gas station, rising in the distance over the treetops.

"Let's go!" Following the tree line again, they came out just behind the convenience store. The pumps seemed far away from the shelter of the trees.

Agreeing to split up, Fiona, Matt, and Salvatore went first, as their tanks were emptier. Dean and Barry stayed under the cover of the trees, watching for any signs of trouble, while Jerrett slumped over, resting. Apprehension gnawed at Dean's gut, as Matt went into the store to pay. If the riders took off without paying, there was no way the clerk wouldn't call the authorities, but if they slipped him a little extra, maybe he would keep quiet.

Dean chewed his glove nervously, glancing between their friends and Jerrett. Finally, Matt came out of the store and flashed them a thumbs up as he hurried back to his bike. The trio made their way into the trees and joined Dean and Barry. Cutting the engines, everyone sat quietly, watching for any Guards. After waiting for fifteen minutes or so, it seemed they were in the clear.

"Dean, why don't you guys go now?" Fiona suggested. Dean got ready, but Matt grabbed his arm to stop him.

"Let me take Jerrett's bike, just in case there's trouble. He can wait here on mine." Jerrett was too tired to argue and mutely climbed off his vehicle.

Matt, Dean, and Barry made their way to the pumps. Dean rested his bike against the column and proceeded to get the pump ready. Scanning the parking lot, he was relieved to only see the clerk watching him from the window. It seemed they'd picked a good time of the day to stop, as the store was empty. The gas flowed with a satisfying gurgle into his tank.

Just as he breathed a sigh of relief, a middle-aged man in a suit pulled into the lot. With a sudden sense of trepidation, Dean swallowed nervously. Glancing over to the others, he saw Barry pull himself up straight and menacing, glaring at the man. Matt was watching, too.

The man climbed out of his car, noticing them at once. He did a double-take at the look of their adapted bikes with all the accessories hanging off them. Staring blatantly, he stopped, as if deciding what to do. Finally, with a determined stride, the man marched over to them.

Dean replaced the nozzle in the pump, readying himself for action.

When the man reached them, Dean could see he was red-faced, with his teeth clenched as he looked them over. "What are you doing here?" he hissed. "Who are you? This isn't your jurisdiction – I'd know, I'm the district liaison. I don't remember seeing any visitor passes! You need to get out of here, we don't want trouble here and I just know that's what you'll bring!" He shook his finger at Dean, the closest target.

As if on cue, Barry stepped between the pumps and inserted himself between Dean and the man. A wall of solid muscle, clothed in menacing black leather, Barry screamed trouble without saying a word. The suited man gulped and took a step back.

"I … I … you can't be here!" he stuttered. Barry took another step towards him, causing the man to back up again.

Having successfully gotten his attention, Barry growled out, "We're getting this gas, and then we're leaving. If you're smart, you won't say a word to anyone about seeing us. You got it?" Leaning into the man's face, he reminded Dean of a big, protective bear more than ever.

Backpedaling, the suited man hastily nodded and then rushed off into the store.

"Let's get out of here, guys. He might call someone," Matt cautioned. Agreeing, they abandoned the station and took off into the trees. When they met the others, Jerrett and Matt switched back and off they went.

The riders had just made it through the populated towns and were back in the woods around the state forest when the sun began to set. Hunting for a safe place to bed down for the night, they finally spotted a secluded glen surrounded by trees. It provided the perfect cover. Sometimes the Guards patrolled with drones or planes. The trees would provide cover for them. They soon had a small fire blazing and were lounging around it.

While resting, Matt, Salvatore, and Fiona were finally able to share their tale. They'd had to dodge Guards and drones every step of the way, and were forced to hide the dirt bikes in an old barn, continuing into the populated areas on foot.

Matt had managed to get into his house, collecting some food, money, and other things, but they were limited as to how much they could carry. They didn't make it into Philly, as the fighting was still raging there. Fiona was upset, worried about her college roommates, but Salvatore had managed to get a call through to his mother. During the short conversation, he'd been reassured that his mother was safe, but hiding out in her apartment in the city. She forbade him from coming to her, insisting she was safe enough and he should look after his brother. It took some convincing, but eventually, Salvatore gave in. The journey back to meet Dean, Jerrett, and Barry had been easier.

Everyone was exhausted by the time they finished sharing their stories and eating. Jerrett was asleep as soon as he lay down. By mutual agreement, it was decided that Jerrett would get a full night's rest while the others took turns on watch.

By sunrise, they were all up, sharing a meager breakfast of berries that Salvatore had found, beef jerky and granola bars. Washed down with water from a creek nearby, their hunger and thirst were slaked temporarily.

Jerrett's color was back, he hadn't thrown up in some time and seemed better since he'd slept and eaten. Though tired, he insisted on heading out.

They rode smooth trails through the state forest. Occasionally they would see signs of campers, possibly people who were hiding out, but were never stopped.

Although they were all experienced riders, none of them had ever ridden for as many hours at a time as they had in the last few days. It would have felt so good to just stay where they were and rest, but they were all being drawn back to the mountains, to their home and families.

Home. Starlight was beginning to feel like that to them. Was it the lure of safety, the loved ones that waited for them, or the new community that was rapidly forming that made it feel as if they were heading home? Or was the realization that their old houses were lost to them – at least for the duration of the war. This trip back had reinforced their loss. Even after the fighting ended, would things ever be the same again?

● ◉ ◉

Jerrett rubbed his head, attempting to knead the headache away. He was ready for this trip to be finished. He needed to be back with his family again. He longed to hold his kids in his arms. He needed to push the images of the soldiers from his mind. They were in his house, *his house*! Would it ever feel like home again? With Gwennie gone, and the soldiers sullying the house, he wondered if it wouldn't be better to just start fresh somewhere else after this war was over. Would it ever be 'over'? Would things ever be the same again? He knew they wouldn't, not without Gwennie, but would his kids ever have a regular life again? His heart filled with longing for his wife and tears pricked his eyes at the thought. He shoved the thoughts down deep and conjured up images of the children instead. Would they get to go back to school, and worry about nothing but homework and motocross races, and not a war looming over their heads?

What would be best for them? He supposed that was something that he'd need to answer at some point, but not now. He just didn't know.

After the lunch rest, the riders continued their journey north. By mid-afternoon, though, the headache and exhaustion had finally gotten the better of Jerrett. He knew he needed to rest, that he couldn't keep going. The others gathered around him, Barry taking his bike, as he sunk down to the ground.

"Sorry, guys. My head's still pounding."

Salvatore appeared with a bottle of water and some painkillers.

Matt replied, "No problem. We knew you might need to rest soon." Though the others understood, the urge to get back to the track was all but palpable in the air. They were so close.

Jerrett could sense the urgency in the group. "Look, we don't all need to stay. Why don't some of you go on ahead? They're probably worried about us. Someone should let them know where we are and that we're OK." Barry, Fiona, and Matt decided to go on ahead. Dean would never leave his brother, and they thought Salvatore should stay with Jerrett to monitor his condition. Dean, Salvatore, and Jerrett decided to nap for a while, letting the pain medicine have a chance to work on Jerrett's pounding head.

As he rested, a sudden sense of foreboding washed over Jerrett, sending shivers up his spine. Where they OK back at Starlight? Had something happened? He tried to shake off the uneasiness, dismissing it as exhaustion, but a part of him still wondered what had caused the feeling. Was it a premonition of sorts? He normally didn't put much stock in that sort of thing, but this felt somehow different.

An hour later they were back on the trail. Jerrett's headache had calmed, but he was still filled with a feeling that something had gone wrong. He didn't say a word, not wanting to spook the others, but he couldn't shake it off. Pushing the dread down, he reasoned that he just needed to see his kids and then he would be fine.

He pushed on, determined to get back.

CHAPTER 22

Bad News

Breaking out from behind the wall of trees, relief flooded over Jerrett as he saw the campsite. Home. Finally. Exhaustion filled him, and his head pounded, but he was happy nonetheless. He couldn't wait to hold his children in his arms again and wash away the memory of what he'd seen. He scanned the gathering crowd for his family.

Pulling up his bike to the Keplers' camper, he spied Matt and the others standing in a clump. They all turned at the sound of the bikes pulling up, but no one raced to greet them, no children scurried from the truck with open arms. Laura Kepler wiped her eyes. Matt met his gaze with a solemn expression, his mouth downturned and eyes full of pity.

Just one look at Matt's face made Jerrett's stomach churn and his breath quicken. He froze. Something bad had happened.

Jerrett sensed Dean pull up beside him, Salvatore on the other side.

"Uh, oh, why are they all staring at us?"

Jerrett couldn't answer; fear gripped him. He cut the engine and slowly, reluctantly, climbed off the vehicle.

Jerrett didn't want to ask what happened, but at the same time, the need to know was overpowering. He stood by the side of his bike, Dean next to him. They watched as Matt broke off from the group and made his way over.

Matt halted in front of him. "Jerrett," he looked at his feet, then back to Jerrett. He opened his mouth to speak, and then stopped again.

Jerrett's heart pounded in his chest. He wanted to tell Matt to spit it out, but he couldn't get anything past the lump in his throat.

"Jerrett," Matt tried again. "It's Troy and Cami. They've … they've disappeared." He squeezed Jerrett's arm in comfort.

The air around him became suddenly still, and Jerrett felt himself sinking to the ground. He willed the dirt to open and swallow him in, burying him from the world. His vision narrowed until only Matt was there, kneeling on the ground in front of him, clinging to his arms. The rest of the world blurred and faded away.

"What do you … do you mean? Where are they?"

Matt started to explain, but suddenly Trevor was there, pushing his way into Jerrett's line of sight. "Jerr, I'm so sorry. I didn't realize they'd gone. I was supposed to watch them, I'm sorry." His face was lined with anguish.

Matt spoke up, explaining. "Jerrett, we think they took the dog and went for a walk. Most of the adults and teens had gone logging for the cabins. Trevor had gone along, to help where he could. He told the kids to stay here, with Laura and Markie, but they must have decided to go down the road. When the ladies realized they were gone, they went searching, but all they found was Jasper's leash by the side of the road. The kids were gone. Jasper showed up a little while ago, but there wasn't any sign of the kids. Saul and Paulo organized the others into search parties and we've been combing the woods all day and night, but there's no sign of them." He paused, and then added, "We think someone picked them up. But we don't know who," Matt finished.

Laura, having gathered close with the others when they saw Jerrett fall, broke in. "I'm so sorry, Jerrett. We were in the RV with Marlowe. He didn't feel well, and when we came out the kids were gone."

"We're going to keep looking. We haven't given up," Saul added, joining the group. Jerrett rose and stepped back, needing space, the air suddenly sucked out of him. It seemed as if a hole had opened inside him, engulfing him in its emptiness. He was drowning in it.

Turning, he staggered away, weaving and tottering, unaware of the others hovering just out of his line of sight. What was he going to do? How was he going to find the kids? Where could they be? He collapsed onto a tree stump and dropped his head into his hands.

His brothers were on him in a minute, their hands grasping his arms. "Jerr, we'll find them. We will. We won't give up until we do," Dean encouraged him.

"I'm so sorry, Jerrett, I shouldn't have left them," Trevor pleaded. "It's all my fault."

Jerrett met his youngest brother's teary gaze. He shook his head 'no', before he dropped his eyes. Trevor reached over and gripped his brother's neck, squeezing it.

A rapid explosion of anger had Jerrett on his feet in seconds, a red haze blocking everything out except the rage. Growling and bursting with the desire to hit something, anything, he smashed his fist into the nearest tree trunk. Thunk! Again. Thunk! Thunk! Harder and harder he lashed out against the limb, until he felt Dean and Trevor manhandling him away from it. Jerrett could barely make out their voices through the red haze, but gradually it faded until he could hear them pleading with him.

The rage vanished as quickly as it had come, and his body sagged with the effort of keeping upright. He felt himself being lowered down onto the stump, hands all around, holding on, holding him up. Dean's voice was there, steady but strained.

"We'll find them. We will ... Jerr ... I promise."

"Jerr ...I'm sorry, so sorry ..." Trevor choked out the words, his body shaking against Jerrett.

Jerrett looked at his little brother and in a brief moment took in the boy's red, swollen eyes, blotchy cheeks, and sagging shoulders.

Jerrett latched on to Trevor, grabbing his brother in a death grip, sobs ripping out of them both. He was only dimly aware of other arms wrapping around the two of them, but knew it was Dean and Dalton.

They stayed that way for some time, drawing strength for whatever lay ahead.

● ● ●

Over the next few days, the community continued to search the area, looking for signs or clues of Cami and Troy. But they found nothing.

Although the residents of Starlight wanted to stay hidden, desperation finally drove Saul to question his nearest neighbor. Leo Castillo lived about two miles down the road from the track. Leo's children had gone to school with Saul's daughters, and so the two men had grown to be friends over the years.

To cover their identities, Saul decided to pretend the missing children belonged to his brother, George, whom Leo had never met. Even though he trusted Leo, it didn't seem wise to advertise just who or how many people had come to stay at Starlight.

Saul made his way up Leo's dirt driveway, his ancient truck splashing through puddles as he went. Soon Leo's farmhouse came into view and Saul parked in the driveway. Climbing out of the truck, he saw Leo appear in the doorway, investigating who it was. Pulling down his shirt where it had ridden up over his belly, Saul waved a greeting and made his way up onto the porch.

As Leo pushed open the creaking screen door, he welcomed Saul with a warm smile that crinkled up the corners of his cinnamon-colored skin. His black hair had turned gray in recent years, but the man was sturdy and strong from the hard work of farming his land.

He reached out his hand in greeting. "Hola! Come in." He stepped aside, ushering Saul into the kitchen. After offering his friend a drink, Leo joined Saul at the table. He studied Saul a moment before finally stating, "Something is troubling you, my friend. What's wrong?"

Saul adjusted his ball cap before answering. He was an honest man, who didn't like lying to his friend, even if it was for the best. "My brother, George, and his family have come to stay with us until things settle down. Two of his children, a boy and a little girl, have gone missing. We found their things down on Maple Road. They were taking a walk, we reckon. Other than that, we haven't seen any sign of them. Have you seen anything? Either of the children? Or anyone hanging around?"

Leo puffed out his cheeks and blew out the air, rubbing his whiskered chin thoughtfully as he shook his head. Saul waited.

Finally, Leo looked him in the eye and said, "My friend, I may have some bad news for you." He paused, reluctant to continue, "Four days ago, I spotted a Guard patrol. I wondered what had brought them this far up into the mountains. We rarely see Guards up here, you know, and so I watched them as they went down the road. They seemed to be just doing a routine patrol, but they were headed your way."

"That is strange. I wonder what would have brought them up here on patrol?" Saul said. "Maybe ... maybe they found the little ones and picked them up. The timing would be righLeo continued, reaching for Saul's arm, "I am so sorry, Saul. I should have called you, let you know they were about, but I didn't realize they were up to no good."

Saul's eyes closed as he attempted to steady himself. He unconsciously ran a hand over his beard, a habit he'd acquired.

Leo added, "Why would they take such young children, though? Surely they were no threat?"

"They've got these camps, Leo, reeducation facilities, they call 'em. There have been rumors about them, people getting snatched and taken there, but I didn't know little kids were a target, either. I would've thought it would just be troublemakers, rabble-rousers, that sort of thing, ya know? But the Guards were here, on the right day and at the right place. Who else would've taken them?"

Rubbing his beard vigorously, Saul knew he had to get back home. Jerrett and his family needed to hear this. He dreaded being the one to tell his friends the bad news. For this to happen so soon after Gwennie's tragedy was unbelievable. He wondered how Jerrett and the others would take it.

"Saul," Leo patted his arm, interrupting his thoughts. "There is reason to hope, don't give up yet. If they were taken by the Guards, then they are alive, not lost or injured in the woods somewhere. They can be found and brought home again, and the love of your family will heal what they have endured."

Saul didn't trust his voice, but looked his friend in the eyes and nodded. Leo was right: there was still reason to hope and that was what he would tell Jerrett. They would find the kids and get them back. Saul vowed to himself, this would not be the end.

Leo walked Saul to the door and they exchanged goodbyes, Leo promising his support in finding the lost children, should Saul need it.

Saul left, his heart heavy with the bad news he would need to share.

DONT TREAD ON ME

CHAPTER 23

What Next?

A week had passed, and luckily most of the effects of his concussion had faded. But that wasn't what Jerrett was concerned about anyway. A whole week had passed and there was still no sign of Troy and Cami. They were gone. Just *gone*.

But not gone from Jerrett's mind.

Thoughts of the children consumed him every second of the day. The community had given up searching the woods, and there was no place else to look. The kids weren't just lost, they had been taken. But there was nowhere to search, no flyers to put up, and no police to call. In the middle of a war, who cared about two missing kids? Jerrett was at loose ends with no direction, just rage. Life was moving on, with or without Gwennie and the kids. It was killing Jerrett.

Night after night, Starlight's residents sat around the campfire, hashing out ideas and theories about where the kids were and how to get them back. The suggestions ranged from logical answers to crazy conspiracies.

All the futile discussions nearly drove Jerrett mad. He was so angry he just wanted to lash out. At anything. He needed something to do to keep himself busy.

That's when he decided to build a cabin.

Even with the trailer and truck as living space, it was still an unbearably cramped dwelling for a family of six and a dog. Combined, it was about the size of their living room back home.

Even a small building would help. Dean, Trevor, and Dalton could bunk there, the trailer used for storage, and when Troy and Cami came back, they would stay in the truck with Jerrett. *When* they came back, not if.

Trevor designed a simple log structure to build next to the truck; it could hardly be called a cabin as it was only one small room, with a steeply pitched roof. It was more like a shack, Dean had mused.

But Jerrett hardly cared. He threw himself into the building project with fervor, pounding out his fury on the nails. He desperately needed the distraction. Every day Jerrett worked from dawn to dusk until he fell asleep out of sheer exhaustion. It was the only way he got any sleep.

Saul loaned them the use of his tractor to haul logs and the sawmill equipment to cut boards. Dean and Dalton worked by his side. Dean wasn't much for carpentry work, but Dalton was proving to be a good worker. He didn't say much, just hopped to whatever task was put before him. Trevor was still limited to one arm, so he used his woodworking skills to direct the others.

All around the camping area, the sound of hammers and busy voices flowed. Many others were building, too. The Carusos and Barry were building a full-sized cabin. Matt and Luke Bradford were working on an outhouse for their community.

During the week, several new arrivals joined them. Two more motocross racers, Drey Boddie and Dylan Williams, had arrived a few days ago. The two men were in their twenties, cousins or something, no one was sure, but they were nice enough and willing to help anyone in exchange for being allowed to stay. Their current residence was the two pickup trucks they'd arrived in.

At the moment, Drey and Dylan were busy helping Jerrett roll a log up a ramp to add to the wall he was constructing. As Jerrett hammered a nail in place, he heard a ruckus from across the clearing. Jennica Bradford, Luke's wife, was running across the meadow, her colorful skirt flowing behind her, calling out frantically. Jerrett watched her run up to her husband, and even from a distance, he could hear the panic in her voice. Luke dropped his hammer and took off towards their RV with his wife.

"Dean," Jerrett called, nodding his head towards the activity. Dean followed his brother's gaze as he moved to his side. Drey and Dylan turned to watch, too.

"What's going on?"

"Not sure. Maybe we should go see." Turning to Drey and Dylan, Jerrett said, "Be right back."

Jerrett and Dean left their tools and made their way over to the Bradfords' RV. Knocking on the door, Jerrett called out, "Hey, Luke, everything OK?" They waited a bit, and when no one answered, they let themselves in. Pushing through Jennica's curtain of beads, they made their way to the back.

Young Marlowe Bradford lay on his parents' bed; pale, sweaty, and coughing – in a half-choking, can't-breathe, sort of way. Seeing him this way was like a stab in Jerrett's heart. Not another child … It killed him to see another young life affected by this madness.

"What's wrong with him?"

Luke turned, answering, "He's really sick. Has been for the last week or so, but it's getting worse now."

"He's having trouble breathing," Jennica choked out, tears forming in her eyes, the worry evident on her face.

"What is it?"

"Pneumonia, or bronchitis or something. He's got a pretty high fever and now he's wheezing, too.

"Do you have anything you could give him?"

"Jenn's been making herbal tea, but he needs more than that – antibiotics, an inhaler..." Luke answered.

Jerrett and Dean exchanged a look. This was bad; Marlowe needed medicine. Salvatore had looked in on him, but there wasn't much he could do. Trying to calm them, all Jerrett could suggest was to talk to the others and brainstorm ways to help.

He and Dean left the RV and met with the crowd that had formed outside.

"What's going on?"

"Everything OK?"

Jerrett held up his hand for quiet, and then explained the situation. "Anybody have any antibiotics along?" When no one did, he added, "Any ideas?"

The questions and comments began to fly. Could they take him to hospital without any questions being asked? How far away was the nearest one? Would it look suspicious to be so far from home without permission? Was there a doctor close by instead that they could go to?

"No hospital will take him without reporting it. Then they'll know where we are. Private doctors are out, too. They have to report a stranger," Salvatore informed them, shrugging. "Doctors won't refuse to treat him, but questions will be asked. They'll want to know why Luke and Jennica are up here and where they are staying. The Guards will probably take them in for questioning."

"And we all know what can happen then," Dean added, thinking of all the people who had disappeared.

Salvatore nodded, then offered. "I can tell you the prescriptions that will help him, if you can get them somewhere."

"But where?"

"I don't know, but he needs help now," Salvatore added.

The group fell silent. A sense of urgency was palpable in the air.

"If we can't get him to the hospital, and there is no doctor who will see him, we will just have to get the medecine for him," Matt announced.

"How, rob a pharmacy?" someone quipped.

Matt's steely gaze met with Jerrett's. "If that's what we have to do. We can't let anything happen to Marlowe. He's one of us."

"Of course," Jerrett agreed. "Look, let's go to the pharmacy in town and at least ask if they'll help us. Maybe they will."

"I think you're dreaming, Jerrett, but we can try," Matt said. "But what's the plan if they say no?"

"Then we take it by force."

The stunned crowd looked on, but no one argued. They would do what they needed to.

Matt called the local pharmacy, describing the dire situation, and the hoped-for help. He was flatly denied. The pharmacist could not give them anything without reporting that they were away from home without permission. Luke and Jennica would need to go to the hospital and admit they were out of their living zone.

They couldn't do that. Luke and Jennica would be arrested, and Marlowe taken away and put in a camp. All the residents of Starlight could be at risk.

When Matt told Luke what was happening, Luke was ready to turn himself in.

"You can't do that!" Matt said.

"If it's the only way to help Marlowe, that's exactly what I'll do!"

Jerrett squashed down his own feelings of turmoil and put his hands on Luke's chest. "Wait, slow down. What if there's another way? Salvatore told us what meds to look for, what if we break into the pharmacy and just take them?"

Luke was already shaking his head, "No way. No, if someone gets caught, it's prison! Or a labor camp! I can't let that happen to any of you, I'd never forgive myself. No."

"How else are we going to get them?"

Luke was quiet for a bit, playing with the fringed edge on his flannel shirt. "Okay, look, I'll go myself. Give me the list, Salvatore. None of you has to be involved."

"No," Matt's answer was firm. "You need a lookout, and someone to help you find the stuff; you need a plan." His voice took on a softer tone. "Let us help you; we all know you'd do the same for us."

"I'm going," Jerrett announced firmly. One look at his grim, determined expression would brook no argument.

The government's forces may have snatched his kids, killed his wife, taken their home, and kept Marlowe from a doctor, but no more! It needed to end, *now*. There wasn't anything Jerrett could do about the other matters, but this he *could* do. It was time to fight for what was right, for a child's life. His kids were out of his reach for the moment, but Marlowe, he could help.

The sudden need to fight back was almost overpowering. Fire filled Jerrett's soul and spread through his body, igniting it like an explosion. They couldn't always win! In some way, at some time, it had to end! This fight wasn't against some pharmacy or a doctor, but against the never-ending martial law they were subjected to. It ran their lives and dictated everything they could do. No more! There was a right and a wrong in this world, and letting a child die due to a stupid law was certainly wrong. In a small but significant way, Jerrett could finally do something.

"It's time to fight back! These bastards have taken enough. It's time to take something from them."

Dean was nodding in agreement, while Matt clapped Jerrett on the back. The fire was lit in all of them.

Luke, Matt, and Jerrett decided to go that night, under the cover of darkness. Matt offered to scope out the drugstore. He left, taking Dylan and Drey as back-up.

The others found dark clothes and rigged up some masks. When Matt and the others returned, they mapped out a plan. Salvatore offered to join them, since he was the only one who knew what to look for.

Once it was fully dark, the four scavengers departed on the muffler-quieted, Mad Max-style dirt bikes. They rode on the trails as far as they could, only venturing onto the roads when they got close to town.

The streets were vacant and dark. The riders crept down a back road through town, avoiding the main drag.

Matt led them through someone's backyard and down an alley. As they followed him, Jerrett was fueled by the need for vengeance. Marlowe was getting that medicine. His anger was misdirected, sure, but he didn't care.

Rounding a corner, they were suddenly confronted by a vicious barking and growling. A large German Shepherd took off after them, snarling and snapping. Jerrett heard a scream of pain from someone, but didn't take time to see who. He just knew all four riders were still upright, so he kept going. The dog chased after them.

"Get rid of him!" someone yelled.

Seeing a broken tree branch dangling ahead of him, Jerrett reached up and yanked it loose. The force of the motion jerked him around, pulling him off his bike.

The dog spotted his prey on the ground and came after Jerrett at once. Swinging the branch around, he missed the dog's head but scared it into backing up. Bracing himself for another attack, Jerrett felt the sweat run into his eyes and his heart thudding in his chest. The German Shepherd lunged at him. Swinging with all his might, he connected with the dog's head.

Whimpering and cowering, the dog backed away, tail between his legs. Jerrett breathed a sigh of relief. He watched for a second longer to be sure the attack was over.

"Jerrett, come on!" Luke yelled. Jerrett glanced up to see his friends watching him. Dropping the stick, he scooped up his bike and kicked it over.

Nothing.

The dirt bike didn't respond. Jerrett growled in frustration, kicking frantically. Lights came on in the nearest house, and voices could be heard. Suddenly Matt was there, next to him.

"Leave it! Get on!" he hollered. Jerrett hesitated for a split second, torn between leaving the bike and getting caught. Then he dropped the offending machine and hopped on the back of Matt's. They raced off before the neighbors could see them.

As they tore silently through the town, Jerrett fumed at the loss of the souped-up machine. Someone was going to have a nice surprise come morning.

They were at the pharmacy shortly. It was a small, independently owned place on a quiet side street. Slightly rundown, they hoped there wasn't much security. According to Matt, the medicines were kept in the back of the store, behind a counter. If there were security cameras, the masks would protect them; if there was an alarm, they hoped to be in and out quick enough to avoid the locals. No Elite Guards were stationed nearby; patrols of the area were rare.

The group shut off the bikes and leaned them against the building.

"Okay, Matt, you stay out here on watch. Bang on the door if you see someone coming – Sal, are you limping?" Luke asked.

"Yeah, damn dog bit me," Salvatore grimaced as he held his right calf, a dark stain spreading.

"Can you make it?"

Salvatore nodded grimly. Grabbing up a brick, Luke led the way to the back door and promptly smashed the glass.

He turned to the others, "Let's do this."

They moved quickly. Salvatore and Luke began rummaging through shelves, looking for medicine. Jerrett filled his backpack with other medical supplies. Aspirin, bandages, ointments, and creams were stuffed in the bag. In the back, he could hear Luke call out softly, asking Salvatore for confirmation of the right drug. Jerrett hurried back to help.

"That's the inhaler stuff. Grab it! And some Albuterol over there. I need to find the right antibiotics. Jerrett, look over here with me," Salvatore shouted to Luke, as he pulled Jerrett along behind him.

Matt poked his head in the door, "Come on guys, hurry up!"

Just then Salvatore called out, "Here it is! I found it!" He thrust some pill bottles at Jerrett, who shoved them in his pocket, and then he helped Salvatore fill his bag.

"Someone's coming!" Matt yelled in the door.

They abandoned their scavenging and rushed out. Mounting the bikes, they tore out of the parking lot. Jerrett glanced back in time to see two men running around the corner after them.

"Go, go!"

The riders cut through a row of trees with low-hanging branches. Ahead of Jerrett and Matt, Salvatore's bag caught on a branch, wrenching it off his shoulder. Turning back for it, Salvatore lunged, but missed, barely keeping his bike upright. He stopped, intending to turn around, but a glance behind Jerrett told him the men on foot were catching up.

"Leave it, go! Go!" Abandoning the bag, they raced on down the street, out of town, and then into the safety of the woods, outrunning their pursuers.

After a trek through the narrow-wooded paths, they were soon back at Starlight. A crowd quickly gathered around.

Bursting from the group, Jennica asked, her voice frantic, "Did you get the medicine?"

Luke met her in a hug. "I've got the inhaler medicine." He handed over several inhalers and boxes to his wife. "And we've got all the supplies in Jerrett's bag. But the antibiotics were lost."

Jennica looked stricken, as she clutched the inhalers to her chest protectively. "Will this be enough to make Marlowe better?"

"Let's go get this started. We'll try everything we can," Salvatore tried to mask his concerns.

Jennica, Luke, and Salvatore disappeared into the RV, as the rest of the crowd gathered loosely around the blazing fire. They were happy at the raiders' return, yet solemn, wondering if Marlowe would be alright. Laura Kepler finally broke the silence.

"What was in the other bag?"

At that Jerrett smiled, happy to have good news to share. He pulled open the bag and dramatically pulled out the items one by one. Excited gasps and comments came from the crowd.

"Cortisone, thank God. These bug bites have been torture!"

"Bandages! And antibiotic ointment!"

"Ibuprofen. Yes!"

Jerrett smiled at the joy spreading around the group. Someone brought out a stew and served it to the raiding party.

After yet another retelling of the evening's events, Dalton commented. "If only the antibiotics had been in your bag, dad."

And suddenly Jerrett remembered. He leaped up, collapsing his folding chair in his haste. He patted down his pockets until he pulled out three orange pill bottles triumphantly.

"I can't believe I forgot! Salvatore handed me a couple of bottles before loading his bag! I shoved them in my pocket." Cradling the precious bottles in his hands, he ran to Luke's RV. "Luke! Luke!"

A confused-looking Luke answered the door, his other children gathered close. Jerrett thrust out the bottles. "Antibiotics, Luke. I forgot Salvatore handed me some!"

Luke's mouth dropped open. "Are you serious? No way!" Laughing, he grabbed Jerrett in a hug and pulled him inside. "Jennica! Come here! Antibiotics!" Jennica burst out of the back room. Salvatore and the Bradford kids burst into laughter, clapping and dancing around.

Luke linked arms with Salvatore and skipped a jig around the room, landing on the couch in a fit of laughter. Jennica caught Jerrett in a bear hug, her hands gripping the precious pill bottles tightly, tears of joy racing down her cheeks.

"Thank you, thank you, thank you," she whispered softly in Jerrett's ear. "I will never forget this."

Finally, something had gone right. Jerrett's spirit sang for joy.

DON'T TREAD ON ME

CHAPTER 24
Evie's Back

It had been only a few days since they'd had the euphoric high of saving Marlowe and already the boy was improving. The camp was aglow with a feeling of victory and triumph.

Dean felt a sense of pride in what they'd done, but for Jerrett, it was merely a band aid on a gunshot wound. The pain of his lost children and Gwennie never let up. Every time Jerrett saw his kids' clothes or toys, a look of pure misery would come across his face. Dean would see him pause, his face going blank and his body freezing in place as he held a sweater of Cami's or Troy's riding gear. Jerrett had taken to sleeping with some of his kids' clothes tucked up against him. Inhaling their scent, he said he could almost pretend they'd cuddled up in bed with him.

During the day, Jerrett wandered about, looking lost and dazed. Dean, Matt, and the others tried to find tasks to keep him busy, but as soon as he was done, the aimless wandering would be back.

Their tiny, one-room cabin was mostly finished, and the brothers had moved boxes and supplies from the camper truck into it for storage. Dean had discreetly tucked away some of the kids' belongings in there, too, so Jerrett wouldn't be tortured every time he saw them.

Dean was organizing the new room when suddenly his phone rang. Cell reception was spotty on the mountain, so he was surprised when the call came through at all. Pulling out the phone, his heart leaped when he saw who it was.

"Evie! Where have you been? I've been trying to reach you forever. Where are you? Are you OK?" The questions tumbled out of him too fast to stop.

"Hold up there, cowboy!" Evie scolded with a laugh. "One question at a time! God, it's good to hear from you. Sorry I haven't called for a while. It's been really rough here."

"But you're OK?"

"Yeah, I'm fine. Just a little banged up ... and a little tired." Evie sounded worse than just tired, more like exhausted.

"I've been thinking about you ...all the time," Dean said, wistfully.

"Aww, Dean, me too. I wish I was there with you. But good news – Mitch says we're coming up to your camp, if it's OK? We need some time to regroup and heal up. We could use that EMT you were telling me about."

Dean's heart leaped for joy, "Really? You're coming?"

He could hear her chuckle and knew she was smiling. "Yes, yes! We'll be there tomorrow if it's OK."

"I can't wait."

"Me neither."

The conversation drifted on to talk about the latest news. Evie said that the militia groups had banded together, along with some vets under an ex-army man – Major Russ Donaldson, a tough old bird, who only had one arm.

The militia ranks were growing, but the government forces still outmanned them. The militia needed recruits, badly. Mitch's group was temporarily relieved of duty to rest and recover. Alonzo Ramirez and Andy Rowland, whom Jerrett and Dean had met at Mitch's meeting, had been shot badly. Few in the group were untouched by injuries, but most were minor.

When Evie asked how things were going up at Starlight, Dean had to tell her about Troy and Cami.

"Oh, Dean, no! I'm so sorry. Do you know where they are?" Dean told her about the camp rumored to be on the Pennsylvania-Ohio border.

"I know that place! It's really there, Dean, I've seen pictures of it. They *are* taking little kids. Adults, too. It's not a good place, Dean.

I've heard, well …" She broke off and Dean knew she was trying to spare him the details. Dean almost demanded she tell him, but realized he didn't want to know if he couldn't do anything about it.

"Do you know exactly where it is? Or how it's guarded?" he interrupted her.

"No, not those kinds of details. But Mitch has connections, he'll be able to find out more … if he's willing to help Jerrett. Those two didn't exactly leave on the best of terms …"

Dean felt a chill creep go through him. They needed Mitch and his contacts! But how could he get Mitch to help? An awful idea occurred to him and he hated himself for even considering it. Before he could talk himself out of it, he blurted it out.

"Tell Mitch he can bring his men here and we'll care for them, but in exchange, we need him to help us get the kids back. If he won't help, then … your group can't come up here." If using the injured men as a bargaining chip was the only way to ensure Mitch would help them, then so be it. It ripped Dean apart to say those words to Evie, when all he wanted was to hold her in his arms, but he needed Mitch to know he was serious.

Evie was silent for a moment, but answered, "I understand. I'll tell him."

"I want you, Evie, no matter what. But Mitch can't come here for help without helping us. It may be the kids' only chance. You understand, right?"

"I do. I really do. I'll get him there, don't you worry." They talked a bit more, then Evie hung up, promising to get back to him with word soon.

This just may work, Dean said to himself. He hoped so, anyway.

● ● ●

It hadn't taken Dean much effort to convince Jerrett and the others to let Mitch's group come once they heard about the plan. In his desperation, Jerrett would do anything to get the children back.

Saul cautioned Mitch not to let anyone follow. He'd advised Mitch to send people in small groups, driving in civilian vehicles so as not to attract attention. If they could come after dark, that would be even better. Saul had gone out to the end of the driveway, where he'd built a blockade of tree branches across the lane, to watch for them.

The first pickup truck rolled in around 10 am. Evie was driving, and two men were her passengers.

Saul pulled away the foliage and greeted her. Her dirty, red hair was pulled back in a messy ponytail. Dark rings circled her eyes and scratches covered one cheek. He could see a bandage poking out from her shirt sleeve as well.

Resting an arm on the window, Saul drawled, "So, you're Evie. Been hearing a lot about you. There's a young man up there who's been mooning for you non-stop."

Evie gave him a tired smile. "I've been anxious to see him, too."

Saul peered around her to the men inside. Blood-soaked bandages were wrapped around them. One spared Saul a pain-filled glance, the other was unconscious. "They the worst injured ones?"

"Yeah. Alonzo and Andy both got shot. I hear you've got an EMT?"

Saul nodded in affirmation. "Yup. Good kid, but he ain't no doctor. This may be beyond his expertise."

Evie glanced at the two men and then back to Saul. "I know," her voice was sad. "But it may be their only chance." She paused then added, "The next vehicle should be along after dark sometime. Look for a red van."

"Red, huh? Couldn't find anything more conspicuous?"

Evie shrugged. "We grabbed what we could."

Saul nodded. "Were you followed?" Evie assured him she hadn't been. "OK, well I'll stay down here and watch for a bit, just to be sure." Then Saul directed her up the lane to the track.

"Thanks, Saul." Evie started up the dirt road.

Despite her exhaustion, she could hardly contain her excitement at seeing Dean again. The smell of honeysuckle wafted in the open window and the birdsong rang out in the air. Soft, gentle breezes tickled her hair across her neck. A feeling of peace and security filled her.

Evie followed the road easily through the woods. When the sunlight filtered through the branches, she knew she was at the encampment. At first glance, she saw little signs of life, but gradually the hidden buildings and RVs came into view. The vehicles and cabins were tucked along the edges, under the trees or draped with tarps and foliage to disguise them. Then her eyes fell onto the dwelling she'd been looking for – Jerrett's truck. She watched as the door opened and out walked the dark-haired, athletic man she'd come to care so much about.

Throwing the truck into park, she bounded out of the door and ran towards him.

Dean met her halfway, scooping her up in his arms and twirling her around. She felt his warm breath as he kissed her. He murmured softly, "You made it," while his arms cocooned her tightly. When at last he set her down, he scowled at her appearance.

"You're hurt." He touched the scratches on her cheek, then lifted her bandaged arm as if he could peer right through it and see the damage underneath.

"I'm OK. Just a little stiff. It's Andy and Alonzo who need help," she gestured to the truck.

Dean didn't look convinced, but conceded. "Alright, we'll get them checked out first, but then it's your turn." Evie felt a flame of indignation and started to protest, but Dean blocked her with his hand. "No argument. You're getting looked at." Evie blinked in surprise. No one told her what to do! But strangely, it felt good to be looked after.

The two of them made their way back to the truck, where a crowd had gathered. Salvatore was already there, and he flung open the door of the truck where Andy rested.

"That's Andy, he's been shot in the leg and it keeps bleeding." Then Evie pointed to the short Hispanic man in the back seat. "He's worse. Shot in the abdomen. Bleeding stopped, but we think an infection is setting in."

"What's his name?" Salvatore asked, shoving someone away and moving to the back door.

"Alonzo Ramirez."

Salvatore pulled back the dressing on Alonzo's stomach. Grimacing at what he saw, he replaced it carefully. "Let's get them moved into our cabin."

The Caruso/Forrester cabin was quickly converted into a rugged hospital. Barry's single bed was occupied by Alonzo, with Andy in one of the bunk beds. Gawkers had crowded in the doorway, blocking the meager light. Paulo quickly shooed them away, leaving only himself and Laura to assist Salvatore.

Evie found herself exiled outside. It felt surreal to be relieved of the responsibility for two men so suddenly. She hugged her arms around herself, lost as to what to do now.

"Are you hungry?" Dean suddenly appeared behind her, his hand on her shoulder.

She jumped at his touch, heart thudding. "You scared me!"

"I'm sorry!" Dean looked stricken. "I thought you'd know I was there." He wrapped his arms around her, and she knew he felt her tremble. "They're in Salvatore's hands, now, Evie. It's time to take care of yourself. Let's get you something to eat. Then I want to clean those wounds." Evie allowed herself to be steered away towards the campfire. She collapsed into a chair, and a plate of hot, steaming food was put into her hands. She inhaled the rich aroma from the plate and her stomach growled. She hadn't even realized how hungry she was. Digging in, she was too tired to take notice of anything around her except her food. When her plate was empty, Dean took her by the hand and led her away from the fire. She stumbled across the ground and past a heavy fabric door on a structure of some kind.

"Let me check that arm, and then you're going to sleep," she heard Dean say through her daze. The light from a lantern swung above her, creating mesmerizing patterns. Dean's face swam in and out of focus as Evie fought to keep her eyes open. He tenderly unwrapped the dirty cloth from her arm. "What happened?"

"Knife cut ... a Guard surprised me ..." she murmured.

"It's not too bad, but let's wash it and rebandage it." Dean drifted out of sight and then returned. She felt his tender ministrations and tears sprung to her eyes. It felt so nice to be cared for. Her eyes were becoming so heavy-lidded she was having trouble keeping them open. She felt herself swaying.

"Here, lay down." Evie felt Dean easing her down on the soft blankets. As her eyes shut, she felt the cool cloth on her face, washing the scrapes. Then, nothing, as a long-awaited sleep claimed her.

● ● ●

Dean couldn't believe how tired Evie was. The dark circles under her eyes told of the stresses of the last few days. He wondered just what she'd seen since they'd last met. What horrors had she witnessed or been forced to participate in? Had she been shot at? On the run for her life? Did she have to kill anyone? Dean shuddered at the thought. Pulling a blanket over her shoulders, he tucked it in tightly around her, then smoothed her dirty hair back from her face. She was tough, that was for sure, and knew how to take care of herself, but he wanted to protect her anyway. She needed someone who was going to watch her back. He wondered where her uncle, Mitch, had been. Was this his way of watching over his niece? Dean seethed inside. First Mitch had planned the violence at the rally that killed Gwennie, his sister-in-law, and now he had let Evie come to be in this ragged state. The hatred and rage that Jerrett must be feeling towards the man became real to Dean, too. Mitch had some explaining to do when he arrived.

Dean's hand lingered over Evie's soft skin, ghosting across her face. She wasn't going into battle again, at least not without him, he vowed. They'd been apart long enough, but not anymore. Where they went next, they went together. If she still wanted to fight, then he'd fight by her side.

● ● ●

That night, under the cover of darkness, the red panel van carrying Mitch and the remaining seven men arrived. Saul had taken up his spot near the barricade again, and let them in.

After instructing them where to go, Saul stayed for another quarter-hour, watching for any tails, then went up to join the rest. He found an uneasy, tense group around the campfire. Jerrett stood by Dean's side, his fists clenched tightly as he fought to control himself. Dean was grilling Mitch about Evie. But Mitch wasn't saying anything back; instead he swayed on his feet, looking as if he could collapse any minute. Saul grabbed Mitch and guided him to a chair.

"Dean," Saul warned, "Now's not the time. They need food and rest. There'll be plenty of time to talk to him later. Now, go on Dean, Jerrett, you too. Dylan, Drey, will you see if they brought some tents along and set them up? You," he pointed to two teen boys nearby, "go help them. Jennica, would you get these men some food? Is there stew left?" He watched to see if his orders were followed. Once he was sure no fights were breaking out, he relaxed and looked around at the new arrivals.

The militiamen had dropped tiredly into chairs or onto the ground. Once Mitch had finished his bowl of soup, he seemed better. He took time to introduce his men to the crowd. The large, muscular dark-skinned man was Ely Monroe, who along with Jude Kinsey – the blond with tattoo sleeves – were Mitch's top men. The other members of the group were Jason Collins and Julian Emerich, who were young and strong, but bloodied and tired. Lucas Grant, a slim, black man with glasses, had a head wound that bled freely. Two red-haired brothers, Pomeroy and Bo Miller, had found lawn chairs and collapsed into them. Soon all were digging into bowls of thick, hot stew brought over by Jennica and her daughters. Laura and Paulo came by, having finished doing what they could for the two men who had arrived earlier and began looking over the newest arrivals. After a cursory exam, only minor injuries were found. They patched up those who needed it and by the time they were done, the tents the militia had brought had been erected.

Saul watched as the militiamen went off to bed. Then he made his way over to the Nolans. Finding Jerrett and Dean lounging in the doorway of the delivery truck, he strode up to them. Trevor and Dalton were inside, sitting at the table. "Hey, guys."

Silent, steely glares met him.

"Look, I'm sorry I sent ya' all away, but them boys is done in. They need a chance to recover before you start in on them. I know there's history there between ya' all, but remember, we need them. Jerrett, you know Mitch can help you get the kids back. And you'll need all those strong fighters. You don't have to like Mitch, but you will have to work with him." When no one answered, Saul shrugged his shoulders and took his leave. He'd said his piece and there was no point in harping on.

"Saul."

He turned to see Jerrett's outstretched hand. Saul knew it was Jerrett's way of saying there were no hard feelings. Saul clasped the younger man's hand and shook it.

CHAPTER 25

Training Camp

After a few days to rest and heal up, Mitch's troops were looking much better. Evie's arm was healing up nicely. The dark circles under her eyes had faded after a few good nights of sleep. Even Andy Howland, with his serious leg wound, seemed better. The only one not showing improvement was the man with the belly wound, Alonzo Ramirez. Salvatore didn't hold out much hope for the man, unfortunately. Infection had set in and there wasn't much they could do for him. Salvatore, Paulo, and Laura took turns sitting with him.

Tents had been pitched along the tree line for Mitch's men. The tents stood out in a contrast of red, blue, and yellow against the green foliage. Saul wasn't happy about the bright colors and lack of camouflage; he was afraid it would be too noticeable from above if a plane or drone flew over their way. Barracks would need to be built for the men, and soon.

After three days to rest and recoup, Mitch's team began the task of logging trees for a shelter. While they worked, Mitch started training the residents of Starlight.

They met in the clearing in the middle of the quasi-village of raggedy dwellings. Jerrett, Dean, Trevor – whose arm had finally healed up – and Dalton, were gathered with Matt, Luke, Barry Forrester, and Saul's three daughters. Evie was there, although Jerrett suspected it was to be near Dean more than anything.

Mitch, along with two of his Lieutenants, Jude Kinsey and Ely Monroe, watched the new recruits as they wandered in. He was dressed, as usual, in camo from head to toe, his squared-off shoulders thrown back, posture erect and his penetrating gaze picking apart the volunteers. A handgun was strapped to his hip, within easy reach.

Jerrett hated even looking at him. All he could think of was the last time he'd seen Mitch, that day at the shop, when he had told them about the violence they expected to occur at the rally and how he welcomed it as a means to get them to the place they were now. Ultimately it had been that permissive violence that had gotten Gwennie killed. Jerrett seethed inside, his blood boiling. He felt a steady hand on his shoulder and turned to see Dean. As if reading his mind, Dean muttered, "Remember, this is how we get the kids back. Keep thinking about that." With a deep, calming breath, Jerrett nodded, forcing back the anger. It felt strange to have hot-headed Dean as the voice of calm and reason.

When they were all present, Mitch stopped his pacing and turned to the group. "OK," he began, "I think we should start with target practice and weapons. Now, how many guns do have amongst you?"

After counting their arsenal, Mitch explained that with Saul and Markie's help, he'd set up a shooting range a way off in the woods. It was far enough from camp to be safe and Markie had even put up caution tape to keep wanderers out of the area.

"What about the sound of the guns?" Matt asked. "Won't the local people wonder what's going on?" He wasn't used to gunshots.

"No, there's a rod and gun club just over that way," Mitch pointed, "and they do target practice all the time. Anyone taking notice would assume it was from them, and besides, with the echo from the mountains, it would be impossible to pin down anyway."

"There's always hunters up here, too," someone else added.

The group was dismissed to get their dirt bikes, as it was a bit of a hike to the new range.

Jerrett pulled out Troy's dirt bike, his own bike lost that day in town when they'd gone for the medicine. He ran a hand lovingly over the frame of Troy's most prized possession. Closing his eyes for a moment, he imagined pushing the grief and pain deep down inside himself. Gritting his teeth and sucking in a deep breath, he shoved his helmet on and revved the engine.

The group mounted the dirt bikes and headed off through the woods to the range.

Mitch had them practicing for the better part of two hours. He seemed pleased with the group's progress, and Jerrett was surprised to see that the man was actually a good instructor. Ely and Jude circulated among them, guiding the trainees.

Out of their family, Dalton was the best shot, better even than his old man, who ranked second. Trevor's arm ached when he shot, so he didn't last long; the strength in that limb would take some time to build back up. Dean picked up the skill well enough and his fierce determination saw him through. Jerrett hadn't found a sport yet that his younger, super athlete of a brother couldn't conquer, especially with Evie to show off for now.

Fiona and Felicia Carrigan were crack shots, but the youngest missed often. The sisters would be an asset on the mission, especially with their woodcraft skills, honed from years of roaming the forest.

Matt and Barry hadn't fired a gun in years, but weren't too bad. Luke didn't do well.

That evening, Mitch announced that for the purpose of this mission and the need for expediency, Luke, Trevor, and Lanny Carrigan would not be used. There just wasn't time to properly train them. If there were hard feelings, no one voiced them. Trevor was disappointed, as he wanted to go along to get the kids, but he understood the reason.

Jerrett had kept his feelings towards Mitch under control all day, and by the time darkness fell he was exhausted and wanted some time alone. Wandering away from the communal campsite, he climbed into the truck. Jasper greeted him with a whimper from the bench. The dog hadn't been the same since Troy and Cami had been gone; it seemed as if he knew something was wrong.

"What's up, buddy?" Jerrett rubbed the dog's ears. "You miss them, too?" He lay back on the bench, the dog instantly snuggling up against him. Absent-mindedly he stroked the dog's belly, feeling the rough hair under his hand. He gazed around the truck, taking in Troy and Cami's plaques hung on the walls, Cami's sandals, and Troy's favorite cap. Clothes littered the floor, mingled with trash and dirt. Four men living together were not really a neat mix, although Dean tried relentlessly to keep it tidy. For the millionth time he wished Gwennie were here.

Jerrett leaned back but felt something lumpy under him. Reaching back, he pulled out Cami's favorite doll – some hideous stuffed monster thing – and tucked it under his arm. It smelled like her, a mixture of jelly, dirt, and sweat; the perfect mixture of sweetness and grittiness. It so perfectly represented his baby girl. He missed her sassiness, her playfulness, and her endearing kindness. He remembered when she'd given her flip-flops to Tori. He missed her stomping around in motocross boots and a tutu. What he wouldn't give to hold her in his arms right now? How she must be missing them! What was she doing right now? Had they let her stay with Troy? Or had they split them up? He couldn't bear the thought of them being alone, so he conjured up an image of them together. In his mind's eye, he saw Troy cuddling his sister, soothing her, telling her a story. Troy could be such a good big brother and he'd be looking after his sister, if he was with her. He'd never let anything happen to her. But he was just a little boy himself. Ten years old, and with a little sister dependent on him. He must be scared, but he would be trying to show a brave face to Cami.

Jerrett found himself wondering if his children would be the same when they found them? Would they be traumatized, maybe even brainwashed?

If he found them …

What if he never did? A chill went through him and tears pricked the corners of his eyes. Jerrett felt his fears running away with him and shook his head to clear the fear. Pushing the dog gently off, he reached in the cooler for a beer. There weren't many left; he'd better make this one last. Taking a long, slow pull of the beverage, he forced himself to relax. It was only a short time now until they got Troy and Cami back. Mitch could do it, he told himself, Mitch could find them and figure out how to get them out. He had to.

● ● ●

It was late that night when Evie finally got away from her duties. She found Dean, rearranging bags and boxes in the lean-to. It was sturdy and sound, but small; the space under the sloped roof was filling rapidly with belongings. A narrow cot stood by one wall, a newly made table with crooked legs on the other side. The floor was packed dirt, with an old sheet laid over it for a rug.

Leaning on the doorway, she smiled and said, "Hey there, handsome."

Dean turned and smiled. A smudge of dirt was smeared across one cheek and his hair, growing out of the buzz cut, was sticking up all over. Quite the look for such a neatnik. Even so, he was sight for sore eyes. "Hey yourself, been looking for you all day." He crossed the tiny space and took her in his arms.

"How's the cut?"

"Oh, it's fine. Salvatore says it's healing nicely."

"Good. I can't stand to see you hurt, ya know. When you pulled up to camp the other day and were all bloody and exhausted looking … I was so worried."

Embarrassed, Evie waved off his concerns, "I'm fine. It was nothing. I'm bound to get hurt at some point with all this going on." Pulling away, she walked around the room, examining the space.

"Well, I'm not OK with that."

Startled, Evie stopped and looked at Dean, her hands going to her hips defensively, mouth gaping open and eyes widening. She was about to protest his possessiveness when he crossed the room and took her in his arms, kissing her. The fight went out of her and she leaned into him, her arms wrapping around his neck.

"Evie," his voice was husky and thick, "I think I love you."

Startled, she pulled back to look at him. He loved her? "You can't mean that. You hardly know me." She pulled away again and paced the tiny space. "What are talking about – you love me? At a time like this? You're going to tell me you love me? We're at war here, who knows what tomorrow will hold! It's not the time for us to be getting involved."

She stopped, looking at him, only to see him watching her with a smirk on his face. "What? Why are you grinning at me like that?"

"Because you love me, too."

Evie was incredulous. "You can't decide that for me! I'll tell you I love you when and if I want to. And that's not now!"

The infuriating grin got even bigger. Dean came closer. "You do love me; you're just scared to say it." He leaned on the wall in front of her, blocking her way.

"Scared! I'm not scared of anything!"

"Then say it."

Evie clenched her jaw. He could be so infuriating! Her blood boiled, her fiery temper ignited.

"I will not!"

Dean just cocked his head to one side, "OK, if you're not ready to say it, fine. But I'm not afraid to. I love you. I think I always will. And I want to stay with you, take care of you, fight by your side, whatever, as long as we're together. I love you … no matter what tomorrow brings."

Evie was shocked to feel the tears pricking her eyes. She never cried! What was this man doing to her? She felt her walls crumbling, melting away with Dean's declaration. Unable to restrain herself any longer, she fell into his arms, clutching him with all her might. No one had ever made her feel this way before. She wasn't sure how to handle it, but it felt good, it felt right. She kissed him again, the passion igniting in her as her kisses became more forceful, more demanding. Dean responded in kind, pinning her up against the wall and returning her fervor.

They found their way to the narrow cot and lowered themselves into it, allowing passion to take over. The heat of their skin was glowing between them as they came together; their kisses became more urgent and forceful, as the desire built up between them and overcame them both.

Afterward, they lay in each other's arms, squeezed together in the tiny space. Dean twirled a strand of Evie's fiery hair around one finger and Evie traced a finger across his bare chest. Their legs intertwined, and their bodies pressed tightly against each other. Evie was overcome with emotion. This man was special to her, unlike any boyfriend she'd had before. Maybe it was the craziness of the times, the sense of impending doom, of fighting, and the war. Whatever it was, she knew at last that this man was for her, that what they felt between them was special. It was a feeling to be cherished for however long they were to have each other.

Sighing with pleasure, Evie rested her head on Dean's shoulder and softly said the words he'd been waiting to hear.

"I love you."

DON'T TREAD ON ME

CHAPTER 26

Clash of the Titans

The next day Mitch decided to send out scouts to the closest government camp, on the Pennsylvania-Ohio border. Mitch knew the general location, but no specifics. The group needed a recon team, so Mitch chose his First Lieutenant, Jude Kinsey, to lead the expedition. The red-haired Miller brothers were sent along as a part of Jude's team, using the pickup truck Evie had driven up to Starlight.

The entire camp came to see them off.

Jerrett hung back and watched as Mitch stepped up to the driver's window to give last-minute instructions. He overheard him remind the scouts to watch the camp from a safe distance and report back on the layout and security, and if children were being held there.

As Mitch finished, he shook each scout's hand and stepped away. Seeing Jerrett in the crowd, Jude, in the driver's seat, motioned him over. Jerrett came forward as Jude reached out a tattooed arm to shake hands.

"Hey, man. Hang in there, OK? We'll find them," Jude offered, tucking a long strand of blond hair behind his ear.

Jerrett grasped the man's hand, clamping the other on top. "Thank you," he answered warmly; it was all he could manage to get out past the lump in his throat. He stepped back, watching as the red-haired brothers waved and Jude sped away.

Swallowing hard, Jerrett turned to the rest of the group. Joining his brothers, he wrapped an arm around his son as they headed off to make breakfast.

Around the camp, others were busy with various projects. Jennica had started a garden, and those not training were helping her. The youngest children were reluctantly attending a school of sorts under Laura Kepler's guidance, partly to keep them busy and out of trouble.

Shooting drills continued after they'd eaten. Several of Mitch's men were there; the rest were occupied with barracks building.

The training group headed out to the range. Three of the teens had not handled a gun before, so Mitch concentrated on them that morning. The others practiced under Ely Monroe's watchful eye. After a break for lunch, Mitch had them gear up and hit the track. He wanted to see each recruit's riding ability. The idea of using the dirt bikes on missions and for scouting appealed greatly to Mitch because they would be able to go off-road. Escaping the Black Bears would be much easier. Carrying a clipboard, Mitch made copious notes about each person's skills. Evie followed her uncle, helping him evaluate the recruits.

Watching the teens fly around the track, Mitch smiled at their natural ability. The younger ones were less cautious, strong, and energetic. They only concerned themselves with how fast they could go, how high they could jump, and how hard they could hit the corners. He could use that.

As they came off the track, he announced to all that there would be a meeting later that afternoon and that all the recruits were to attend.

Jerrett, Matt, Dean, and Barry stood together at the back of the crowd.

"He calling the shots now?" Barry wondered quietly, a trace of annoyance in his voice.

"Guess he thinks so," Matt supplied.

Jerrett snorted in frustration, "Not on my watch. He'll get someone else killed." He clenched his jaw, remembering Gwennie, the familiar ache rising in his chest. "I guess we better go, though, to see what he wants ... and to keep him in check." Murmurs of agreement echoed his words. If Mitch thought he was going to roll in here and tell them all what to do, he had another thing coming, Jerrett thought with vengeance. *I'll make it my personal duty to stop him from organizing another operation that ends up in slaughter.* As they walked away, another thought invaded Jerrett's thoughts, warring with his desire to keep everyone safe: rescuing the kids. He'd do anything to get his kids back, even if it meant working with a madman. Mitch was highly skilled and well connected, but dangerous all the same.

With a sense of unease circulating among them, the men agreed to meet up later and hear what Mitch was planning. Then they broke apart, wandering off to eat lunch and rest.

That afternoon, the meeting took place under the trees in the center of the camping area. The cluster of tall pines had become a gathering place of sorts, as it was almost dead center of their little makeshift village. A faint drizzle had begun, causing everyone to huddle under the trees near each other. Jerrett and his brothers were together, standing with Matt. Jerrett fidgeted with nervous apprehension. Just what was Mitch going to announce? He looked around to see Dalton standing with the Bradford kids, an arm leaning on Woody's shoulders. The kids looked indifferent; faintly curious, but not sure why they were there. All of Mitch's men were there also.

Mitch hopped up on a stump, Evie stood by his side, clipboard in hand. His beady, penetrating eyes took in the crowd. Once he seemed satisfied that all were in attendance he cleared his throat and began.

"After the last few days of watching, I think I have an idea what we're going to do. We've got some decent shots here, and the skills you all show on dirt bikes will be invaluable. I want my guys to learn to ride if they can. Jason Collins and Ely Monroe already ride street bikes, so if someone could show them the finer points of dirt riding, I'd appreciate it. Then we can work on the other guys. You teenagers," He motioned to the kids scattered around the crowd, "You guys and gals are amazing on the track. You throw around those machines like they were part of you. I want to use that ability.

You guys are young, strong, and have enough energy to do what we need."

The hairs on the back of Jerrett's neck were standing up. What was Mitch getting at? Just how would he want to use the kids? A few were as young as fifteen. Jerrett's brow furrowed as he listened.

"I was thinking you all would make good scouts. Ride on ahead, see what's happening and ride back to report what you see," Mitch continued, oblivious to the grumblings that followed. The crowd was looking at each other, heads shaking and whispering, but Mitch continued anyway. "That way we can save the fighters for the hard work, and not wear them out so much. We'd be better prepared for what we'd be facing." He paused and noticed the angry glares from the parents in the crowd. His brow wrinkled in confusion as his head swiveled. Evie looked at him, her eyes wide, shaking her head frantically at him and pulling on his arm to silence him. He ignored her, brushing her away. "They'd be helping our country! We'd be giving them a chance to make a difference! They want that, I'm sure. We can use their talents –"

"They're only kids! What the hell are you talking about? What's wrong with you?" Jerrett interrupted. He couldn't hold his tongue any longer. "You want to put fifteen-year-old kids on the front lines? Are you crazy? You'd be sending them into God knows what situations!"

"What if they get shot at? How will they know what to do?"

"They aren't trained for this!"

"Are you crazy?" Angry voices from the crowd rang out, protesting.

"Are they disposable to you?" Jerrett demanded to know, pushing his way forward. "Are they? Do you want to send them in to save the fighters? What are you thinking? You think you're gonna send my kid in there?" He was face to face with Mitch now, hostile and enraged.

"Jerrett, that's not what I meant!" Mitch countered, backing up slightly, "They'd be able to ride away before they got into any danger! They're stealthy, they can do it! We need them!" He stepped off the stump, into Jerrett's space. "It's their future at stake here: they should have some part in protecting it! You want me to send out a seasoned fighter? We need every man we've got for the long haul. I can't afford to use the militia as scouts if I don't have to!"

"You're going to have to, cause you ain't using a kid for that job! I won't let you!"

"You won't let me?" Mitch was incredulous. "Who put you in charge of this chickenshit outfit? You aren't going to tell me what to do!" Spittle flew out of Mitch's mouth as he continued. "You want my help? Then you do what I say!"

Jerrett's hands curled into fists. "Never!" His jaw clenched in rage, he shook his fist in front of Mitch's face. "Not if it means putting any more people in danger – for your benefit! You got my wife killed in your damn rally! These kids won't be doing any scouting!" The muscles in Jerrett's face tightened, his lips were pulled back and his teeth bared as he glared at the man.

Shouts of agreement rang out from the crowd.

Mitch's face was red with fury. "I didn't get your damn wife killed, she –"

Jerrett's fist smashed into Mitch's face.

Screams rang out all around. Mitch crashed to the ground, Jerrett following. His fists connected with Mitch's head and torso. Rage poured through Jerrett, turning him into a madman. Others joined in the fray, though Jerrett didn't notice, his anger blinding him.

Eventually, Matt managed to pull Jerrett off Mitch, pinning his arms to his sides. Mitch staggered to his feet, wiping blood from his face. He turned to Jerrett, hostility pouring off him in waves. He lunged at Jerrett, landing a solid punch to his cheek. Matt was thrown off balance and dropped to the ground, Jerrett falling with him.

Mitch was on him instantly.

Jerrett felt the blows rain down on him. Tangled up in Matt's limbs, he couldn't get up. He tucked his head under his arms.

Someone screamed. Bodies collided with each other in grunts and gasps.

Using his only defense, Jerrett kicked out his foot at Mitch. He heard Mitch grunt in pain as he connected, but he barely paused in his attack.

Suddenly the barrage stopped and Jerrett looked up to see Barry, his arms locked around Mitch, pulling him back.

Jerrett leaped to his feet, fists raised, but Barry had thrown Mitch to the ground and was kicking him. He glanced around him, and saw bodies all over the ground, the fighting dwindling. Looking back at Mitch and Barry, he saw Ely Monroe had restrained Barry and pulled him away from Mitch. Mitch crawled along the ground, holding his ribs, blood streaming from his face.

Suddenly Mitch's men, Jason Collins and Lucas Grant, whose glasses were sitting askew on his face, appeared between Jerrett and Mitch. Jason held his hands up in a peaceful gesture and Lucas straightened his crooked frames. "Enough, man. He's had enough," Jason was saying.

Jerrett could feel the rage leaving him. It seemed to sink right down his body like water in the shower, to pool at his feet. In its place exhaustion and pain took over. He raised a hand to indicate he was done and hunched over holding his head.

Turning his back to his opponent, Jerrett straightened and looked around him. People were picking themselves up off the ground. Dylan and Drey leaned on a nearby tree, Dylan bleeding from his head. Evie was helping Terra up off the ground. Dalton and the rest of the teens stood off to the side, looking scared and shell-shocked. Others were scattered all over, picking themselves up.

Dean was rubbing his bloody knuckles as he stood over Julian Emerich, one of Mitch's men. Barry, still raging and swinging, was being held in check by the huge black man, Ely. Matt was trying to calm him.

Jerrett gasped and grabbed his side as a sharp pain made itself known. He could feel blood trickling down his cheek, and various aches and pains all over his body. His only consolation was Mitch. *As long as he's hurt worse*, Jerrett consoled himself, *then I won*. The victory was short-lived, however, when his breath hitched and he had to reach out to support himself on a tree.

"Dad," Dalton materialized by his side, hands gently gripping Jerrett's arms. "You OK?"

Jerrett glanced over at his son's worried face. Despite the pain, he suddenly realized he felt more alive than he had in some time. It was as if all the pain and grief that had been building inside him had suddenly found a release. As the adrenaline left him, a peaceful calm took its place. He wondered if this is what Dean felt after a fight.

His face cracked into a smile and he straightened. Swinging an arm around Dalton's thin shoulders, he said, "Yeah, I'm OK. It's over. Let's go home." Dalton returned the grin, and the worry faded. They stopped to gather up a bloodied Dean; obviously, his brother had jumped into the fray to support him – like he always did.

Jerrett draped his other arm over Dean's shoulder and the three of them walked away, leaning on each other and connected as one.

CHAPTER 27
The State of Things

Over the next few days, training resumed, albeit at a slower pace since so many were still recovering from the brawl. The militia and mountain dwellers had made peace, but it was an uneasy alliance.

Jerrett felt as though he'd been through a meat grinder. His eye was swollen shut, and he had a jagged cut across his cheek, which Salvatore had butterflied. His ribs were bruised, and it hurt to move around much.

There were no serious injuries, but many people were cut up and bruised. The worst injured was Mitch; Barry had worked him over. Barry could be a ruthless, dirty fighter when angered and Jerrett was glad they were on the same side.

Just that morning, Jerrett had passed by Mitch. The man was walking hunched over, a grimace on his bruised face. A feeling of satisfaction swept over Jerrett to see the man suffer. He deserved what he got and more.

The two of them tried to avoid each other and if they couldn't, their conversations were terse and clipped.

The others were on the mend as they went about their duties. Andy Howland, who had the leg wound, was up and hobbling around the camp. Unfortunately, his injured comrade hadn't fared so well. Alonzo Ramirez had finally succumbed to his wounds and passed away the day after the brawl. Saul had chosen a clearing in the woods for his grave, and a hasty funeral had been arranged. Andy, a devoted churchgoer, had spoken a few words over his friend and offered a lengthy prayer. When the funeral was over, everyone went back to camp and to work. There was much to be done.

Jerrett found himself remembering Gwennie and the quick funeral they'd had for her in the backyard. The similarities were disturbing. He wondered if this would be the new way of handling their dead. It was a gloomy thought that haunted him the rest of the day, even as he went about his work.

The barracks were nearly finished. Only the gaps between the logs needed to be filled in with mud, but it was easy work and the children were assigned the task. They enjoyed the work, which often turned into a game, as the mud was flung at each other. It was good to hear the laughter of the children, but it made Jerrett long for Troy and Cami.

Jerrett's truck was emptier now, as many of the tools and supplies had been moved to the lean-to, along with Evie and Dean. It had officially become their space now. A second cot had been found for Evie and the two of them had put down a plank floor. A real door and windows were next on the construction list. It brought a smile to Jerrett's face when he thought of how happy his brother was. He deserved it. Jerrett remembered Dean's last serious girlfriend and how she'd broken his heart. It had taken a long time, but it seemed Dean was finally healed.

Around the rest of the encampment, life continued as this became their new 'normal'. Jennica's garden was coming along well. Lanny Carrigan, Trevor, and Luke Bradford were usually hard at work there. The digging was proving to be a good exercise for Trevor's arm.

Laura had managed to corral the younger children for a few hours each day to have a kind of school. She had few materials or books, but she did what she could to keep the kids busy and engaged. There were about eight children most days in her camper, ranging from the oldest – Barry's daughter, Caitlyn – to the youngest, little Maggie Kepler. It worked out surprisingly well, and the older ones helped with the youngest. The children seemed to thrive on the routine and familiarity. Saul's wife, Markie, helped often, teaching the children about woodcraft.

In the evenings, Salvatore and Paulo taught the others first aid, since they could no longer go to the doctor. Doctors had to report anyone out of their zone without a pass. Those who had helped patients without reporting it to the authorities had been turned in by nurses and other personnel so often, that few took the chance anymore.

This feeling of settling into their new routine was comforting to most of the camp, but Jerrett was still plagued by the uneasy sensation that nothing was right in his world. He still didn't feel equipped to do everything Gwennie used to do. He could barely recall if he'd fed the dog each evening, much less keep an eye on Dalton, Trevor and Dean's wellbeing. Gwennie had made it all look so effortless. He wondered if she'd known how much he'd appreciated her. Had he told her enough? A pang of regret struck his heart. If only she were here now, and he could make up for all the times he hadn't said how much he loved her. Maybe if he got the children back – no, not if! When! *When* the children were back, maybe then they could finally create a new normal for themselves and begin to heal the giant hole Gwennie had left in their hearts. Someday …

Jerrett resumed his work, since keeping busy was the only way he knew to deal with the overwhelming sadness and despair that threatened to overtake him.

He bent over to yank a long, thick branch out of a tangle of undergrowth. As he gathered the firewood, he spied the Carrigan house peeking through the trees. He let his thoughts drift towards his old friends.

Saul and Markie, so giving and generous, were maybe rethinking the idea of letting the militia settle there. It had opened a can of worms, Markie had said, that they weren't expecting. Jerrett worried that they'd brought too much trouble to the kindhearted couple's doorstep. He'd never forgive himself if the Guard caught up with the Carrigans and punished them for the shelter they'd given.

When his work was done, he found himself wandering across the meadow and down the gully to where Saul and Markie's house stood.

They'd built the sturdy, wooden two-storey house themselves. These days it housed Saul, Markie, and their three daughters as well as Saul's brother, George, and his wife, Irene, and children.

Now, however, there didn't seem to be anyone around. The only sound that broke the peaceful silence was the crickets and birds chirping in the trees surrounding the home. The back of the house butted up to a gentle hill, which hid the building from the view of the track. A large deck stretched out by the front door, with potted plants and flowers scattered all around. Muddy work boots lay by the door and a rusted metal chair sat next to the window. A lazy tabby cat sprawled on the steps. The grass around the house hadn't been mowed for some time, but lay trampled in a path from the deck to the driveway.

Jerrett followed the well-worn path up to the deck. Pausing to pet the cat, he continued up to the door.

Markie Carrigan answered his knock. Her long, brown hair was pulled back in a messy ponytail, her denim shirt and jeans streaked with dirt. But her face lit up in a warm smile when she saw Jerrett.

"Hello! Come on in!" She held open the door and gestured for him to enter. "Pardon my dirt; I was just taking a break from the garden. I was going to have some lunch. Care for some soup?"

"Oh, no, that's OK Markie. I just came by to talk to you and Saul."

"Well, Saul and George are out at the sawmill just now. "

"Are the others around?"

"Not right now. I think Irene took a walk and the younger children are with Laura at school. I don't know where my girls are. Not here anyway." She smiled and shrugged. "But what's troubling you? Let's sit down and talk."

Markie pointed to a bright yellow chair at the kitchen table. She sat in a purple one. Each mismatched chair was gaily painted a different color. The kitchen was filled with artifacts from the woods around them – snake skins, antlers, deer heads, and wood carvings.

An ancient wood stove stood in the corner. Jerrett loved the warm, homey feeling the room gave him. Markie pushed a cup of coffee in front of him.

Wrapping his hands around the mug, he lifted it to his lips, savoring the flavor. Setting it back down, he said, "Markie, I need to talk to you." He paused, gathering his thoughts. "I'm afraid that we put you and your family in danger. When I asked to come here, it was to hide out for a little, get our bearings. I never thought we'd be here this long, or that our house would be overtaken. I just thought it'd be a week or two, ya know? And now there's all this going on. The militias are here, we're fighting and causing trouble, we have had to cut down so many trees to build our cabins. When you said yes, you didn't know it would be yes to all of this. And now I don't know when we'll be able to leave, or when we'll ever find the … kids…" His voice broke and he couldn't continue.

Markie reached over and laid a sympathetic hand on his arm. "You'll find them. Jerrett, you will. Keep positive thoughts." She patted his arm and sipped her coffee. Setting down her mug, she continued, "As far as the village you've got going on up here – listen, Saul and I have talked about this. You and yours are always welcome up here, Jerrett, and for as long as you want to stay. We wouldn't have permitted you to come otherwise. As for the others, well, we're in the middle of a second revolutionary war here, Jerrett. Did you realize that?"

"I … I guess so, Markie. It's hard to think of it that way."

"Well. That's what this is. It's a monumental moment in our country's history. America is on the cusp of something we've never seen, a chance to make it what it should be again, what our forefathers intended all along. I'm an old lady, and Saul's an old man –"

"You aren't that old!"

She chuckled, "No, I guess we aren't, but we are too old to fight in a war. But this, we can do. We can shelter those that can fight, and we can shelter our friends and family. The woods can provide a safe hiding place. They can give us logs for cabins, fresh water, plants, and food. We can hunt. We're pretty well off up here in terms of self-sufficiency, you know. Sharing what we have is our way of contributing to the fight."

Jerrett spared her a small smile. "But I'm afraid we've brought danger to your doorstep, Markie. If they trace us here, you could all be arrested for harboring people out of their zone and aiding the militia. I couldn't live with that."

She patted him sympathetically. "That's not on you. That's on us. It's our decision and ours alone. This is our way of contributing and don't you dare try to take that away from us." She shook her finger at him sternly. "Now listen, what you need to do is work on getting those kids back. That's it. Don't you give Saul or me another thought. And those girls of ours, well, if the militia hadn't come here, they'd have gone to them. They were bound to find a way to join up somehow."

He could see she meant what she was saying and when she got like that, there was no use protesting. The twist in his stomach relaxed and his frazzled nerves felt soothed. He smiled at her; she and Saul were truly amazing people. He would still worry that one day trouble would come to Starlight, but at least he knew Saul and Markie's position on the matter.

They chatted a bit longer, enjoying the coffee and the conversation. When it was time to leave, he wrapped Markie in a warm, tight hug.

It was with a lighter heart that Jerrett returned to the camp.

● ● ●

That afternoon the adults in the camp gathered. Mitch had decided they needed to talk things out after the melee, and he had new information to share. He enlisted Matt to run the session, knowing that anything he said himself could easily be misconstrued and cause another ruckus. He hoped Matt could be an impartial third party.

Stepping up on the stump, Matt could see over the crowd. Waving his arms, he cleared his throat to get their attention.

"OK, everybody. We need to talk. We've got some things to clear up." He waited for silence and then continued. "I think we all agree that the teens aren't going to be used as scouts. They aren't going to be allowed in such a dangerous position as that."

Matt saw heads nodding and voices murmuring in agreement. He continued, "But Mitch was right in some things. These kids should have a part in this … revolution. We're doing all this to make things better for their future. They are young, strong, and healthy, with riding skills that can be very beneficial to the militias." He paused, trying to judge the reaction he was getting. "Mitch has come up with the idea that they could be used as rear guards. It would keep them away from the front lines, but also put their skills to use. They can be trained by Salvatore and Paulo in first aid and be used to care for the wounded. They could drive wounded soldiers back to camp on the dirt bikes and carry messages from the headquarters to the field. This is something they could do without being in as much danger. It would be a great benefit since the government has put such restrictions on the communication systems, and the mountains constantly interfere with our cell signals. Each family should take some time to talk and decide if they will allow their teens to participate."

Matt had to raise his voice over the muted conversations going on throughout the crowd. He noted the concern on many faces, but was happy to see some were nodding in approval. "On another note, Mitch has informed me that he's heard from the leader of the resistance. He is a retired Major and he is the official bigwig of the United Militia Revolutionary Army. That's the new name of their outfit. He's united most of the militia groups, along with some vets and civilians. He wants a few things from us specifically. What's his name again, Mitch?"

"Major Russ Donaldson; a one-armed bastard."

Stunned, Matt didn't know what to make of that comment, so he just ignored it and continued.

"Umm, right, he's the leader of the resistance now," Matt continued, relaying the information Mitch had supplied. "The Major wants to use Starlight as a safe haven – a place for the wounded and non-combatants. Troops would not be stationed here, except in emergencies, so it should remain safe to house our families here.

"Saul and Markie have already confirmed they want to do their part and have agreed to this proposal. It means a greater risk for us to be discovered, as there will be more people coming and going, but we also get a better security system. The Major will station a small number of troops here to protect us and the wounded."

"What else does he want?" someone called out.

"The militia needs new recruits, fighters. Major Donaldson wants to know if any of us want to join, to do their part?" Matt felt a swell of patriotism. "Look, guys, you can't ignore the significance of this. It's the second American Revolution! We have to ask ourselves, do we sit by and watch, waiting to see what happens? Or do we help to make things right again?" Matt paused, watching the crowd of family and friends. He felt the need to back off. "I don't want to convince anybody of anything. We each must decide for ourselves. It's too important a decision to go into lightly."

"What would it entail? What would be committing to?"

"Yeah, we're not soldiers."

Mitch stepped forward and answered the question. "You'd be mostly giving support to the fighters, providing supplies, gardening, medical care, respite, scouting, and supply runs, but some of you could be used in combat if you have the skills needed. Especially vets." He paused, then added, "You don't have to let us know right now, but please think about it. How can you help? What can you do? We need everyone we can get to turn this around. Let me know as soon as you reach your decision." He shook Matt's hand and then left the area.

Murmurs of discussion could be heard all around. Most people were going to take their time thinking things through and talk it over with their families, but a few chose to join up right away. Dylan Williams and Drew Boddie, who were both young, single men without families, followed Mitch, intent on signing up right then.

The Nolan men gathered together. Each said their piece, in turn. Jerrett had no desire to commit to anything just yet. His focus was on getting the kids back; everything else could wait. Dean felt a strong urge to join up; he wanted to do his part and remain close to Evie, but of course, the kids came first. Jerrett understood the patriotic pull, he felt it himself. Trevor was content to follow whatever his brothers decided. Dalton had wanted to join the militia long before, but the way he'd lost his mother had forced the boy to grow up quickly. He wouldn't rush into another battle like the one he'd witnessed at the rally. He knew what it was like to have someone die in his arms. No argument was heard from him on the decision to wait. They were patriots, yes, but some things took precedence over that. Troy and Cami were too important.

⦿ ⦿ ⦿

After dark, everyone gathered around the communal campfire. The size of the crowd had grown, thanks to the militiamen. Jerrett watched Matt teasing his littlest daughter and smiled along as she exploded into giggles. It made him miss Cami. He desperately wanted to hear her laugh again. The hollow place inside him exploded into a hole big enough to swallow him and he couldn't stand to see Matt and his child any longer.

He'd just gotten up to head back to the truck when the noise of an engine wheezing up the drive became apparent.

"Someone's coming!" he yelled. Everyone leaped up at once. Matt and Laura kicked dirt over the fire, Jennica hurried the kids inside and others ran about dousing the lights. Jerrett, Dean, Evie, and several of the militia grabbed weapons and ran down to the drive.

"You three, take cover on that side, we'll be over here!" Ely Monroe whispered urgently. They shrank into the bushes on either side. Jerrett knelt, his brother and Evie by his side, heart pounding with anticipation. They watched silently as headlights came down the drive.

"It's Jude!" a shout rang out.

The scouts had returned. Those in hiding emerged from the bushes, waving their arms and flagging down the truck. Jerrett shook with anticipation: what had they found out? Had they seen his kids?

Ely beat him to the question. "What did you find out?"

Jude pushed his windblown hair out of his eyes. "Look, I don't want to tell it over and over. Jump in the back. Let's head up to camp and tell everyone at once." Ely nodded in agreement and they hopped into the bed of the truck.

But Jerrett grasped Jude's arm through the window, halting his progress.

"Did you see my kids?"

Jude shook his head sadly. "Don't know, man, but there are kids there. Just don't know if they are yours. Jump in, I'll tell you all I know."

The ride back to camp was short, but it seemed like an eternity to Jerrett. Dean seemed to sense his anxiety. He slung an arm over Jerrett's shoulders and kept it there the entire ride back.

Reaching the camp, a crowd quickly gathered, asking questions all at once.

Mitch smiled at the return of his soldiers as he made his way to the truck. "Welcome back! Are you all OK?"

Jude answered him quietly and exited the truck, followed by the red-haired brothers, Pomeroy and Bo Miller. Jude led the crowd to the communal fire pit.

"OK Jude, tell us what you saw," Mitch commanded.

Jude looked around at everybody for a moment. "Well," he began, "First we stopped at the nearest town, to kinda scope things out. There's no love for the Elites there, that's for sure. The old-timer at the local bar was chatty, told us where the camp was exactly. Said anyone rounded up west of Harrisburg got sent here – our area included." Jude clarified, then continued. "We left the truck about a mile away from the camp and hiked in. Elites were patrolling all around the area, so we stuck to the woods. It took us a while to get close, but the tree line is thick near there, so there's good cover.

"The camp's got about six big metal buildings; they kinda look like garages, but without garage doors. They each have a door that faces into the middle of the camp. The buildings are set up facing each other, three on each side, with a wide path down the middle."

"What's security like?" Mitch interrupted.

Jude continued with his briefing, "There's a chain link fence, topped with barbed wire."

Bo Miller spoke up, "With a Guard tower –"

"– in the front," his brother Pomeroy added.

"Yeah, we were thinking we could maybe cut the fence somewhere, avoid the tower completely," Jude continued.

"Could we climb over?"

"Nah, not with the barbed wire on top."

"Oh yeah, forgot about that."

"Well…" Jude began again, infuriatingly slow, "I don't know how many Guards they got exactly, but it didn't seem like too many. Maybe cause it's kinda secluded there, they don't need many."

Jerrett couldn't hold his tongue any longer. "What about the prisoners? What did you see? I know you didn't see my kids, but what kind of people have they got there? Men, women, or kids?"

Jude looked up at him with pity in his eyes. "Sorry, we didn't see your kids, man. We just couldn't get that close. But there were definitely children there. There were women, too, and some men. They seemed to be milling around, kinda aimlessly, like there's not much to do. But then, later, they all gathered in the middle when a loudspeaker came on."

"What was that all about?" Dean wanted to know.

Jude paused long enough for Pomeroy to jump in, "It was creepy, man. The stuff they were saying over it."

Bo added, "Brainwashing, like. They were saying stuff like we should be grateful to the government for taking care of us –"

"– feeding us, clothing us, giving us security and stuff –"

"– went on and on, filling their heads with nonsense –"

" – creepy, like I said."

Jerrett was getting tired of tracking the brothers' conversation as they constantly took turns interrupting each other.

"And they all just stood there, listening to it all, no one making a move to leave."

"Yeah, till it was over, then they all just went back to whatever they were doing to begin with," Pomeroy finished up.

Jude took over the conversation, "It was really weird, like they said. Like they were all conditioned to stop and listen whenever the loudspeaker started up."

Dean looked over at Jerrett with concern. He looked shook up. Dean didn't feel much better, thinking of Troy and Cami in such a place, subjected to that

"So ...what do we do now?" Dalton broke the silence. All eyes turned to Mitch, their de facto leader in all things military.

Mitch took his time answering, but when he did it was with an air of authority. "Now we get them out."

CHAPTER 28

Preparing

The next two days were filled with frantic planning. Jerrett wanted to leave immediately, but Mitch overrode him, wisely declaring that they needed to plan first. Mitch estimated a ten-person team would be ideal to mount a rescue and provide cover fire. The group could then be split up into smaller fire teams as well, if needed.

Evie would be Mitch's second-in-command. Ely Monroe, an ex-marine, was an obvious choice to go along. After that Mitch chose Jude, Bo, and Pomeroy, since they had seen the camp firsthand.

The next task was not going to be an easy one.

Reluctantly, Mitch approached Jerrett, who was heating soup over a propane camping stove.

"Jerrett, do you have a minute?"

Recognizing the voice, Jerrett clenched his jaw and threw back his shoulders before he even turned around. Raising his head high, he turned and greeted Mitch with a simple nod.

Mitch suddenly seemed uneasy, as he looked at his scuffed boots and shuffled his feet. The silence was deafening.

"Just spit it out, Mitch. I don't have all day."

At that, Mitch's head snapped up, anger flaring in his green eyes. The color was just like Evie's, Jerrett couldn't help but note, though lacking in warmth.

"OK then," Mitch's tone was cold. "I will get right to it. I don't think you should come along on the mission. You – "

"Stop," he held his hand up. "There's no way I'm not going."

"Be reasonable, Jerrett. You're not a soldier, you've got no woodsman skills and you're not that great of a shot. Heck, your kid can shoot better'n you – if he wasn't so young, he'd make a fine soldier." Mitch held up a hand to stave off Jerrett's argument. "I can only bring so many people along; you and your brothers would just be dead weight. Besides, I just can't trust you to keep a level head. What's going to stop you from rushing in at the first sight of your kids and wrecking the whole plan? I can't take that chance!"

Leaning forward and squaring his shoulders, Jerrett lowered his chin and glared at Mitch, his body tense and rigid. "If you think for one second I'm staying back when my kids are in there, you're crazy! Those are *my* kids, and no one is more determined to get them out than me."

"I'm going too," Dean's voice broke in. Jerrett turned his head to see his brother and Evie. With his voice raised, he hadn't even noticed them approaching. Dean continued, venom leaching out with every word. "You aren't leaving either of us behind." His fists were clenched and his muscled shoulders taut.

"They need to go, Uncle Mitch," Evie added.

"Now look – " Mitch began, "We're not sightseeing here!"

Jerrett moved so fast no one could have seen it coming. He had Mitch's shirt bunched up in his fist and the man up on tiptoes in seconds. Spittle flew from his clenched teeth as he spat out, "Sightseeing! You bastard!" He shoved the man, causing Mitch to stumble backward. "Those are my *kids!* No one cares about them like we do!" Jerrett stepped back, ran a hand through his hair, and took a deep, steadying breath. "How do we know you won't get spooked and turn tail? That you won't abandon the mission if there's a snag? Me and Dean," he pointed to himself and his brother in turn, "We'll get them out – no matter what. I can't say the same about you." Jerrett paced back and forth, seething for a minute before he stopped and continued. "We'll stick to the plan – as long as it doesn't involve leaving the kids behind. You can count on that. We're not stupid enough to blindly run into an armed camp.

Trevor and Dalton will stay here. They're too young. But Dean and I go. That's final."

Mitch, red-faced with embarrassment and anger, threw his hands in the air, conceding the argument. "Fine! Have it your way." He started to walk away but then turned back. "I still don't agree that it's a good idea. I think you're putting the whole operation at risk, but I can see I'm not going to convince you, so have it your way. The team's lives are on you, not me." Mitch's arm shook with anger as he pointed at Jerrett and then himself. He turned on his heel and marched away.

Jerrett watched him leave and then turned to his brother. "Thanks for that."

"Anytime, every time, brother. I've always got your back."

To Evie, he said, "Thanks for standing with us. But I don't want to be the cause for hard feelings between you and your uncle."

Evie tossed her red hair and smiled grimly. "You're not. It's been coming for a long time, but this is the final straw. No one cares about those kids more than you two and it's only right that you come." She added quietly, "They're going to need you after what they've been through."

His anger left him suddenly and a cold shudder went through Jerrett. What *had* they been going through? He was chilled to the core and filled with an urgency that he couldn't contain. He scrubbed at his hair and dropped into a chair.

Dean, sensing his brother's sudden change of feelings, squatted by his side and wrapped an arm around his shoulders. Evie knelt on the other side.

"We're almost there, big brother. We're getting them back. Soon. Just hang in there a little longer."

Jerrett clasped Dean's hand in solidarity while Evie hugged his neck.

@ @ @

In the end, Jerrett, Dean, and Evie went on the mission, along with Mitch and his soldiers. Fiona and Felicia Carrigan were chosen for their crack shots and woodsman skills. Some felt a medic might be necessary, and Salvatore was added to the roster. Eleven in all.

The militia fighters were prepared in no time, with their gear and weapons stowed in the red panel van. Evie helped the others figure out what they would need. Ely and the Carrigan sisters would be riding ahead as scouts on their dirt bikes. Dean and Jerrett would be leaving their bikes behind on this mission, so they could ride back in the van with the children – assuming they could get them.

As Jerrett took one last look around his truck, he snatched up Cami's worn-out security blanket and inhaled the scent before he stuffed it in his backpack. He missed the kids so much it hurt. Would they be there? Would they be OK? *They'll be there,* he told himself, *and they'll be OK, and we* will *get them out.* Soon they'd all be back here, safe and sound. Turning, he headed out of the door, only to be met by Trevor and Dalton.

Trevor came up to him and wrapped his big brother in a hug. "I wish I could go." Jerrett could see the pain in his eyes. "I'm sorry … I'm not strong enough."

Jerrett grabbed Trevor's face so he could look him in the eye. "You are one of the strongest people I know. Don't ever think that. I know you'd be there if you could. For now, you stay and take care of Dalton. I don't want him to be alone. Keep the home fires burning for us, will ya?"

Unable to speak, Trevor just nodded. Releasing Trevor, Jerrett crossed over to Dalton next and grabbed his older son in his arms. "I love you, son. I'll be back soon with them soon, ya hear?"

"I know you will, dad. I love you, too. Tell Troy to hurry back so I can race him, will you?"

Jerrett nodded in affirmation and stepped back. Dean swooped in to hug them both, Evie following with a kiss on each boy's cheeks. "You guys take care of each other, now, OK? We'll be back with Troy and Cami soon." With that, the three newfound warriors turned and left their family behind.

CHAPTER 29

So Close, Yet So Far

It was a tight fit in the panel van with eight people. They hadn't had time to paint it, so the bright red was still there, and the thought of it attracting undue attention had Mitch nervous.

The Carrigan girls and Ely rode ahead on their dirt bikes, scouting the way.

Jerrett shifted uncomfortably in the back of the van. Driving in the rear of a vehicle had often given him car sickness as a child, and it still resurfaced from time to time. There were no windows to look out of, other than on the rear doors. But the alternative would be to switch seats with Jude up front and that meant sitting next to Mitch, which appealed to him even less than throwing up. So he suffered in silence, trying not to think about how he felt and instead concentrating on the mission at hand.

After the team had been selected, they had brainstormed ideas on how they were going to complete the mission, but without positive identification of the children or a visual of the camp, it was hard to know exactly how to proceed.

Jerrett was jittery and could hardly sit still, his mind swirling with scenarios and plans. He pictured the camp in his mind's eye, the buildings, the fence, and the prisoners. He wondered what kind of cover there would be, how attentive the Guards were, and the different ways they could get in. Were his kids really there? If they weren't, he had no idea where else to look. He was going to scour every corner of that place to find out. Jerrett felt as if he could take on the Guards with his bare hands. If his kids were there, nothing would stop him from getting them back.

He tightened his hand around the gun strapped to his side. It was heavy, but its presence was comforting.

Looking around him at the others, he could see Dean and Evie tangled in each other's arms, whispering. A pang of jealously coursed through Jerrett. How often had he and Gwennie done that? He wondered what she'd have thought if she could be here now. Would she forgive him for losing the children?

Resting his arms across his chest, he willed himself to rest and conserve his energy. He daydreamed about home with Gwennie and the kids.

After a while, he heard Dean calling him, "Jerr, we're getting close."

Jerrett sat up abruptly, his senses alert. All around him, the team was in motion. They were loading weapons and strapping on gear. Jerrett pulled his pack closer and opening the top flap, glimpsed Cami's tiny blanket safely tucked inside. Running a finger over the worn fabric, he stuffed it back in and closed the flap tightly.

Jerrett heard the arrival of the dirt bikes outside the van. He felt the truck pull over to the side of the road and saw Mitch roll down his window.

"There's a patrol up ahead," Ely's voice called out. "What do you want to do?"

"It's time to ditch the van and walk the rest of the way. Easier to hide that way. Grab what you need," Mitch called back to the others. He said something to Ely, then steered the van off the road into the trees.

As they all climbed out, they could see dusk settling over them as the sky faded to gray. The evening air was crisp and cool, a relief from the summer heat. Jerrett saw trees lining either side of the road and mountains rising in the distance. The sight of them reminded Jerrett of Starlight and brought him a feeling of comfort and warmth.

Swinging his pack onto his back, he made his way to Mitch. "What now?"

"We've got to cover the van up," Mitch answered. Then casting his voice a bit louder, he said, "OK everyone, grab some branches and let's get this thing hidden."

The team scrounged for broken limbs, which they handed over to Pomeroy and Bo. Jerrett could hear the brothers squabbling as they arranged the branches.

Red paint peeked out through the leaves.

"I can still see it, Mitch," Evie pointed out.

"Yes, but it will be dark soon. Unless someone looks very closely, they won't see it. We'll be gone before the sun comes up."

"It's this way, everyone," Jude motioned. "Be ready to duck into the brush if you hear a car."

"Ely, you and the girls go up ahead on the dirt bikes. See what you can see and come back and tell us. How far away was the patrol?" Mitch asked.

"'Bout four miles," Felicia cut in.

"Don't let yourself be seen."

"Never," she grinned widely. "We're invisible."

Ely turned to Mitch and said, "We'll stick to the tree line when we get close, hide the bikes in the woods if we need to." He shook hands with Mitch, and the three scouts took off. The others watched until they disappeared around the bend.

Along the edge of the road grew waist-high weeds, which extended to the tree line. A person could crouch among them and be nearly invisible. It was the perfect cover. The team walked in single file along the edge of the road, ready to throw themselves in the scrub at a moment's notice.

Bats flew in and out of the trees, hunting for bugs in the twilight. Darkness lurked beyond the trees and the woods were eerily silent.

Mitch was leading, but they all heard the noise of an engine at the same time.

"Down!"

Dropping into the tall weeds and flattening himself, Jerrett could sense the others all around him, though no one made a sound. Heart pounding, he twisted around silently to watch what was coming; it somehow felt better to see what it was, even if he could do nothing about it.

A canvas-covered army truck sped by, the weeds whipping violently in its wake. Jerrett held his breath, praying that the militia members were invisible in the rapidly fading light.

The truck showed no signs of stopping.

Once it was around the bend and out of sight, the group began to cautiously pick themselves up, scanning in all directions. Mitch waved an arm, indicating they should move.

Jerrett hitched his pack, swallowed nervously, and started walking. He could feel the sweat trickle down his back and every sense seemed heightened.

After walking for what felt like forever, they heard a quiet whistle. Jerrett turned his head and could barely make out the outlines of Ely, Fiona, and Felicia, sitting astride their silent dirt bikes, hidden in the trees.

The group gathered close, excited to see them.

"Did the transport pass you?" Fiona asked.

Mitch nodded. "Yeah, but it didn't see us."

Ely gave a half-grin, "Good." Then he added, "We need to leave the dirt bikes here. Just up ahead is the camp and there are Guards stationed at the main gate. We can't see the rest of the camp without working our way around the perimeter, so I don't know where the rest of the Guards are stationed."

Mitch looked thoughtful, "How's the cover?"

"Sparse. It'll be hard to get in. Definitely need to wait a little longer till it's fully dark."

It was agreed that they would move in closer to the camp by creeping through the woods. They could spy on the camp from under cover.

Once that was decided, Jerrett could wait no longer. "Let's go, then!" He hissed at the others. Without waiting, he plowed through the trees.

Dimly aware of footsteps following him, he still jumped when a hand dropped on his arm.

"Slow down, brother," Dean cautioned softly. "We can't go charging headlong into something we don't know about. We go together, silent and slow. If we give away our position, they'll be after us in no time and then there's no way we get the kids." He moved his hand up to Jerrett's neck. "Steady, Jerr. Steady," he cautioned. Jerrett knew Dean could tell how close he was to coming apart. To be this close and not be able to rush into the camp was killing him. He shut his eyes for a moment and took a deep breath. In, out, in, out … he willed his heart to slow. When he felt under control, he opened his eyes and nodded to Dean.

The group continued through the woods, quiet and careful. Full darkness had descended and cloud cover hid the moon. It was a perfect night for the mission at hand.

The eleven teammates spread out, keeping within eyesight of one another, treading as silently as possible through the half-mile of woods. The undergrowth was thick, except for a few narrow trails scattered here and there from the deer. Eventually, the woods began to thin out and Mitch signaled for them to slow down. Stooping to a crouch, they crept up to the edge of the tree line and looked out over an expanse of empty space.

The complete lack of cover took Dean's breath away. How would they ever get to the perimeter fence without being seen? He kept one eye on Jerrett, hunkered down beside him, half expecting him to make a run for the compound. Dean resisted the urge to grab onto him.

They studied the camp silently.

Surrounded by a chain-link fence, topped with coiled barbed wire, and only one entrance, it was formidable indeed.

Dean was handed a pair of binoculars. Nodding his thanks, he pressed them to his eyes. He counted six rectangular buildings facing each other in rows of three. All the structures were of steel, cold and functional.

How would they ever find the right dwelling that the kids were in?

Dean could see light from a fire burning in a barrel outside the nearest building. Dark figures passed by the light, some small enough to be children. He passed the binoculars to Jerrett, whispering to him, "Look by the barrel fire. There *are* kids in there!" He felt his brother stiffen beside him.

After everyone had a look, they melted back into the trees, instinctively gathering close to Mitch.

"OK, I saw multiple civilians wandering around, including children. The main entrance is out – too much focus on it. I've got another idea." When he had everyone's' attention, he laid out his plan.

CHAPTER 30

The Rescue

The militia members and motocrossers were in position, hunched in the woods near the rear of the camp. The wooded area ran parallel to the side of the camp, separated by an empty no man's land the size of a football field. The trees had been cleared for visibility, leaving only scattered stumps.

Felicia, Fiona, and Salvatore were positioned near the camp entrance as a rear guard to the militia group. They were assigned to watch for anything unusual coming in the front gates and to contact Mitch via cell, if necessary.

Jude Kinsey would be the point man, clearing the way. Then the others would enter the camp. Dressed in civilian clothes, with weapons concealed beneath, the militia members hoped to blend in with the prisoners.

Once they got inside, they would split off in twos to search for the children. Since Jerrett, Dean, and Evie would be able to identify the kids, they were each paired with a soldier. The Miller brothers would guard the extraction point by the fence.

"You ready, Jude?" Mitch asked.

Jude had on a black shirt like the rest of them, and mud smeared across his face. He adjusted the strap holding a large pair of bolt cutters to his back and rested his hand on his knife in its sheath. He nodded tersely to Mitch.

The group watched from the woods while Jude began his journey across the open expanse. He crawled out of the cover of the trees and over to the first large stump, ducking in behind it. Waiting a moment for the searchlight to sweep past, he resumed his trek across the field to the fence. He ran as fast as he could, zigzagging when needed to avoid searchlights that swept the area in a regular pattern.

In the dark, it was nearly impossible to see exactly what Jude was doing as he neared the fence, but that was just as well: they all knew what he was going to do with that lethal knife.

The minutes stretched out forever before Mitch's phone began vibrating in his hand.

Mitch talked softly into his cell. Then turning to the group, he announced quietly, "Jude cut the fence and took out the Guards. We're good to go."

A few at a time, the group made their way across the expanse, covered by Jude with his silencer and pistol. Each ran at a full-out sprint as fast as they could.

When it was Dean's turn, he began his run straight for the fence. Jerrett had thought Dean's timing had been perfect, but it had taken longer than they thought to reach the fence line. As he and Evie raced across the expanse, the flood lights suddenly swung back through no man's land and headed straight for them. Jerrett could see Evie grab Dean and the two of them froze, dropping to the ground, just as the circle of light swept past, not more than three feet away from them.

The entire group held their breath, waiting for a siren to wail. But the light continued on its way, and Dean and Evie leapt to their feet and raced the final distance to the fence.

When it was Jerrett's turn, he watched the searchlight carefully for his opportunity, not wanting to get caught out in the open like Dean and Evie. He sprinted across the space.

Gasping for breath, Jerrett reached the fence line. Looking over his shoulder, he saw Dean and Evie just beside him. Dean clapped him on the shoulder and gave a big sigh.

Jude pulled back the fence for them to pass through. Silently, the group headed out, splitting up as Mitch pointed out which way each should go. The Miller brothers took up the position of the rear guard, making sure the exit was secure. They tried to look nonchalant as they lounged against the corner of the nearest building.

Jerrett exchanged a long look with Dean, wishing he could speak. Dean seemed to read his mind and flashed him a hang loose sign, before turning away with Ely.

Jerrett and Jude picked their way around the outside of a long, steel building. They shuffled along slowly, hunched over, trying to blend in with the defeated prisoners.

Groups of people huddled in clumps around various barrel fires. As he and Jude scanned the groups, a few people looked their way, but none seemed particularly concerned. A camp this size should be big enough that no one would know all the captives.

Suddenly loudspeakers rang out, startling them both. They stopped as a prerecorded message boomed out. Only half-listening to the propaganda, Jerrett went back to scanning the smallest of the captives. He and Jude worked their way around the next building.

Slipping silently around the corner, they were startled by the sudden appearance of a slight woman in a dark coat. She looked thin and ragged, and gasped when she saw them. She froze, her body tense. She pulled her coat tightly around herself and her face was a mask of fear. Jerrett could only imagine what kinds of things happened to a young woman alone in the dark in these places. He extended his hands and called out softly, "Hey, it's OK. It's OK. We aren't going to hurt you."

She looked at them through guarded eyes, stepping back and hunching her shoulders as if to disappear.

Jerrett could tell by her shabby clothes and demeanor that she'd probably been here a while. He wondered if they could get some information out of her.

He approached her cautiously, his hands still held out.

"Maybe you can help us," Jerrett said. Jude hissed at him and nudged him roughly. Jerrett knew Jude didn't want him to tell her why they were there, but Jerrett went ahead anyway. "We're new here. We don't know our way around yet. I'm Jerrett and this is

Jude. We're looking for my kids. We think they might be in here somewhere."

The women relaxed just a little. "Did you come in on the prisoner transport today? What makes you think your children are here?"

Deciding not to correct her, he said, "We were told they brought anyone west of Harrisburg here. My children vanished in that area."

Her expression softened a bit and she stepped closer. "Tell me about them. Maybe I know them."

Jerrett relayed their names and descriptions, praying for good news.

The women looked on him with something akin to pity, "I'm sorry, I don't know them, but they could be here somewhere. How did you get separated?"

Jerrett glanced at Jude, who shrugged, leaving it up to Jerrett how much they should tell her. Jerrett was stuck between a rock and a hard place: he didn't want to reveal much, but they needed some help. Instead of answering her, he asked, "What's your name? How did you get here?"

The woman looked defensive again, but answered, "I'm Angie Timmons. I didn't do anything wrong ...I just ... I was out ...after curfew. My children were at their father's house, and he was ... drinking too much. They called me and I had to go get them. The Guards grabbed us on the way back." She stiffened up and nudged her chin toward them. "What about you two"? she asked, bravely.

Summoning up his courage, he said, "We snuck in to get my kids. We didn't come on the transport."

Surprise lit up her face, "Do you have a way out?"

Jerrett nodded.

Her demeanor changed in an instant. She lunged forward and grabbed his arm. "You've got to take me with you! Please! I'll show you where the unoccupied children stay. But I've got to get my kids out of here. Please!" The anguish in her face was more than Jerrett could stand. This was no spy. Without looking at Jude for permission, he nodded. He heard Jude sigh behind him and could picture him rolling his eyes with annoyance.

"I don't like this, Jerrett. We shouldn't be telling anybody why we're here!" Jude snarled.

"It's my call, they're my kids!" Jerrett hissed back.

The woman smiled with obvious relief and said, "Oh, thank you! Thank you so much!" as she clutched Jerrett's arm. Stepping away, she motioned for them to follow, and she took off in the direction of the buildings. Jerrett and Jude trailed along behind.

Steering around large clumps of people, they made their way towards one of the buildings along the front of the camp. Waiting until the Guards had passed by on their rounds, the trio crept up to the door and slipped inside.

DON'T TREAD ON ME

CHAPTER 31

The Reunion

The huge room was well lit and orderly, with rows of bunks stacked along either side of the building. Their headboards butted up against the walls and there was very little space between each set. It reminded Jerrett of military barracks. A wide pathway stretched down the middle, where several picnic tables had been placed. Women and children were scattered everywhere, some sleeping in bunks and others lounging at the tables. They looked dirty, raggedy, and resigned.

Jerrett and Jude looked at each other and wordlessly started down opposite sides of the building. Angie talked to the people sitting at the tables. Jerrett and Jude searched every bunk, scanning for anyone that looked the same size as the children. Reaching the end of the bunks, they meet with Angie again. No luck. They hurried out of the building and on to the next one.

Two more buildings were searched in the same manner and with the same results.

"I don't understand," Angie looked defeated. "I thought all the unoccupied children were kept in the first building. I can't figure out why they'd be anywhere else."

Jude reluctantly sighed and dropped a hand on Jerrett's arm, "Maybe they aren't here."

Jerrett started shaking his head, "No! They have to be here somewhere!" His voice rose.

Jude shushed him frantically, "Shh! I'm just saying it a possibility!"

Jerrett pulled Jude up to him by the shirtfront. "Jude, I'm going to search every corner of this camp! We aren't giving up. You can help me or get lost!" he growled.

Jude put up his hands. "Jerrett, chill out! I'm with you all the way! If we're searching this whole camp, we better quit yakking and get going. Come on!"

Jerrett nodded his thanks, and they slipped out of the building, none of them noticing a young man with a blond mohawk, who had snuck out behind them and followed them.

Angie led them over to the next building. It was an exact replica of the others. They ducked inside the door just as a silent vibration of Jerrett's phone went off. Jerrett spared a glance at the screen.

"Mitch just texted. Extraction in 15 minutes." He looked at the other two. They didn't have to say anything. If they didn't find the children in this one, they wouldn't have time to search any more.

"We're going have to wrap it up, Jerrett."

Jerrett snarled at him, "I'm not leaving until I find them!" Then he softened his voice a bit. "Look, if we don't find them here, you take Angie and get out. I'll stay on my own and keep searching. It's not on the rest of you."

Jude started shaking his head, but Jerrett cut him off. "We're wasting time. Move!" Jerrett split off without another word and nearly ran down the left side of the barracks, scanning as fast as he dared.

There were only a few bunks left. Looking across the room he saw Jude had reached the end of his row. Jude looked up and met Jerrett's gaze with a look of pity and shrugged his shoulders. Angie was still questioning the people at the table.

Turning back to the task at hand, he saw a figure in the next bed, covered with a blanket. That was the right size for Troy, wasn't it? And there was something about the position, the way the right arm was thrown over the head – that was how Troy liked to sleep.

And then he heard it.

A soft little voice, one he knew so well, singing ever so gently, "You are my sunshine … my only sunshine…"

He rounded the end of the bed, heart pounding.

The sight before him took his breath away.

Cami was sitting cross-legged on the floor next to the bunk, tracing a pattern in the dusty floor with one hand, while the other held onto a slightly bigger hand trailing out from under the covers on the bunk.

Jerrett froze, unable to move, absorbing the scene before him.

"Cami," he breathed out, tears filling his eyes.

A little dirty face whipped up. "Daddy!" she shrieked, and in a whirlwind of energy, she leaped off the floor and was in his arms.

Jerrett felt her latch onto him in a death grip, his own arms returning the hug so hard and with such desperation, he was afraid he would hurt her. He breathed in her scent, the smell of dirt and sweat and ... *Cami*. "I'm here, baby! Daddy's here!" He cradled her against him.

She suddenly pulled back and squirmed out of his grip. "Daddy, it's Troy. He needs you." Taking his hand, Cami led him to the figure on the bed.

Jerrett's breath caught and he dropped to his knees. *His son* ... "Troy ... it's daddy." Jerrett carded his fingers through Troy's dirty hair, grown long and shaggy. His face was colorless. The smell of sickness was in the air. Troy didn't react, lying still and silent. Jerrett felt his heart stop. Oh God, was he ...?

The boy moved. Jerrett sprang into action. "Troy!" he called loudly, "It's me, daddy! Come on son, open your eyes!"

"He's sick, daddy," Cami materialized by his side. "He's been sleeping all day and he's really warm. Been puking all over the place."

Jerrett spared his little girl a glance, giving her a slight smile. "It's OK now, baby. Daddy's here. We'll get him all fixed up." He saw Jude and Angie coming up behind them. "It's them," he said needlessly.

Turning back to Troy, Jerrett shook his child's arm gently. The boy's eyes flickered open. Closed. Open. He stared in disbelief. "Dad?" he croaked out.

Jerrett smiled, "Yeah, bud, it's me. I'm here."

"Dad!" Troy reached for his father, tears springing to his eyes. Jerrett cradled his son carefully; the boy felt so frail and gaunt in his arms.

"What happened to you, Troy? Are you OK?" He could feel the heat radiating off his son's body.

"I've been sick ... throwing up." The glazed, feverish look in Troy's eyes worried Jerrett. He scooped the boy up in his arms, surprised by how much weight he'd lost.

Turning to the others, he said, "Let's go. Come on, Cami." He started down the center aisle. Jude scooped Cami up and ran past Jerrett, to scan the doorway.

"OK, it's clear. Let's go!" They crept out of the building and Angie resumed her position in the lead. Jude and Jerrett followed with the children. Angie stopped at the door of the next building.

"Wait here, I'll just be a second." She disappeared into the structure.

The men waited outside anxiously, Jerrett squatting to the ground with Troy balanced in his lap. "You OK, big guy?"

Troy nodded mutely. "I can try and walk, dad."

"Save it for later, when we get out of here." Jude set Cami down and she leaned on Jerrett's shoulder.

Minutes later Angie emerged from the building, with a boy, a girl, and two other women following. "These are my kids, Dakota and Gabriella."

"Who are they?" Jude snapped, jerking a thumb in the direction of the two women. "You just said it would be your kids?"

Angie drew herself up defiantly, "Linaya's my friend," she explained, pointing at a woman her age, and then to the older woman, "Willa helped me look after my kids. They're coming too."

Jerrett just shrugged as he picked up Troy and led them away. The boy wrapped his arms weakly around Jerrett's neck. Cami held onto his shirt-tail and the others followed.

Suddenly a siren pierced the night, and floodlights came on all around them.

"Oh dear! They must have seen you!" Willa called out as she pressed her fist to her mouth. Angie hugged her kids to her sides protectively as she looked all around.

"What do we do, Jude? We'll never get out through no man's land now!"

"They must have realized we don't belong here. Or they saw the Miller brothers."

"Whatever. Doesn't matter now. We've got to get out of sight." Jerrett looked all around them.

Linaya spoke up. "There's a storage shed over there," she pointed. "We could hide in there!" Jerrett followed where she pointed, and the group hurried off in that direction. He trusted that the rest of the rescue group would be seeking cover as well.

They made it to the shed, but it was secured with a padlock. Jude grabbed up a rock and smashed it over and over until the lock gave way. Jerrett was momentarily thankful for the blaring loudspeakers that blocked out the noise. They hustled inside, easing the door shut behind them. Jude had his pistol ready as he peered out of the corner of the window. The rest huddled as far back out of sight as they could.

"Now what?" Jerrett whispered to Jude, who spared a look back at him and shook his head. Then Jude turned back to the window.

After a minute or so, he hissed, "Look at this, Jerrett." Jerrett peered out the window and saw a young man with a blond mohawk leading a group of Guards past the shed and around the next building.

"That's Andre. The rat! He must've seen you all and alerted the Guards," Angie informed them.

"Why would anyone do that?" Jerrett wondered.

"You'd be amazed what people will do for extra food rations," Willa informed him.

"What'll we do?"

Jerrett glanced around them. "Look around everyone. Maybe we can find something we can use as a weapon." The group made their way along the edges of the shed, searching diligently. Jerrett spied a shovel behind some boxes and started to force it out of the pile.

Then Jude called out softly, "Hey, lookee here! This might be our ticket out of here." Jerrett and the women gathered around to see what Jude had found. He was pulling open the door of the electrical panel next to the door.

"Which one do you think we should try?" Jerrett asked.

Jude didn't bother to answer, but instead started flicking the circuit breakers frantically. Within seconds the camp lights went out, the sirens stopped, and everything was plunged into darkness. A few seconds more, and the screaming started as people stumbled their way around, running into each other and objects in their way. "C'mon!" Jude said, yanking open the door.

The group hurried out of the shed. "Hang onto each other!" Jerrett called, grabbing each of his kids' hands in his. There was no way he'd lose them in this chaos.

People were running in all directions, shouting and crying. No one knew what was going on. Jude led the way, his gun out at the ready. They stumbled through the dark, tripping over unseen obstacles on the ground. Linaya hung onto Jerrett's shirt from behind and Jude had Cami's other hand, forming a line.

Suddenly a body slammed into Linaya, breaking their connection. Jerrett felt her fall, but what could he do? He didn't dare let go of either child's hands. "Get up! Grab onto me!" he called. There was a noise, a struggle, behind him as he assumed they were untangling themselves from each other. A yank on his shirt told him Linaya was back on her feet and reconnected. "Hang on! Go, Jude!"

They continued forward at a painfully slow pace so as not to lose each other. When Jude touched the cold metal wall of one of the buildings, he followed alongside it. "This way!"

Jerrett hoped they were moving in the right direction. Just ahead, he discovered he could make out the faint outline of the fence. Jude led them along as he followed the fence, leading in the direction of the rear of the camp. There were fewer people behind the buildings, by the fence, and so it was easier to maneuver. They soon made their way to the back of the compound. Jerrett risked letting go of Cami's hand so he could scoop up Troy as he scanned the area.

At first, Jerrett saw nobody there, until suddenly a voice called out from the shadows, "Jerr, you found them!"

Dean emerged, a smile busting across his face. He ran over and scooped up Cami.

"Uncle Dean!" she squealed.

"Shh!"

Dean hugged his niece tightly, then turned to the bundle in Jerrett's arms. "Is that Troy? Is he OK?" Dean's voice was frantic with worry as he peered over Jerrett's shoulder, Cami still in his arms.

"Hi, Uncle Dean," Troy answered weakly, barely lifting his head off Jerrett's shoulder. Dean used his free hand to ruffle Troy's hair and then planted a kiss on his head.

"Hi yourself. You OK? Ready to get out of here?" Troy smiled and nodded lethargically.

Evie joined the group and Dean passed Cami to her, readying his gun to protect them if needed.

"Let's go, people," Mitch ordered. "We're attracting unwanted attention." He indicated three prisoners, all men, who were watching them from a short distance away. Looking around, he suddenly noticed Angie and her crew. "Who are they?"

"They're coming, too, Mitch. They helped me find the kids," Jerrett hastily explained. Mitch didn't argue.

Pomeroy and Bo Miller met them at the fence and led them out of the gap.

Once they were all through, the three men who had been watching them hurried over to the fence.

"Where are you going? Can we come? We need to get out of here!" The man was middle-aged and chubby. The other two were younger, just out of their teens by the look of them. All three were dirty, their clothes torn and stained.

"Come on," Bo answered, holding up the fence. Pomeroy nodded his approval. Once they were through, they moved quickly to join up with the rest, leaving the fence hanging loose. Maybe others would find their way out before the Guards sealed it up again.

The group scurried away, across no man's land, to the cover of the trees, running as fast as possible. Speed was of the essence now. Jerrett found himself falling behind with his heavy burden. His shoulder blades itched with the sensation that a bullet could hit him at any second.

Dean and the Miller brothers dropped back to cover him. They zigzagged across the open land. Jerrett watched as Evie and Cami ducked under the cover of the trees.

In that instant, the floodlights burst on, breaking through the darkness. Jerrett and the others froze as the lights flowed in every direction.

"Go Jerr, go!" Dean yelled. Jerrett took off in a run, trying to weave around the circles of light. He could sense Dean, Bo and Pom following him. "Go! Go!" Dean implored.

At last Jerrett crashed through the undergrowth and into the relative safety of the woods. The sound of gunshots broke through the night. Jerrett and the others whipped around in time to see prisoners streaking out of the breach in the fence. As the captives raced away from the compound, Jerrett saw several shots find their targets and people fell to the ground. One woman lay still in the circle of light. Jerrett gasped and turned Cami towards him. He jumped up and pressed further into the woods.

They went on until the camp was out of sight and the tangle of the tree branches shielded them. Allowing himself a moment of respite, Jerrett dropped to one knee and rested Troy on the ground. Salvatore appeared by his side, as if by magic. As he looked over the boy, Jerrett glanced around, mentally counting heads. They were all there, even Fiona and Felicia. Evie had a hold of Cami, Dean was by his side, and everyone else was catching their breath.

They could hear the alarms ring out and bullets behind them, but none seemed to be coming their way.

Relief flooded Jerrett's soul and he felt weak with the sudden emotion. They'd done it! His kids were safe, back in his arms. Tears spilled down over his cheeks and he heaved a great sob. Dean made his way to Jerrett's side.

"We did it, Jerr! We got them!" Dean grabbed his brother in a powerful hug. Jerrett hugged him back, too overcome to speak.

After only a few minutes, Mitch announced they needed to move. He asked about Troy's ability to walk.

Jerrett wiped away the tears and forced himself to focus. They weren't out of the woods yet, so to speak.

He eyed the uneven ground, with the roots and branches just waiting to snag the unsteady boy's feet and trip him up. "How 'bout a piggyback ride, Troy?" The boy nodded weakly and climbed up. Dean helped Jerrett to his feet.

"When you get tired, Jerr, we'll switch out."

As silently as possible, the group made their way through the woods.

CHAPTER 32

Journey Home

"**W**e need to move!" Mitch ordered. "Back to the van!"

"Wait, who are these people?" Fiona wondered aloud, looking at the eight newcomers.

"Fellow escapees. They're coming with us." Jerrett explained.

"Where is it that you're going?" the middle-aged man from the camp asked. Fiona offered him a hasty explanation. Mitch cut them off with an order to move.

As they stumbled through the woods, they could still hear the uproar from the camp, but it was fading into the distance. The group hurried through the woods as fast as they dared.

Jerrett's heart thudded in his chest. Adrenaline propelled him onward, just as it did when he was racing. Resisting the urge to look over his shoulder, he continued his plunge through the trees, following Dean.

Had they been spotted? Were the Guards moving in on them? There was no way to tell.

As they traveled further away, the sounds from the camp became muffled.

Mitch and Felicia led the group, while Fiona and Ely took up the rear guard. If there were any fighting, it would come from behind.

The half-mile to the dirt bikes seemed to take forever.

When they finally reached the bikes, Jerrett allowed himself a breath of relief as he sat his son on the ground, his arms and back aching.

Mitch issued orders. "Ely, you and the girls need to ride back and get the van – if the coast is clear. Throw one of the bikes in the back so one of you can drive, and then come get us." They agreed and sped off.

The rest of the group sat hidden in the trees, resting and sharing water bottles. Jerrett sat with Troy reclining beside him and Cami in his lap. He couldn't stop staring at them, reassuring himself that they were really here.

Before long, the scouts reappeared, Fiona driving the flashy red van. "It's clear. No sign of soldiers," Ely announced.

"Then let's go, people," Mitch commanded. The group hastily pulled themselves up to their feet. Bo and Pomeroy quickly moved to help Fiona unload her dirt bike. Once it was out, the others quickly piled inside.

Like before, Mitch and Jude commandeered the front seats, and Ely and the Carrigan girls resumed their positions as scouts. The van was so crowded, that Pomeroy crouched on the floor between the front seats. Jerrett found himself leaning on the rear doors, Dean and Evie beside him, the children sprawled across their laps. As he looked around at the tightly packed group, he met the gaze of Angie's friend, Linaya. A soft smile spread across her face and she nodded at him. Jerrett couldn't help but smile back. She was a pretty woman, even with a dirty face and uncombed hair. She held his gaze a moment longer, then ducked her head shyly, refocusing her attention on one of Angie's children.

Jerrett smiled to himself, heart full. He tucked his face in Troy's hair, kissing the boy's head, and tightened his arms around both the children. They'd done it! They were here, in his arms again. At times he'd been afraid he'd never hold his children again. That they'd be gone forever, just like Gwennie.

But here they were, safe and sound.

As the van lurched around a corner, he held them tightly, struggling to keep them from bouncing around. Dean offered Troy another bottle of water and helped him keep it steady as he drank.

"Look there!" Jude's voice suddenly cut through the din as he pointed something out.

Jerrett craned his neck to see as Dean called out, "What's going on?"

"Our scouts are coming back, and fast." Jude's strained voice called back.

Mitch stopped the van and rolled down the window. He leaned out to talk to Ely. A minute later, he turned back to those in the van. "We got trouble! Scouts report a patrol ahead, coming our way. They must be looking for us," Mitch called back.

"Tell those riders to get out of here! They have zero protection," Jerrett called out, rising to his knees.

"He's right. Go! We'll meet up with you later," Mitch ordered them. The three bikers vanished quickly. "Jude, find me a route, now!"

"These damn back roads. They crisscross all over the place. The Guards must have circled around to get in front of us." Jude was frantically punching in data on the GPS on his phone. Mitch bent over the device, with Pomeroy trying to look over their shoulders. Finally finding what they were looking for, Mitch whipped the van around and tore off down the road.

"What are we going to do?" Someone called.

"Run."

Mitch stomped on the gas pedal and whipped the van down a side road.

Those inside held on to anything they could as they bounced off each other. Cami cried out in fear.

"It's the wrong way!" Angie yelled. "We're heading back to the camp!"

"Only for a minute, there's another turn soon that takes us away again. These back roads loop around all over the place. Let's hope we can lose them," Jude told them.

Mitch took the next corner so sharply that the occupants flew into each other. Cries of pain followed.

The van came to a turn which took them in the opposite direction, then a Y where they veered off to the left. The scouts on their dirt bikes were nowhere in sight.

They raced down the road, but the old, overloaded van was no competition against the military vehicles. All too soon Jerrett spotted the military convoy coming up behind them. He called out to Mitch. Mitch sped up, whipping the van around. Jerrett watched through the window as the convoy came closer. A soldier with a bullhorn leaned out the window of the truck in the front. Jerrett could hear the man yelling for them to pull over, but of course, Mitch ignored them as he spun the wheel to the right, taking another road. The truck followed them, a jeep trailing after it.

What he saw next, made Jerrett's heart stop. The man replaced the bullhorn with a high-powered rifle and leaning out the window, aimed for the van.

"Get down!" The occupants of the van scattered to the floor, screaming and crying. Jerrett pushed his children down and spread his body over them. He didn't have time to do anything else as the bullets ripped into the van, piercing the sides.

Return fire could be heard and Jerrett looked up to see Jude, leaning out of the window, rifle in hand. His face was deadly calm as he took aim at the vehicle behind them. His long, blond hair was strung out behind him, caught in the wind. The tattooed arms held the gun steady and Jerrett knew their lives hung in this patriot's hands. He was not the image someone would picture when they thought of a patriot, but that was exactly what he was. Jude's bravery, steadfastness, and loyalty mirrored those of their ancestors who had also fought for freedom from tyranny.

Jerrett would forever remember that moment and the image of the modern-day rebel, fighting for what he believed in.

Jude turned to Mitch, a wide grin splitting his face. The sounds of cheering filled the van, pulling Jerrett back to his senses. Wondering what had happened, he twisted around to peer out the rear window, just in time to see the military truck careening off the road, the glass in front of the driver riddled with bullet holes. The jeep veered around its comrades, continuing the chase.

"Jude, the jeep!" Pomeroy yelled, handing the man another fully loaded weapon.

Jude switched out guns with Pomeroy and resumed his position. Firing on the jeep, Jude fought to maintain his balance as he leaned precariously out the window.

With a sudden shriek, he fell from his perch, landing on the floor between the seat and dashboard. Blood splashed across the inside of the windshield.

"Jude!" Mitch yelled as Pomeroy scurried into Jude's seat and took over his position, firing behind them. Salvatore grabbed up his medical bag and crawled over the bodies in the van. Someone yelped as they were stepped on.

Pomeroy's gun found its target and the jeep veered off to the side.

"I got him! Did ya see that?" Pomeroy shouted. He climbed down off the seat to give Salvatore room to work.

Bo greeted Pomeroy with a hug, his face radiant with joy. "You did it!"

The passengers were all talking, crying, and shouting at once.

Jerrett let his attention sway from the redheaded brothers to Salvatore. He had pulled Jude up onto the seat and was bending over him.

"Is Jude OK?" Evie called. Salvatore didn't answer, but they could all see him bandaging Jude's arm.

Suddenly one cry rose over all the rest. All eyes turned to Willa, the gray-haired older woman, as she leaned over a body. Jerrett pushed through to her, gently moving her away as Salvatore appeared beside him.

It was one of the young men from the camp, laying still and unconscious, a wound in his temple seeping blood and a puddle rapidly forming under him. Cami screamed. Jerrett turned her against him, trying to prevent her from seeing.

"Oh, God!" Willa moaned. Salvatore leaned over him, feeling for a pulse, but soon straightened, shaking his head. The man was dead. Willa covered her face and cried.

Someone passed over a jacket and it was laid over his face.

Silence filled the van. "Who was he?" Ely finally asked.

"Did anyone know his name?"

The chubby middle-aged man answered, "Sebastian. I don't know his last name. Didn't know him at all. We just bunked next to each other for a short time." Looking around at each of them, he said, "I'm Charlie Payton, by the way." He turned to the other man who had come with him. "Mateo, did you know Sebastian better?"

Mateo was a black-haired, short young man. He shook his head sadly. "He was new. Told me his last name once, but I don't remember it. Sorry."

They all stared at Sebastian, hidden under the blanket, and sorrow overtook the joy of the moment before. He was a young man, his whole life had been before him and now he was gone, a victim of this senseless war. Worst of all, they had no way to let his family know what had become of him.

Jerrett feared there would be many more tragic stories like this before the war was over. Sliding back into his spot, he wrapped an arm around the kids, drawing them close. The others settled back down, resuming their positions. Silence fell over them all.

They drove on that way for several more miles, silently lost in their thoughts.

"Damn it!" Mitch suddenly yelled out as he steered the van to the side of the road.

"What's wrong now?" Dean asked.

"Engine's overheating. Bet we took a bullet to the radiator," Mitch growled. He climbed out of the van, followed by several others who joined him to peer into the engine compartment.

After searching for a bit, they announced that two bullet holes had pierced the radiator, causing the overheating. With no way to fix it, they were left with only one choice.

Walk.

Gathering up their supplies and weapons, the raggedy crew abandoned the red van. Sadly, they realized they had no choice but to leave Sebastian behind. Willa and Mateo paused to say a prayer over the body. Mateo was the last to turn away, crossing his body reverently.

After consulting their GPS, they decided the best way to go was a shortcut through the woods. They should come out on the other side onto a road called Fox Lane. It was still quite a way from the track, but they were heading in the right direction. They sent a text to Ely, telling him to meet them there, but few of these little back roads had street signs. It didn't help that Mitch's phone kept losing signal, either. They could only head in the right direction and hope they could find the scouts later.

The woods were pitch dark, however, and the going was excruciatingly slow. Those who had flashlights or phones lit the way as best they could for the others. Even so, the tree roots tripped people up non-stop and Jerrett wondered how they were ever going to get through. Troy stumbled frequently, even with Jerrett and Dean holding onto him.

"Hey, here's a trail!" someone called out. Following the trail made the trip much easier, but there was no way to tell if it would take them to Fox Lane. Mitch tried to follow their progress on his spotty GPS as best he could.

They stumbled blindly through the undergrowth, scraping and bumping into the rough bark of the trees as they attempted to follow the deer path. After about a half-hour, the trees finally gave way. Stumbling out of the dark woods, they could see the clouds had lifted and the moon provided a trace of light.

Though they couldn't tell exactly where they were, it was a relief to be out of the suffocating darkness.

Jerrett looked over his family. Troy was pale and tired, his eyes only half-open. He needed rest and a warm bed. He couldn't walk any further, that was for sure. Cami was uninjured and healthy, but how far could a seven-year-old walk? He wondered how Angie's children and the older lady, Willa, were faring.

Dean looked up and met his brother's gaze. "Jerr, what'cha worrying about now?" he chastised. "It's OK. We got away from the convoy and we've got the kids. That's all that matters, right?" He spared Jerrett a smile.

The grin was infectious; Jerrett found himself smiling back. His brother was right, they had the children back, they hadn't gotten caught and they were on the way home. That *was* all that really mattered.

When the rest break was over, he scooped up his son in his arms, prodded his daughter to her feet, and led the way down the road. He was tired, his arms ached, and they had a long way to go, but none of it mattered. His heart was light, joyous, and free for the first time in months and that carried him on.

● ● ●

They walked for miles until they were too tired to even talk to each other. There still was no sign of the scouts on the dirt bikes. The children slogged along, dragging their feet, pulled by the adults in turn. The group, now numbering thirteen adults and four children, spread themselves across the dark, lonely road.

They were past worrying about the camp patrols; they were too far away now and on a road so obscure that their only fear was if they stumbled onto another group of Elites entirely. But it didn't seem likely this late at night and so far from anywhere. Jerrett was still carrying Troy on his back, not willing to let anyone take a turn. Dean had resigned himself to keeping close to his brother and letting him go as long as he could. Who knew what Jerrett was telling himself to keep going? Whatever it was, it was working.

● ● ●

One step. Now another. Another. The weight on Jerrett's back was so heavy. But he pushed on anyhow. He didn't hear the voices around him anymore. His throat ached, dry and scratchy; his ears buzzed, his muscles cramped. The road blurred in front of him, the inky blackness so thick that he could barely figure out where the surface was. His footfalls were becoming heavier ... and heavier. Another step. Another step. Don't stop ...

Suddenly, the weight was lifted from his back, and he stumbled off balance, crashing onto the pavement. He felt hands gripping his arm. Cold water splashed across his face, shocking him to his senses. A water bottle appeared in front of him, and he grabbed for it eagerly. Chugging the water down, its coolness soothed his parched throat. His surroundings slowly came into focus. He was aware of Dean hunched by his side, his arm heavy on Jerrett's shoulder, worry etched in his face. He smelled the fragrance of the pine trees along the road, saw the moon sliding out from behind a cloud, and the people resting on the ground all around him.

"Where –" his voice cracked, and he tried again. "Where's Troy? Cami?"

"Right here, Jerr. You just carried Troy for four miles. I think it's my turn now, OK, big guy?" Dean patted him reassuringly as Jerrett craned his neck to see the kids. They were sitting just behind him, Salvatore checking them over.

Salvatore made his way over to Jerrett next. "You OK there, superman?" Salvatore looked Jerrett over carefully, noticing the bloody scrapes on his knees from where he had fallen. "No major harm done. Drink that water up. You need it. Rest up and let your brother carry the kid for a while, OK?" Jerrett could only nod; he was too tired to do anything else.

Dean reappeared. "Guess I can't pick on you anymore about not being in shape, huh, big brother? You trying to outdo me? You know you don't stand a chance," he grinned.

Ignoring the ribbing, Jerrett grasped Dean's shoulder, pulling him close. "De'n …" he mumbled through his exhaustion, "You al-always got my back. Always there when I need ya …what would I ever do … without you?" He grabbed Dean in a crushing hug.

Dean returned the embrace. "That's what I'm here for, right? To watch out for you. Ain't that what brothers are for?"

A nod was all Jerrett could manage.

Mitch soon announced they needed to be on their way. Evie and Dean pulled Jerrett to his feet. He tottered a bit before regaining his balance and felt Cami's hand slip into his. Bo and Pomeroy lifted Troy onto Dean's back and they started off.

They hadn't gone more than a mile down the road when they all heard the telltale sounds of dirt bikes. A cheer went up from the tired crowd as their companions sped into sight.

Grinding to a stop, Fiona pulled off her goggles and called out, "Where have you guys been? We've searched for you forever!"

Felicia and Ely pulled up beside her.

Ely cut in, "We thought maybe you'd all been captured. What happened?'

"Where's the van?" Felicia added.

Mitch explained what had happened when they were pursued by the camp Guards.

"Well, now that we found you, some of you can ride double with us and take a break from walking."

Mitch nodded in agreement. "Good idea. Put the boy on there." Dean sat Troy down on the back of Ely's dirt bike.

"Ely, you ride on ahead to the Starlight and get someone to come back for us," Mitch ordered.

Ely agreed, and Mitch continued, "Take one of the girls with you for backup. The other one can stay with us and scout out the road ahead."

After a brief discussion, Fiona insisted her sister go on ahead while she stayed back. Jude was chosen to ride with Felicia since he'd been hurt, but he resisted.

"There is no way I'm riding back while there's kids and an older lady walking. I'm fine. Pick one of them." The determined look on Jude's face told the others not to debate the matter.

Willa, the oldest at 62 years old, was obviously tired and worn out. They put her with Felicia.

Standing silent, Jerrett watched as Troy and the others rode out of sight. He didn't take his eyes off them until they rounded the corner. Then, resigning himself to the hike, he took his daughter's hand and started off, the others following. Though they were tired, the journey seemed easier now that they knew help was coming. It was with lighter spirits that they finished their journey home.

CHAPTER 33

New Beginnings

They'd been home two weeks and things were going fairly well. Jerrett didn't know when he'd started calling Starlight home, but it felt comforting

Troy and Cami had been quiet the first few days, but they were beginning to come around. Troy was regaining his strength after a few rounds of IVs had reversed the dehydration. Both kids were having bad dreams. Though he didn't want them to have nightmares, he found he loved the feeling of those warm little bodies cuddled up tight against him.

Jerrett wondered what changes he would see in the children in the weeks and months ahead. He had no illusions that their time in the camp could have a lasting impact on them.

Trevor and Dalton were overjoyed to have them back and guarded them constantly. Rarely were the two children out of sight of either one of them.

After breakfast, Jerrett found himself looking over the little village that had sprung up. They'd taken to calling it Starlight Town lately, as it helped to differentiate between the village and the track. An eclectic group of homes could be seen from Jerrett's vantage point. There were several small cabins in the process of being built. Barry, Caitlyn, and the Caruso brothers lived in one; Angie Timmons and her children in another; and Linaya and Willa in the third. They were tiny, with one room and a loft, but cozy and private. They must have been similar to the early pioneer cabins.

An old school bus had been found in a local junkyard and hauled up in the dead of night. The residents had parked it in the middle of the new town, wedging it between clumps of trees to hide it. After that, they'd painted the bus in an eclectic pattern of green and brown, camouflaging it. Everyone had gotten in on the job, and it had turned into a town painting party. After it was done, they'd dragged some netting and tree branches over it. The effect was pretty good, considering. Charlie Payton and Mateo, from the camp, were in the process of gutting it. Drey and Dylan were helping out and the plans were for the four of them to share the space, with extra room for new arrivals if needed.

The two motor homes of the Bradfords and Keplers stood side by side, representing the 'high end' lodgings of the town. Everyone joked that they were in the rich suburbs and the rest of town were the slums.

Jerrett's truck, trailer, and lean-to stood across the clearing from the motor homes. It looked shabby in comparison, Jerrett thought with a chuckle. Trevor and Dalton had been bedding down in the trailer, Jerrett and the little kids inside the truck, and Dean and Evie in the lean-to. The couple had installed a real door now and wooden shutters over the open windows. It was shaping up nicely.

Two outhouses stood at either end of the town like sentinels, far enough away from the homes that the smell wasn't too noticeable. The militia barracks were finally finished, housing row after row of bunks for the soldiers. It was a long, one-storey, narrow, building along the tree line. In the center of the town, by the clump of trees, there were rough benches for meetings. Down the valley, at Saul and Markie's house, Saul's brother George and his family were still bunking with them. It was a bit cramped but manageable.

Jerrett walked the length of Starlight Town, crisp red and yellow leaves floating down all around him. He zipped his coat against the slight chill in the air. Fall was on its way. He headed to the right, down a trail into the woods. A hundred yards or so down the path, he paused at a small clearing that had become the town's graveyard. Alonzo Ramirez was the only body there, but a second cross marker had been placed in memorial, bearing the name 'Sebastian', after the young man who had died during the escape.

Jerrett paused for a moment in respectful silence, then continued on his way to the logging site.

A gaggle of rowdy kids passed by him on the narrow trail and he had to duck to the side to avoid being run over. Young Marlowe Bradford, fully recovered from his life-threatening bout of pneumonia, led the pack. Jerrett laughed to see him so active again. Cami waved hello to him as she buzzed past, slipping him a tiny smile. He smiled back, missing her exuberance, but happy to see even a little smile. It was a start.

Reaching the clearing of the logging site, he saw the village's adult residents scattered before him. The meeting had been arranged late last night when an unexpected guest had arrived.

Making his way through the crowd, Jerrett came face to face with the quasi-famous figure of retired Army Major Russ Donaldson. He stood with a hand on his hip, his empty right sleeve folded up and pinned. His shaved head was covered with a black ball cap, bearing the name of his military squadron. He wore a gray t-shirt and black jeans with boots. Somehow he looked out of place in civilian clothes, as if he'd spent most of his life in a soldier's uniform. And he probably had.

The residents of Starlight Town were mingling about, chatting with Major Donaldson and his men. The Major, being secretive in nature, did not want to meet in the town center. Some of the closest neighbors now knew that people were staying at Starlight. Even though they had no fears that the neighbors would tell authorities, it was still better to keep what went on at Starlight as private as possible.

Even before he started his speech, Jerrett knew why he was there. The revolution needed soldiers.

As the crowd gathered close and quieted down, the Major started talking. His booming voice rang out loud and clear.

"Hello!" he began. "Thank you for letting me come up here to talk to you. I've heard from Mitch Carson all about your recent mission to rescue the folks trapped in one of those horrible camps and I must congratulate you! What an accomplishment for your first mission! Imagine that – taking a squad of non-military folk and going after one of their camps! Excellent job. You got yourselves in right under their noses, from what I hear, and rescued your people. Good for you! You are just the kind of soldiers the Revolution needs.

Now you all know we need more people in this fight. If we can get people involved, I believe we have a chance to win this thing. I've got a meeting in a few days with a group of active military members who want to help our side. I'll know more after the meeting, but imagine what we could accomplish with the military on our side. We could turn this whole thing around! But we need you. We need soldiers, sure, but we also need folks who would be nurses or doctors, messengers, cooks, camp aides, and the like. If we all do our part, we can make a huge difference out there. We've got a job to do, people, and I know you have the courage to do it. Like Harry Truman once said, 'America was not built on fear! America was built on courage, on imagination, and an unbeatable determination to do the job at hand.' Well, we've got a job to do and we need everyone's help. Now, who is ready to stand up and commit themselves to the cause? We need you.

"If you are ready to do your part, please sign up with my aide, Bernie." He pointed to a short, nervous-looking man in wire-rimmed glasses. "Tell him any skills you have, where you feel you could best be of service, and what you're good at.

"Let me say again, we need you! Your great country needs you! A person, fighting for his rights, makes the best soldier on earth. Stonewall Jackson said something to that effect and it's still true today!" He paused for effect, then continued, "If you are ready to help, please come forward…"

Jerrett's body moved as if pulled by an invisible force. He knew what he had to do; there was no more talking himself out of it, no more hemming and hawing, it was time. He was dimly aware of others moving around him, following him to the table set up near Donaldson's aide.

As much as he'd celebrated the victory of infiltrating the camp and rescuing the children, he knew there was still much to be done. They'd struck a blow to the enemy, but it was far from over. Avenging Gwennie, protecting his kids, supporting his brothers – that was what mattered now, and he finally knew how he was going to do it. He stepped forward, and Major Donaldson's aide peered up at him.

"Sign me up. I'm ready."

☻ ☻ ☻

Love Your Book

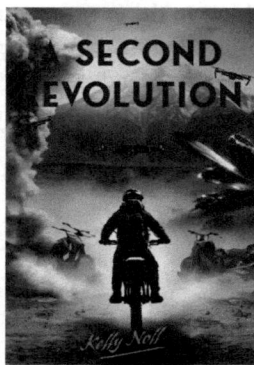

A Second Revolution

TIMELINE

JULY 2024

Soft-back book printed from paper that has been carbon offset through the World Land Trust Scheme.

PRINTED by Hobbs the Printers Ltd
at Southampton, United Kingdom

PUBLISHED by Cybirdy Publishing
London, United Kingdom

CYBIRDY
Publishing Limited

SPECIAL EDITION
Autographed by the Author

Kelly Noll

KELLY NOLL

WHO are you?	WHO did you obtain the book from?	WHEN did you obtain the book
FIRST GUARDIAN		
SECOND GUARDIAN		
THIRD GUARDIAN		
FOURTH GUARDIAN		
FIFTH GUARDIAN		

Born and raised in Lancaster County, PA, **KELLY NOLL** was a preschool teacher for over 25 years. Kelly's family is deeply embedded in the sport of motocross, and she has combined her love of writing with her knowledge of the motocross world. Along with her husband and son, she owns and manages a motocross track, Rocket MX, in the Pennsylvania mountains. She has written three children's books, titled A Day At The Track, The ABC's of Motocross and the 123's of Motocross. Kelly was privileged to star in an episode of Makeup2Mud which aired in 2020 during a pro supercross race on NBC sports.

A Second Revolution is her first novel.